MY EVIL EYE

A.L. HAWKE

PHANTOM HEART, LLC

Copyright © 2022 by A.L. Hawke

All rights reserved. No portion of this book may be reproduced, distributed or transmitted in any form or by any electronic or mechanical means, including information storage and retrieval systems, without permission in writing, except by reviewers who may quote brief passages for a review.

ISBN: 978-1-953919-20-5 (paperback)

ISBN: 978-1-953919-19-9 (ebook)

Library of Congress Control Number: 2022946454

This is a work of fiction. It all comes directly from the imagination of the author's mind. This includes names, characters, places, and incidents. Any public names are used solely for creative purposes. Any resemblance to actual people, living or dead, or to companies, institutions or locales is entirely coincidental or accidental.

Line edited by Stephanie Marshall Ward

Proofread by Alexa B., alexabooks.wixsite.com/authors

Cover © 2022 by Regina Wamba of MaeIDesign.com

Published by Phantom Heart, LLC

27702 Crown Valley Pkwy D-4, #201

Ladera Ranch, CA 92694, USA

Printed and bound in the United States of America

First printing October, 2022

Learn more about A.L. Hawke at www.alhawke.com

Correspondence: contact@alhawke.com

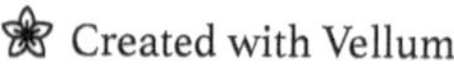 Created with Vellum

1

FUGU TIME

They always look at me funny. Whenever I roll my cart down the aisles shelving books, readjusting my glasses over my nose, or even just typing on the computer, boys look at me weird. Somehow they know I don't quite fit in. I know. I don't. But you know, to monsters, it's the normal people that are the weirdos.

There's one now. Look at him. He's just leaning against a wall with his sweaty armpit over the nose of a poor blonde in a cute sky-blue university sweater who's trying to study. She doesn't look like the type that normally studies—neither does the jock—but this is dead week, when students actually have to. She's trying to humor him by looking up and smiling, but I know she really wants him to leave her alone.

Don't look at him. Forget about him.

I shake my head and shelve a heavy textbook.

I'm in the main hall of Sunland University's library. It's a grand retro-nineteenth-century hall with loads of walnut columns and bookshelves and a vaulted dome ceiling. On one side is a waterfall. Yeah, an actual waterfall. And they have plants surrounding it, which I love because with the lighting and foliage, it makes me feel I'm outdoors and it's daytime. I like to read here late at night when I finish work early. On the other side of the hall is a bunch of offices behind windowed walls. Everything's lit by modern-looking chandeliers.

Shit, there's another creep bugging the girl. This ape won't stop fucking slapping her shoulder. I always perk up when guys act like this. I was violated in Sarpedon eons ago, you know. Even a little playing around is *not okay.*

Hey, don't look at me. Don't do that!

What a bunch of assholes.

Calm down, Gorgi.

Well... Don't fucking look at me!

He turns. Then he leans over and whispers something to her. I move my wigglies back from my ear to snoop.

"Come on. You want the stuff or not?"

"Give it to me or just leave me alone, Carl."

The guy standing over her looks right at me.

Keep your eyes off me!

My gaze is deadly, you know. It's like Fugu. Do you know what Fugu is? Fugu in Japanese translates to "fortune." It's the puffer fish. The puffer fish is a delicacy that tastes wonderful but, if not prepared just right, the poison doesn't give you good fortune. I've tried Fugu. It's not *that* great, even when prepared right. I've had it prepared wrong too. (It tastes the same, by the way.) Anyway, my eyes are like Fugu. They lure you in, entice you, but if you enjoy too much...bye, bye. Hey, what a coincidence—I'm shelving a book on Japanese cuisine.

"Excuse me?" Someone is tapping on my shoulder.

I whirl around. Being an A+ apex predator, it's rare that someone sneaks up on me, but I was distracted by the jerks.

"Can you help me with my book search?" he asks.

It's this tall guy with wavy golden hair thrown to the side. His face is a little sunburnt. He's wearing a button-down and baggy pants. He's got broad shoulders and strong arms. He's grinning. And he's cut and he's, *uh, hmm,* hot.

Oops. He opens his eyes wide. Did he see my cursed eyes? No, he's looking over at those two assholes laughing at the girl.

"I—" He coughs. "I figured you work here?"

"I do," I say, looking down at the floor.

"Can you help me? I'm in this Western Civ class, and the professor's asking for us to check out a book. I think she thinks it's like an inside joke. I mean, who checks out books at a library anymore when there's the web? No one. It's kinda stupid."

"There's lots of stuff in books you can't find online."

"Oh," he says, looking flustered. "Of course, *a librarian* would say that." He stops talking. I think it's because I'm staring at the ground.

Yep, he leans down to look into my eyes. I turn away.

"Are you okay?" he asks.

I nod. But I don't look at him. I want to. I really do. I already caught a glimpse of his strong jawline, five o'clock shadow, perfect teeth, and kind smile.

"I was just saying we could google it," he continues, rubbing his neck. "But the professor wants us to use the library. I've seen you working here before. You're one of the librarians. Right?"

"Yes."

He smiles again. He has such a cute smile. It's telling me he's not really here to search for books, you know.

Shit, did he catch a glimpse of my Fugu? Is that it? I wear these thick spectacles with special lenses to hide my golden gems, but they're not perfect. If a guy gazes straight into my eyes, it's Fugu time. Particularly if my gold gems turn green.

Sometimes somebody catches a glimpse from the side. Many years ago, I went to an optician to fit me with trick glasses that would be clear for me but blurry straight on for wandering eyes. I've tried lots of ways to hide my cursed eyes. Opaque shades work too, but Charlie, he's my boss, wouldn't take kindly to his librarians wearing sunglasses at work.

"Can you help me?" Oh yeah, the blond guy's still talking to me.

He follows me down three steps into another part of the library I love, with the gorgeous fountain I was talking about. The fountain has lovely trickling water. It's made of white stone and, I mean, it's not the Trevi Fountain, more of a tacky bozzetto, but I absolutely adore it. It was here decades ago when I applied for the job. I think it's what sold me. And tables circle the fountain, with computers where you can search for stuff. Students also sit on the three steps, but they're nearly always empty when I work here at night.

I sit down in front of a large antique monitor.

"What would you like to search for?" My eyes are focused on the screen.

His sunburnt hand is beside mine. Mine, peeping out from my ugly thick furry brown sweater, hovering over the keyboard, is tanned, always the same olive color, sun exposure or not. I don't burn—or, when I do, it just goes back to the same color. He has strong hands. Cute, nicely groomed strong man hands.

"Genghis Khan," he says, leaning over my shoulder.

"Genghis Khan," I say, typing fast. "This is similar to a google search. It's easy. You just type your word. You get the location here and the ISBN. Get it?"

"What's an ISBN?"

"It's an identifier. All books have them."

I feel tingles sitting near him. And I hear his heart jump a little. And his scent, his essence is... *like ...*

"Excuse me for not knowing what an ISBN is," he quips.

"Well..." I brush my bangs from my eyes with a smile. "Once you find the location, you can look for it by subject. We use the Library of Congress classification system here, not the Dewey Decimal. See, this shows a map of our library and where each category of books is shelved. And here's a call number for a book. Easy, right?"

"Easy for you."

He is staring at my profile. I turn a little so he doesn't see my eyes.

"You really like this stuff, don't you?" he asks.

"I love books."

"*Come on!*" snaps one of the meatheads in a forced whisper. I had totally forgotten about them. "*Hand it over or forget the whole thing.*"

"*Just leave her alone, Carl.*"

"*Let me go. Here's the money.*"

Let me go?!

I look up. I can't see anything past the fountain, but I can smell them. With my nose, I sense a hand yanking his prey's arm. My wigglies fight to break out from their cage in my hair. I press down on my bun. Then I glance back at the boy beside me. He's none the wiser, but he's squinting at me.

"Genghis Khan?" he asks, raising his brow.

"Oh." I start typing fast again. "Here's a directory of over twenty books on the subject. Just go to the third floor and find this section." I tap the screen. "I'll print out a list of call numbers for your report."

I quickly get up, looking toward the commotion.

"Can you show me the location upstairs?"

"What?" I ask, turning back to him with a laugh. "It's easy."

"Easy for you."

"Let me go! Where are you taking me!"

That fucker is tugging her arm! Can you believe this? That fucking dick is pulling her! I sense the whole building like a green schemata in my mind. And the angrier I get the clearer the image becomes.

I've had enough. I rush up the steps from the fountain back up to the main hall.

"Oh...well, thanks," blurts the student.

"Let me go, Carl!"

Let me go?!

I hear the struggle through the walls. They've left the main hall. No one else has any idea this commotion is going on. The struggle isn't loud; it's more like forced whispers. But the girl's panic rings in my ears.

When I was in Sarpedon, I was tricked by the slick, sugary tongue of Poseidon. And the horror began when the god grabbed my wrist. It's been thousands of years, but as the girl is dragged, I feel her pain as if he's dragging me by the arm.

I need to calm down. I can't change in front of these kids.

But he touched her. He's forcing her!

My hair is aching to escape its hair tie. My incisors are digging into my lower lip. I grasp my hands tightly, trying to distract myself, telling myself not to change—not to do that in front of all these students. But I want to hurt him.

I hear a body being thrown against a wall. It's a faint sound. My eyes are burning like green flashlights through my spectacles. Bright emerald. I shade my eyes as I break out into a run.

I hear a shirt tear. And she cries out as he twists her arm again.

Oh, you going to do that? Huh? Okay, you know what I'm

going to do? I'm going to dislocate your wrist, pull your hand from its socket, and stuff it down your motherfucking throat!

I rush down a hallway that connects the library to a nearby lecture building. A girl by the library exit, who's standing by a table reading, stares up at me as I sprint past her. Her human ears probably don't hear the struggle.

Everything turns dark and empty as I enter the corridor into the lecture hall. I follow their scent into another hallway. Then one more turn. And then...

I throw open the door to a boy's bathroom. It's empty. But there's movement in one of the stalls. I rush over and pull at the stall door. It's locked. I easily break the metal door open.

The asshole has the girl bent over facing the toilet. He doesn't even stop groping her—he's locked in predatory mode. Her shirt is torn, revealing bare breasts, and he's dropped his pants. He looks over his shoulder. Actually, they both do.

What a sight I must be. I'm not covering my green eyes anymore. Their bodies are illuminated in green light.

"Go," I say to the girl. "Get out of here."

The girl nods, clutching her torn shirt over her chest. She runs past me to the exit in tears. I turn to the creep. He's such a pompous ass that he faces me, still bathed in green light, with his cock wagging.

I'm feeling pain in my wrist. Is it my ancient memory of Greece? Or is it my empathy for the girl?

She's gone. It's over. Just let him go.

Uh... Nuh-uh.

I smile lasciviously at the boy. I remove my ugly brown sweater. I take off my shirt and bra and lay them gently by the sink. I take my time getting naked in front of him. Let him relish my poison. He's frozen after seeing my eyes.

"Is this what you wanted?" I ask. I slowly back away. "A nude girl?"

He gazes at my body with wide eyes. He doesn't seem to care that I look like a demon from hell right now, with fangs, sharp fingernails, and green, glowing eyes. He wants a taste of my body. A taste of my delicious Fugu. And, boy, is he gonna get it.

His body, though frozen, trembles.

"Who are you?" he asks, struggling to move his mouth. "*The librarian?*"

"I'm the devil."

I walk up to his ear and lick it. Then I brush my palm along his bushy beard and brush my tits against his side. "You want to sin? Sin with me. I'm not innocent. I can show you a good time."

"Sure," he purrs.

I run my hand along his shirt. His hands are weak, so I help him lift it. Then my hand runs over the bulges of his huge pecs. I pull the pants, still bunched around his ankles, away from his feet. Now he's naked and dirty, just like the filthy motherfucker he is.

But I freeze for a moment. I clutch my head in my hand... What am I doing? The girl's gone. She's safe. I can just stop. Right?

NO! He was bending her over like a dog! You gonna let a man do that? After all that's happened to you?

I run my lips along his. Then I slowly wrap my fingers around his wrist. I twist. I could yank his hand right off with one more turn. Oh, it'd be so easy.

Cut it off and stuff it down his motherfucking throat!

No. I... I can't do that.

He winces and writhes as I twist. Then he shrieks. His body jerks to nurse his injured hand, but he can barely move.

"Why'd you do that?" he asks.

I giggle.

"What's your name?"

"Medusa."

My tongue comes out, forked like a snake's tongue, at the utterance of my ancient name. It licks his cheek and ear. But my long serpent tongue doesn't bother him the slightest bit. I reach back with my free hand, as I continue to stroke his cheek with the other, and finally free the bun from my head.

Oh, what a relief! As the bun unfolds, my black hair falls, freeing my friends, and the snakes thicken, slithering and slinking over my face. I take a deep breath as my beasties are let loose. Some of the black snakes run along his face. A couple even loop around his neck. I could choke and suffocate him. I've done it before. He's already too far gone to resist.

I should just snap his neck and be done with him.

No. Tease him. Make sure he's just conscious enough to feel the pain he brought her.

"You naughty, naughty boy," I whisper in his ear. I run my forked tongue along his ear. "How could you do that to an innocent girl?"

"Oh, she's not innocent," he says with a chuckle. My forked tongue enters his mouth and wraps around his tongue. I could constrict it and remove it.

Don't. Not yet. Play with him first.

I pull back from his lips, but it takes all my will to not pull out a chunk of his face.

"She was cheating on me," he says.

"Cheating on you? A virile young man? I don't believe it. So you were going to force a fuck?" At the word *fuck* his body shakes. "Because she deserved it?"

He chuckles nervously.

"Did she force the other boy to have sex too?"

"They met at a hazing," he says. His head is immobile. Only his mouth moves. "My friend met up with her after to study." I run my hand along his thick beard again. I hear his heart beating like crazy. "Next thing I knew I saw them screwing on my bed. So what I did was I planned this whole deal. I wanted to teach her a lesson and show her who her true boyfriend really is. My way. I figured the bathroom was private." He looks at my eyes, but I don't meet his gaze. There's enough green from my eyes in the room to entrance him. A little more and he wouldn't be able to move his mouth and finish his stupid excuse. "I guess... not so private."

"Touch my hair," I say. "Go on."

He lifts a shaky hand and runs his fingers along my hair. My vipers coil around them. Perhaps this would be enough? I can sever his fingers and leave him with a maimed hand? That would teach him a lesson, wouldn't it?

No. Kill him! Kill him!

"Well, you told me your story, my boy, why don't you let me tell you mine?" I cuddle his head on my breasts. "I'm going to give you quite a whopper."

"It was three thousand years ago. I worked in the temple of Athena. I was a priestess. Every day I toiled hard maintaining the goddess's great temple. I was a model priestess. Of course, I was a virgin. All those who worked the great temple of Athena were virgins. God forbid we were ever *fucked*..." His body shakes again. "Or defiled by horny boys."

I guide his hand along my side, and his fingers somehow manage to twitch along the crack of my ass. It makes me almost furious enough to finish him.

"I'm not done," I say, moving his hand from my butt. "Listen. One day, as I was out to gather water from the well, I was surprised by a voice. It was a stranger flattering me over my beauty. I had always known I was pretty. In fact, many think I am the most beautiful woman in the world. In fact, it was my beauty that drew so many other virgins to the temple. That was good for business, but bad for the goddess Athena's jealousy."

"Yes, you are hot," he mutters stupidly.

"Aha. The voice was Poseidon's. The god had seen me alone and came to me when I was vulnerable. The god grabbed my arm and tore off my sacred white robe and fucked me right there by the well. He fucked me like no man had ever fucked before. He was a mighty Olympian god, after all. He showed her who was boss, just like you were doing to that poor girl. Right?"

I laugh. There's really nothing funny about that. But it's too bad for him that he's too entranced to join me in my mirth. If he chuckled, that would be another reason for me to finish him off. Instead, the fucker finds the strength to lower his head and run his lips around my nipples.

Go ahead and suck. That's fugu too.

"Well, the very next morning, I ran. I ran from the temple because I had been defiled. My mere presence dirtied the sacred ground, and it was a grievous insult to the goddess Athena. I didn't get far. Athena came to me personally. She tripped me with Apollo's snakes."

I grab his cock. I pull a little, like I pulled his wrist. He winces. He leaves my tit and leans into my face, pressing his lips into mine. Apparently, he didn't notice my sharp fangs and slithering vipers.

"She turned me into one," I say with a shrug, between his kisses. "Ever since then, I've borne witness and left alone all sins. I turn my eyes from theft, adultery, even murder. But never, ever, ever do I avert my eyes from one sin. Do you happen to know what that sin is?"

He shakes his head.

"Rape," I say. "Rape is one thing I will never witness

again. When Poseidon pinned me, and the stars sent me no mercy, and when, instead of judging a god and punishing Poseidon, the gods turned on an innocent young girl and ruined her, I realized there is no one in this whole fucking world that cares about me. I have been discarded. Trash. For me, I'm done. But for another, no. I vowed to never, ever, ever, let that happen to another lady in my presence. Do I make myself clear?"

He nods with a smile, looking at me—full of desire—thinking somehow, weirdly, that I'm going to have sex with him. If someone were to walk in now and witness my fangs, my moving hair, and my glowing red eyes beside him, they might think this is funny. You do, right? But it really isn't amusing, is it?

He deserves punishment. Punish him.

The snakes in my hair move in a fury, hissing wildly. My eyes glow a brighter green, illuminating his whole face. When I am ready for the kill, I lose all attractiveness. But the boy seems too deep in his trance to notice.

"Now, tell me, what were you doing to that poor girl?"

He laughs. Then he gazes into my eyes and a shadow seems to fall over him. That's what I was waiting for. Realization. With my seduction, I've unleashed the lamia of his destruction. I am revenge. He loses all mirth. Well, like I said, there was nothing funny here. There never was. I reach down and grab his penis and...it's all over.

Look into the eyes of Medusa. Gaze into me as I ravish you. Keep your eyes on mine as your skin tears from your neck, shredding muscle and sinew, leaving your chest bloody and back bare. Your flesh I rip. Your arms and legs I tear. I dismember you into the heap of shit you are.

Still awake? Good. Feel more... Pain!

I should just leave him. She's gone and...

Take his hand and shove it down his throat!

His screams are muffled. His cries seem to be coming from so far away, as if in a faraway tunnel. At this point, I'm far into a trance myself.

And...

I black out. But, in my periphery, I watch a body fall to the floor—in pieces.

In the back of my mind, I recall screaming. Is it a memory or is it happening now? I'm not sure.

As I awaken further, I take a deep breath. I feel dizzy.

I walk to the bathroom mirror. Red is splashed on my face. I wash my face. As the crimson washes away and the snakes recede, my face is absolutely beautiful again. The prettiest face in the world. I arrange my hair back in a bun.

The metallic stench of his blood has taken the place of piss and shit and fills the bathroom. I walk to the door and realize I crushed the doorknob after the girl ran. Then, as I awaken more, I realize a bunch of people are banging on the door.

My God, what have I done? In my periphery, I see crimson flesh smeared and heaped against the white tile. There's only a mound of meat on the floor, no recognizable body.

There's a window on the other end of the bathroom. It's just big enough for us to slither through.

Go, Medusa! Run!

2

———

CORA

"I FUCKED UP."

I put my head in my hands. I'm about to totally cry, but that would make me look weak. And my friend Cora isn't weak. She's the strongest woman I've ever known. Cora is the goddess Persephone, my best friend in the whole world, and I want her to respect me, not think I'm weak. Well, she makes me feel worse with her sad face. Above her frown her lovely bright blue eyes shine—azure eyes I once despised more than anything in the world, until I met her.

She reaches across the table and her pale hand squeezes mine. We're in this seedy all-blue diner at a booth by a window. If it were daytime, we'd see the beach. That's why I wanted to meet here. Cora loves the beach. But it's after ten o'clock at night.

Cora's long hair is blond tonight. Sometimes it's red, other times black. You never know. She's fun like that. When she got to the booth at this diner, she was carrying a motor-cycle helmet and wearing a tight all-black leather jumpsuit. She had told me she was coming by plane. Her private plane. Then by private motorcycle, I suppose. She's so fun.

Unlike me. I'm wearing the same boring thing I wore in the library—my brown wool grandma sweater. And my hair's in its usual bun. So I look beautifully ugly. But, see, that's the thing about my friend. Cora struts her feathers and acts tough, but somehow she still loves me anyway.

"I fucked up."

"Tell me what happened," Cora says.

"You look good," I say. "Your husband Danny passed, huh?"

"I'm not here for me," Cora says with a shrug. "You sounded desperate on the phone. What the hell was so secret that you were worried about being tapped, Gorgi?"

"I've been happy. You know I've lived here for years in peace. But I just got myself into a whole heap of trouble."

"Well?" Cora asks, lifting her eyebrow. "What is it? Are we talking money? You need a loan?"

I shake my head. "I have lots of money."

"Men?"

"No," I say with a chuckle.

"Do you two know what you'd like?" interjects a gray-haired lady. She's dressed in a classic diner outfit.

"No," says Cora, gesturing for her to go away. The waitress obeys and returns to the counter by the kitchen. Cora lifts her eyebrow again, leaning forward, and whispers, "Murder?"

"Sort of."

Cora's eyes open wide. "You're so crazy, Gorge."

"I was working. I... you know, it was late and, you know, it's finals on campus. So the library was full of students studying, even though it was late. I was just minding my own business, shelving books. Honestly, I was looking forward to getting done early and opening up that new book by E. L. James."

"I finally got through *Fifty Shades of Gray.*"

"Yeah? Did you like it, Cora?"

"Yeah, I liked it."

"Well, the library was quiet until there was a commotion. This frat guy was manhandling a sorority girl over a drug deal, tugging at her and making lots of noise. She was telling him to stop, but he wouldn't."

"Uh-oh," Cora said, turning to the window with a nod.

The waitress comes back and hands us glasses of water. "You know what you guys want now?"

Cora ignores her.

"Not yet," I say, but I don't give her eye contact either.

The waitress is rapidly blinking her eyes at Cora and me. She probably thinks we're both total loons. Well, we are. Right? But as she's walking off, I say to the waitress, "Oh, can you get me a cup of coffee?"

She gives me an even weirder look. It's almost eleven o'clock at night. But that's morning for me. Or maybe she thinks I'm weird because I'm wearing dark sunglasses. I don't know.

"Who'd you kill, Gorgi?" Cora whispers, leaning forward.

"He was raping her! He was fucking raping her, Cora! I couldn't let him do that. I mean, you know what that shit does to me. I followed them into the men's restroom. And the bathroom was in an adjacent building, it's supposed to be private. It was late. There was no one else there. And I barged through the stall door because I heard a commotion. He was leaning over her with his pants off and I just... I completely lost it, Cora. I went crazy. Things took over, you know, got hold of me and all hell broke loose."

"How did he die?" Cora asks quietly.

"In pieces."

Cora nods very slowly.

I mean, it's not unexpected, is it? I'm a wretched monster. I've lived centuries learning to accept that. And I hardly would have bothered my friend Cora if nothing had happened.

The waitress hands me the cup of coffee with a tray of sugar and cream. I drink from the cup with a very shaky hand. Then I open the bag of sugar and pour the granules into my mouth. Cora shakes her long blond hair back and peers at me with those gorgeous blue goddess eyes. She tries to smile.

"*He deserved every fucking bit of it!*" I exclaim, hitting the table with my fist.

"Quiet down. It sounds like he did."

"It brought it all back. You know it always does. I can handle anything, any sort of thing, even murder. But that. No. No, I can't, I won't stand for that. Never." An old couple about two booths away looks over at my outburst.

"I know. You said he was *in pieces*?" Cora's talking quietly. "Did you do what was possible... with a small knife?"

I shake my head.

She turns back to the window with a long sigh. This time she puts her head in her hand.

"I petrified him. Then I had him suffocate in his own fucking blood."

"Keep it down."

"Cora, he was going after an innocent girl!"

"Keep it down," she says, whirling back. "Shush. You need to be quiet."

"He had torn the girl's shirt. He was pinning her against the toilet like she was a piece of shit! You know no asshole will ever do that in my sight again. No one. No matter what the cost. I had to teach him a lesson. So I did."

Cora points at her eyes and then at my glasses. I look at the mirror. Even through the thick fake shades, green is shining around my face. I lower my head, pull off my sunglasses, and cover my eyes.

"I've been so happy." I say, shaking my head in my hands. "I don't know what to do. I fucked up. I fucked up real bad. I'm in so much trouble. I didn't know where else to turn. Everything was finally quiet. I was happy. Really, I was. I had all the books in the world to read and no one to bother me. Then this happened. You know when they investigate, it's gonna bring Imada."

"It will."

Yeah. So I wonder if Cora will just walk out. I mean, why help me? She could get in trouble herself.

She told me she had moved far north, to Toronto, Canada, and found this handsome new guy to spend another lifetime with. She's settling into a new life after her husband was murdered. Now this. If she helps her favorite monster, she could be abetting a murderer. Then I wonder... perhaps I could have just hurt the guy—instead of killing him. Maybe I should have just scared him off. Just hurt him a little.

NO! He deserved every fucking thing I did to him!

I cry. I can't act tough anymore. I haven't slept in days. I just cry and cry and cry in my hands.

I know how this works. It's only a matter of time before I'm called into the police station. Then they'll throw me in a dark cell. In the Middle Ages, they'd torture me, if they could. There were many times they didn't know what I was; they figured I was a witch and tried to burn me, only to find me creeping up behind them and tearing them limb from limb.

I feel a hand on my shoulder. Cora's sitting beside me now.

"Shh," Cora says quietly. "Calm down. It's okay, Gorgi."

"It isn't."

"I'm your friend."

I nod.

"This creep. You're positive he was raping her?"

"Yes!" I pull away from her. "Of course I am! Are you crazy?"

"Then stop crying." She sighs and sits up straight. "You gave him justice. Not Imada justice, our justice. From what you're telling me, you should have cut his goddamn dick off."

"I did."

"*You did?*" Cora asks, opening her eyes wide.

That does it. Cora's speechless, which is very rare for her. What does she expect? You get it, right?

She turns to the window again, and this time her eyes are bright red. She covers her eyes because, unlike me, she's not wearing shades. See, our eyes change color when we're under stress. Hers turn red, mine green. Usually it's when we're angry, but I think Cora is overwhelmed by how absolutely fucked up I am. I mean, she's crazy too, but she probably wouldn't do what I did. Or maybe she would? I don't know.

"You're crazy, Gorgi," Cora says, shaking her head. "Nuts."

That only makes me cry more.

"Oh, stop it. It's okay." She gently lifts my chin and brushes my hair from my forehead. "Stop crying." She forces a smile. "I'll help you. But it's gonna take some time to clean this up. You did some gnarly stuff. Just lay low. Call in sick for the rest of the week. Otherwise they'll question you."

"They'll question me anyway. You know how this works. And I always get nervous when I have to talk in front of a lot of people."

"You saved this girl," Cora says. "If they call you in, be Medusa. Be confident and know you did nothing wrong."

"I can't be Medusa, Cora," I say, shaking my head. "Just like you can't be Persephone."

But I wipe my tears and try to cheer up. I drink the remains of my cup of coffee. It's not like I'm going to sleep when morning comes anyway.

"Laying low means no fun," Cora says with a forced grin, folding her arms. "This foils my plans tonight. We can't go clubbing."

"It would have been fun."

"Yeah. Listen, don't worry. Seriously, you did no different from a cop shooting that guy. You're more like a hero."

She gets up and sits on the other side of the booth again. Then she wrinkles her nose, looking around the diner. "Well, we can eat. That's laying low here."

I wipe my eyes and look at my friend and nod. Aside from her rueful grin, she looks good. Real good. She always does.

"How is your new boyfriend in Toronto?" I ask. "I'm sorry to hear about Danny. You liked LA, didn't you? How's Hashan?"

"Hashan is boring as always. I love him to death. And Gabe's an angel from heaven. Toronto's cold."

"I'm so happy for you, Cora."

"Yeah, don't worry 'bout me. Everything will work out, Gorgi. All right?"

"I've been so happy over the past few years. Lonely, but happy."

"Don't worry. Look, if they take you to prison, I'll spring you."

"But I don't want to lose the home I've made. It took so long to get comfortable. I think I'll go crazy if I have to rebuild my life again."

"You won't."

I force a smile.

Cora nods. "Hungry?"

"Yeah. They have good food here."

"Hmm, seems like a dump. But if the food's good, why not?" She flags our waitress, who's behind a counter.

"We're ready to order," Cora says. Her eyes are beautifully azure blue again, so it's okay. And mine aren't bursting with emerald light.

"I'd like steak," I say, staring at the table. "Raw."

Cora is looking at me funny in her peripheral vision. She smiles wide.

"You mean... rare?" the waitress asks, lowering her head, trying to see my eyes.

"No, raw," I say, quickly shaking my head. "Don't cook it."

"I'll have what she's having," Cora says with a laugh. "A raw steak. Just serve it raw with some nice seasoning. With a Coke."

The waitress opens her eyes wide. Then she just nods.

"Oh, I'll have a Coke too," I add as the waitress makes her way back to the kitchen.

"I love you, Gorgiana," Cora says with a laugh. "You're so freaky."

3

LAYING LOW

I'M SITTING ON MY ROCKING CHAIR ON THE PORCH OF MY SMALL one-story house. It's dark and close to midnight. The only light is coming from a streetlight, but my beastie eyes are strong enough to read the book on my lap. Occasionally I catch a drunken kid laughing and stumbling by me on the sidewalk but, although I'm within walking distance of campus, this is a pretty private neighborhood. I'm alone and it's after midnight. I'm laying low, like Cora told me to do. But I'm not about to just stay indoors.

Another college kid rides by on my sidewalk on his bike.

I'm reading a book called *The Guy That Loved Me and Then Died*. I like the title because it's funny as hell. It's about a spy and it's got a bit of Cold War intrigue, and what makes it super funny is I don't think it's supposed to be funny—but I'm not sure. I think the title is a play on words from that old James Bond movie I also love, *The Spy Who Loved Me*. It's an old book. I like all those James Bond flicks. I'm a bit of a movie buff, you know. I spend lots of Friday nights alone on my sofa with a blanket, eating microwave popcorn and watching VHS movies. I have lots of VHS movies. Some

DVDs. Do you remember that rental movie place, Block-buster? Shit, they knew me by name.

The MC, that means main character in heavy-reader lingo, who's being followed by the spy, is now making love to the girl in the snowy woods after they slipped off a ski lift. I told you. Funny.

Here comes another guy riding a bike by my streetlamp. But this one stops on the sidewalk by the house. That's weird. My nares flare and I sniff. He's squinting toward me. He's about fifteen yards from my porch. Very weird. And he's walking right up to me. He smells familiar. He's just squinting up into the darkness.

"Hey," he says, his foot on the first step of the porch. "Is that you?"

I jump—not because I'm startled, but because I've learned over the centuries to act my part. A regular human girl being approached by a stranger while sitting alone on her dark porch, in the middle of the night, might jump too. Hey, it's that cute guy I ditched, who was pretending not to know how to look up books in the library! What the hell?

"Hi," I say.

"I didn't mean to startle you. You live here?"

Uh, yeah.

"I ride by here all the time on my way to lectures," he says.

"Hi."

"What are you reading?" he asks. I can see that cute smile in the shadows.

"It's a book titled *The Guy That Loved Me and Then Died.*"

He laughs. "Is it a comedy?"

"No, it's funny because it isn't."

I like that I can look into his face in the darkness. I can look up at him like a "normal" human being. He's got that blond hair thrown to the side, thoughtful, gentle eyes, with eyelashes that are almost feminine, but there's nothing femi-nine about his chiseled jaw or broad shoulders. He's got a little bit of stubble, which is adorable. He's tall. If I were a normal girl, I'd be going nuts right now. But I'm not normal. Am I?

"Where'd you run off to that night?" He climbs to the third and last porch step. "You left before the library closed. They shut the whole place down. The library's reopened now, but it was closed for days. I looked for you, but you never came back."

"I had to use the bathroom."

"Oh. You like what you're reading?"

"Love it," I say with a shrug, looking at my lap.

He's fishing for a topic of conversation. Maybe he's a spy for Imada? Imada is a secret organization run by the remnants of the gods of Olympus. And they detest Cora and me. He smiles again. Maybe he's been following me? Maybe he's seen that I live here. Or he has a crush on me? Could he have caught my gaze? My eyes can make some men feel as if the attraction is from me, not my Fugu. I still have to get rid of him. Especially now that he knows where I live.

In centuries past, I'd let a snake or two drop from the curls of my hair. It used to work better when people were more superstitious. Having two or three serpents scurrying in your hair used to scare the shit out of people. They'd think I was in league with the devil.

I could flash my green eyes? Perhaps make him think I'm a vampire by showing fangs? Of course, these days I like to rely on my thick, furry sweater, large fake glasses, unshaven arms, and unshowered smell to keep people away.

"Do you take classes at college?"

"Huh?" He's still talking. Can you believe this? "I just work in the library."

"Oh."

He puts his hands in his pockets and looks very uncomfortable.

"I'm a sophomore," he adds. "You look about my age. I thought you were a student working in the library to pay for school?"

"Not smart enough," I lie. Maybe it's not a lie? I don't know. I never went to college.

"You look smart."

"Thanks."

"May I?" he asks, gesturing to a chair beside me.

No!

There are two rocking chairs on my patio beside the porch. He sits on the one closest to me.

I'm an idiot. I should have stayed indoors. Cora told me to lay low. But not being around people over the past few days was driving me crazy. What were the chances that the guy I saw in the library would come tonight?

I smell him. I'm not referring to his cologne. I'm talking about his phenome, his essence. It makes me clench my hand tightly. His maleness being this close makes me lust for him. Heat rises in my back, along my chest, and between my legs. Like I'm in heat. The lamia side of me even makes me lick my lips, and I feel my front incisors grow sharper. I'm ready to jump him right now. You like him too, don't you?

Calm down, Gorgi!

When I lived in Sarpedon in ancient Greece, after I became a monster, if prey had been presented like this, it would have been all over for the man. I couldn't control myself. I was a complete pervert, enjoying sex, using my powers of petrification, and giving in to every desire. It's like how vampires like to suck the blood out of people. I wanted to throw men into a trance, fuck them, and then kill them. Thank Athena for that sick, perverted shit. But long ago, I stopped doing it to nice guys. After reflecting on what I was doing to good souls, I stopped. Except those committing rape. I've never stopped tearing rapists apart.

"Can you show me?"

"Show you what?" I ask, brushing my hair back.

I feel a little wiggly. Even in the dark, my snakes are coming out, being this close to a virile young man. And he's acting coy, which is really bad, because that's acting like prey.

"The book?" he asks, pointing to it.

"Oh." I hand it to him.

He's wearing a black button-down with a T-shirt and khaki slacks. It looks preppy. I'm thinking he went to a party. I smell a slight tinge of alcohol on his breath.

He looks at me and smiles. Then he loses his smile. Why? *Shit!* When I leaned forward to hand him the book, I was facing the streetlight. I think it reflected my eyes. Worse, they could have flickered green. I cover my eyes and look at the floor of my wooden deck.

"What's the matter?" he asks, bending down.

"I have to go." Like back into my house. Like away from this yummy guy. He should get the hint.

"Of course," he says, standing up. He shakes his head, as if recovering his senses. He walks back to his bicycle.

"You want to borrow my book?" I blurt out.

I don't know why the hell I asked him that, but it seemed like a nice thing to say to make up for my rudeness. He looks over, as confused as I am.

"You're not done with it."

"I... read a lot of books," I say with a shrug. "I already read the ending. I can read the beginning later. A story's a story, you know, and I don't believe it matters whether you enjoy it the same way every time. Sometimes it's better starting at the end. You can tell me if the beginning is worth reading."

"You're really weird," he says with a chuckle.

Yes, I am.

"Okay," he says.

What! Really?

With his youthful energy, he sprints back up the three steps of my deck and reaches for my book. "Sounds like a deal. I'll check out your book right now, librarian. I'll let you know if the beginning is worth reading."

And there it is. That look. I'm looking down, but in my periphery, I see his face. It's lust. Yep, I ensnared this guy that night with my eyes, and he's hooked. I must have. That's all. Fugu. I'm so stupid. Once a man is hooked it's hard to shake him off. I was actually thinking he liked me or something.

"When will you be back to work?" he asks. "I can give it to you then."

"I'm on extended leave. I'm not sure."

"Oh... well, I know where you live." Yeah, that's not good. "I'll come back and give it to you here."

"Okay."

"Hey, my name is Asher, by the way. What's yours?"

"Gorgiana."

"Georgiana?"

"No. *Gorg*, like gorgeous. Gorgiana."

"Gorgiana," he says slowly, as if tasting the name. He furrows his brow. "It's pretty and..." *Spine-tinglingly-weird?*

"It's my name," I add with a shrug.

"I like it. I'll see you soon, Gorgiana. After I start reading your book. It was a pleasure meeting you."

"Bye, Asher."

"Call me Ash. My friends call me Ash. And thanks for the book."

I watch him get back on his bike.

"Ash, you know," I holler, "you know the book's ending kinda sucks."

"I'll let you know how it begins. Maybe the beginning's better?"

"Maybe," I say with a chuckle.

What a weird boy.

4

———

MEDUSA

I give it a week. Cora said lay low, but I can only take so many movie nights alone. I have to get back to seeing people, even if I don't talk to anybody. I've been checking out the library from afar. It's gone pretty much back to normal. Anyway, I'm a voracious reader. I want to check out a few more books to read at home.

It's eight o'clock. That's when my shift at the college university library begins. I don't really need to work, you know. I've collected enough money over the years from my relics to not work for a century. I even have places here and there that only I know about where I buried gold bricks. I pick cemeteries because cemeteries are places people don't like snooping around—except in the olden days when there were grave robbers. But now they have all these expensive security cameras. Anyway, I don't see people bothering graveyards much anymore. Not to mention, I'm not an idiot. I bury it in multiple sites. But I still have to work because otherwise I might go completely crazy.

I walk through the sliding glass doors and head up the escalator to the main hall. Maryann, this sweet old woman, knows to leave my work on a cart for the evening. She collects books lying around and stacks them on my cart for me to shelve. As I stand on the escalator, I think about library catalogs. That makes me think of that guy again. Ash. Was it Fugu or was it me?

Stop nightdreaming, Medusa.

I hope it was me.

I suppose now is the time to remind you why I'm the most miserable wretch to walk this earth. I am famously more beautiful than the goddess Athena. Aha, that's why she cursed me. Some say, though I've only caught a glimpse of her from a distance, that I'm cuter than Aphrodite. You believe that? Well, I am. I'm arguably even prettier than my good friend Persephone. At least Cora tells me so, because she's nicer than hell. I can tell you one thing. If you stack me up before a bunch of super models, I'll give them a run for their runway. And that's with the wigglies roaming in my hair.

So, now that I've elevated myself in your eyes, let me ask you this. What if every guy in the world froze when I walked by? What if I could have any one I wanted, but couldn't control my animal instinct and threatened to tear every guy apart? The thing about Medusa turning people to stone is complete bullshit. I mean, I can do that, but so what? That's not the problem. Being a lamia is my problem. Even if he doesn't fall into a trance, any handsome hunk that falls for me runs as fast as he can when he sees my hair thickening and turning full-on cobra. Can you blame him?

Then again, let's consider the opposite extreme. Let's say I were fertile and I could have a baby. I mean—what the fuck? A house full of kids? Really? I'm like a fucking lamia. Don't you know what lamia are? They're famous for eating babies. Gross. Anyway, some kid isn't about to run into momma's arms while her hair's slithering—with fingernails sharp as knives and bleeding fangs, looking like a total fucking Nosferatu. I mean, really.

So I'm wretched and alone. You get it. That's why I talk to you.

Giggles.

Hey, what do you know, I've got a note on my stack of books. It's my boss, Charlie.

I'm still here, Gorgiana. When you get in, please come by my office. We need to talk.

Am I getting canned? He's never, ever here late. That's one of the perks of my job. I think the last time I saw my boss was four years ago.

So I walk over to a bunch of glass offices beside the main library hall. One of these is his office, and I see him through the window, sifting through paperwork at his desk. I knock on the glass. The door's unlocked.

"Hi, Gorgiana."

He's in a button-down and slacks. It's supposed to be formal, but he looks sloppy, with dark unkempt hair.

I yawn and excuse myself. Charlie's office really sucks. He has no privacy; all the students can watch him at all times. Then again, watching students is probably part of his job.

"Hi, Charlie," I say, readjusting my spectacles and looking down.

"Gorgiana, how are you?"

I shrug.

"There was an incident on campus during your shift last week. Did you hear about it? The authorities are asking to talk to all the employees who were here that day. Do you know what happened?"

"I heard a student died."

Charlie loses color for a moment. Then he flashes me a very ingenuine grin. "The poor kid was torn up. Yes, Gorgiana, he died. I've never heard of such a thing in my life. His body was dismembered. The police are coming tonight to talk to people who weren't already questioned. They want to talk to you."

"I'd rather not. Can't I just fill out a written report?"

"They need to talk to you in person."

"I don't like talking in person."

"I know. But you have to."

"I'd rather not."

"I know you're shy. But you have to."

"Okay. Fine."

"Tell me this..." He leans forward and steeples his hands, running his fingertips along his lips. My gaze creeps up just a tad. "Why weren't you here that night when they were questioning us? I didn't know how to answer that. I've never seen you miss your shift."

"I had a family emergency."

"That's why you've been away?"

I nod. And he believes it because, when you really think about it, I've been laying low for the past three decades. I'm not suspicious. I'm mundane.

I jump at the sound of a commotion behind the glass windows. What the hell? About ten men in black suits and sunglasses are moving up the escalator. The commotion isn't from them; the agents are stone silent. It's from all the students still studying for finals, turning their heads and murmuring to one another. It's as if the president of the United States has decided to visit the library and this is his cavalcade of Secret Service agents. One of them, this large broad-shouldered dick who's bald and has a goatee, is walking in the center. He's the only one without shades. I know him well. I loathe him. His name is Hades. Nowadays he's called Orcus. "Orcus" means death. Like killer whale. "Orca." Get it? Orcus totally fits him.

I like killer whales by the way. They're fierce predators, even better than great white sharks. Love great whites too. I swam with a great white shark once. You want to wager on who won? Well, talking to you about deadly marine predators is a fantastic distraction from the more pressing situation at hand. Hades is also a leader in the Central Intelligence Agency. Once, though Cora wishes to forget, Hades was Cora's husband. The brute's a lot of things. But right now, he means just one thing to me. Trouble.

"*Medusa...*"

Hades whispers the word as he walks in the center of his cavalcade. The guards probably don't even hear him, but he knows I do.

"*Medusa. Don't scurry off like the capricious slithery snake you are. You're better off talking.*"

"I have to go," I say to Charlie.

But he's not listening. He's staring at the black suits too. "They're here again," he says, shaking his head.

"*Medusa...*"

I'm running. I have no interest in listening to this asshole. I've been working at the library for over twenty-five years. I'm not going to lose this gig.

Having worked here so long, I know every turn and every corridor of the library. I think Hades saw me run, but I don't turn back to look. And I try to drown out his stupid voice by listening to as many students as I can. But he keeps whispering:

"*Medusa...*"

I throw open a door to a private stairway and run down

the stairs, leaping down the last five steps. Then I burst through a side door and run outside.

It's cloudy. The full moon shines between the clouds. It's hot and humid even though it's dark.

They're after me. I hear their footsteps running out of the library. I look back. I shouldn't have. A group of them are sprinting down the steps under walkway lamps, chasing me. Shit. I mean, *fucking shit!* He's going to ruin everything!

But I'm fast. I'm quicker than any human. The problem is there's still a lot of students out tonight, studying for finals, and they're seeing me run as fast as Jesse Owens. I met Jesse Owens in Nazi Germany once, you know. I've been around. Okay, that's random. There I go trying to get my mind off the fact that Orcus, once known as Hades, the God of the Underworld, is still infernally whispering:

"Medusa..."

Shut the fuck up! Get out of my head!

If he catches me, he's gonna take me down and leave me buried in the earth forever. He's done it to Zeus, he's done it to Poseidon, and he's done it to Hermes. Why wouldn't he do it to a snake like me? He can't stand me. Could you imagine being buried for an eternity? Living forever awake—buried in dirt, but awake? Isn't that worse than hell? Or maybe that is hell?

I'm hurdling bushes.

As I zoom past dark classrooms, I enter a woodsy area. There's a famous lagoon on campus. It's small, only about the size of half a football field. It's the home of an alligator mascot that the students call Allie. I really don't fucking care about alligators right now. Actually, I love alligators, love Allie, just like I love killer whales and great white sharks, but all that's immaterial at the moment, isn't it?

I'm splashing in the cold, dark water. Of course Allie the

alligator is swimming toward me. She'd better be careful because when I'm cornered, I get pissed off.

I submerge under the dark water and pray—not to God, because I'm an atheist, but...shit. Whatever.

Shut your mind off. That asshole can probably read it with his demon ears.

Medusa...

Well, I don't hear him anymore. I just can't stop hearing his voice over and over in my head. I really can't hear a thing now. My ears are submerged in freezing water. And it's cold.

I hear the alligator swimming closer to me. I laugh underwater because Allie actually thinks *I'm* her prey. I could snap her in half with my bare hands.

Yellow lights are flickering above me on the water's surface. *Shit!* Flashlights. They know I'm here.

The pain is entering my lungs as I tread on the muddy ground underwater, drowning. The water won't kill me, but it hurts a lot. Then there's splashing. And with my mind, I can locate all of them jumping into the water. I know the exact location of each agent in the pitch blackness.

Allie changes direction and goes after one of the poor bastards. Ha, ha! She takes down the agent and rolls him. I'm wondering if these CIA agents knew that there's an alligator in this lagoon? They do now. Okay, I get it, that's mean, but really, they deserve it.

I'm in trouble. One of them found me and is splashing in the water, coming close. I mean, a couple are prying their friend from the grasp of the alligator's choppers, but one's heading right over.

I hear a gunshot.

Did they just kill poor little Allie? Really?

Why you motherfuckers!

I stand up on the shallow edge of the lagoon. My hair is slithering down—thick cobras running about my face. My skin is wrinkling and tightening. And my eyes shine forth like green flashlights. My front teeth are pressing down over my lower lip. All the agents crouch and hide from my gaze. Except one. One walks right up to me, not averting his eyes at all. Hades pulls out a pistol from under his jacket and points it at the center of my forehead.

"Will you come quietly, Medusa?"

"*NO!*"

He turns away from my shriek. The sound of my voice is so shrill that it forms a wave of water, which splashes over him. I hear another exploding gunshot. Then...

5

MY CELL

I wake up sitting in a cold metal chair, head on bent arms over a wooden table, rubbing my forehead with this awful splitting headache. It's like I have a hangover, but I wasn't drinking. I look up and squint at this super bright light over me. Then I look, blurry-eyed, across the small room at a dirty gray wall. Ugly gray walls surround me. Even the floors are tiled gray.

Where the hell am I?

BANG.

The sound reverberates in my head, and the pain is almost enough for me to black out again. My head feels like it's going to split open. I realize the pain is caused by the memory of a head injury, because when I touch my forehead, it's not wet or sticky. No blood. No gaping hole.

Then I cringe at the creaking of a metallic door opening. This burly guy walks in and slides a metal chair across the floor. That's terrible. The sound pounds in my skull, making me wince and clutch my head.

He drops a very thick folder of papers on the table, just to make my head feel worse. Then he looks at me with his bright blue eyes—they're azure blue just like Cora's, but perverse and sickening.

"How is Cora's pet?" Hades asks.

"I'm not her pet!" I wince. "Fuck!" Raising my voice at him hurts *so much*. "She's my friend! Don't call me that!"

"How's your head?" the brute asks more gently.

But I'm not going to answer him. Being kind is just an act with this creep.

I look around the room again. Now I recognize it as one of those interrogation rooms in police stations. I knew I'd end up here eventually. I used to be interrogated quite often, a few decades ago. I'm guessing this station is not far from campus. I'm also wondering if I was unconscious for long. Fatal injuries like bullet wounds, even to the head, knock me out, but the effect is transitory.

"How's Allie the alligator?" I snap back at him. Then I cringe as the pain squeezes my head again.

"Oh, was she your relation, Medusa? The university can get another mascot. It took a bite out of one of my operatives, though. We shot it dead. It doesn't have a thousand lives like you."

I put my head in my hands. Not because I'm upset. *Every... single... word... he says ... hurts.* I raise my eyes from my hands; he's stupidly smirking.

"What do you want?"

"When you took that boy's life in the bathroom last week," he says, "you left something of yours. Your neon-green milk. Your tits secrete a special unique toxin during an attack. Lovely though you are, you fuck like a praying mantis. The murder was investigated by the police. Then they took it higher up. After the remnants of his body were studied, it caught the interest of the FBI. And then the CIA. MI6. The DGSE. Everyone. They didn't know—"

"Can you please talk slower. And...quieter."

"Oh, I shot you in the head, didn't I?"

I nod. The movement hurts even worse.

"They didn't know where to turn because your poison doesn't exist anywhere but inside you. So eventually Langley sent an inquiry to the organization that deals with the unknown. Of course I had already gotten a call from Kore, before the inquiry, telling me how distraught you were about the killing."

"I didn't want her to tell you."

"How do you think she was going to help you? She said you were scared because you accidentally dismembered and beheaded one of your fuck toys. I told Kore that's to be expected when your good friend is a monster. Lovely though you are, you're a very nasty creature. I told her it's simply in your nature."

"I don't like you," I say, relishing my ability to look right into his eyes. "And you don't like me."

"No. No, we don't like each other, Medusa. We don't like each other at all." Then he leans over and squints into my eyes. He says slowly and in a really shitty way, "*Nobody should like you.*"

I put my head back in my hands. I'm not crying. I just don't want to see or hear him.

"Or course, his crumbled stone dick was a feat of sheer brilliance."

"*He was raping her!*" I hammer the table with my fist, cracking the wood. But Orcus doesn't back down. He just smiles smugly.

God, I hate him. This god is male, and he's a despicable male at that. He even resembles his brother Poseidon, the beast who violated me. Arrogant. Wicked. Cruel. Disgusting. He calls me a monster, like the alligator he shot? I tell you, that gator now floating dead in the pool is more humane than this motherfucker ever could be.

"Sit," he says. He gestures to my metal chair. "Sit down."

I shake my head.

"Sit down, Medusa. You're going to make me mad."

I stand and enjoy defying him. He rolls his eyes and shakes his head. I look down at my clothes. I'm wearing a white robe, as if I just got out of the shower.

"Did you dress me?"

"Don't worry," he says with a laugh. "I mean, I would have loved to. Your body is irresistible, when you're not a raving lunatic."

"*What do you want?*"

My headache's gone. My rage and the slithering snakes are soothing it.

"Sit," he repeats, gesturing to my chair. "You're getting ugly." He gestures at my hair.

I growl like the beast he says I am. But I slowly sit down. I brush my hand along my head, petting my thick slithery friends. Then I flash him the same infernal smirk he's flashing me.

"We need your help. I'm not here to bind you. If I wanted that, you'd already be chained. I'm also not here to question you. There's nothing I need to know that you can tell me."

"What then?" I take a deep breath and throw my hair back. I feel the wigglies receding again. "How can I *help* you?"

"When you killed that boy—"

"He was raping a girl."

"Cora told me."

"He was and you know it."

"I'm not arguing. The girl was questioned. Her story fits. You saved her. That's not the problem. Let me finish. When you changed—becoming ready for your kill—the poison from your breasts dripped on the bathroom floor. It came to the attention of the National Intelligence Center in Spain.

And from there, Imada. You're smart, Medusa, you get where I'm going with this."

"Athena heard about it."

"Indeed. And you have an eternal feud with her. So do Cora and I. All three of us hate her."

"I hate her more."

"Irrelevant. The point is that the timing of your attack is absolutely perfect for Project Orcus."

"What the hell is Project Orcus?"

"Me." He thumps his chest with a finger.

"You're so pompous," I say with a laugh.

"Medusa, your timing was perfect. You've been hiding for decades. Both you and Kore have been quiet. But as of late, over the past five years, Cora and I have been trying to lure Athena off her island near Ibiza. Recently, after a nasty business between Imada, Cora, and me, we accrued enough evidence in Dellon's old hovel to incriminate her. And now she's planning to go after you. I want to use her to trap Dellon."

Dellon is the modern name for Apollo. Minerva is the modern name for Athena. I hate them both with every fiber in my soul.

Hades frowns. At first, I don't get it. I think he's mocking me. He looks like he feels sorry for me. But the thing is, I felt my body shake when he mentioned Athena.

"I'll help you," he says. "If you help me. We need to work together."

"And if I don't?"

He taps the thick dossier on the table. "Then your first impression is correct. I will incarcerate you. Perhaps, if you are lucky, I'll simply jail you like a human. If you're unlucky, you'll awaken under the ground, in the remnants of Tartarus, shackled to Gaia near my two brothers. I might even chain you to Poseidon."

I growl at him more loudly than ever. I jump up in a rage, ready to tackle him. He doesn't flinch. He merely squints his eyes.

"Rumor is, you sick fuck," I snap, "you pinned Hermes for an eternity suffocating in his own blood!"

"Keep that as rumor."

"I'm supposed to trust you? You want to help an animal you think isn't better than Allie the alligator? I hate you. Just like Cora hates you. You're a vile beast that should go to a Christian hell."

"Yes, but that's irrelevant," he says, raising a finger. "Think of what you just said. Cora might not care for me, but we work together to fight our enemy. Minerva, Athene, is my enemy and she is most definitely your enemy. If you help me, I can keep you comfortable in your prosaic world. You can keep up the silly ruse of being a meek librarian. Cora can visit you, and you two can go copulate on campus. And I can see to it that a fresh new alligator keeps you company in the school lagoon."

"You're such a dick."

He laughs. Then he raises a finger again. "But I need help. If you treasure this life—and, frankly, I'm being snide because I don't get why—you're going to have to help me. Us. You are going to have to work for Project Orcus. Kore and I help each other. Now, as Athena's goons cross the pond, you have a chance to work with us too. The war's back. And you are going to have to take a side."

"What will you do to Athena if you catch her?"

"I have enough legal evidence to go after her the mortal way. Maybe imprison her. Dellon is the real prize. But now Athena knows where you are. She's going to come for you. If I can capture her on US soil, I might get Dellon. She'll tell me everything I need to know. She's squeamish and, I dare say, more of a coward than you." He shrugs. "You're a beast.

But you're a brave snake. If I let her go after you, she'll lead me to our real prize. Apollo. He heads Imada. Dellon leads Imada. Illuminati. The pariah of our world. Perhaps more of a monster than even you."

"But you'll let Athena go free? She was involved in killing Cora's husband, Danny, but you'll let her go after you use her to get to Dellon? Figures. That's just like Athena's own Greek justice."

"Shut up. I told you more than you need to know. We will keep in contact." He turns from my gaze and runs his hand along the stack of apparently incriminating files on me. "You will continue your day-to-day boredom. Read your books. Watch DVDs at home. But report to me. If I don't hear from you, I'll know she's come for you. That is why you must inform me of your location every night."

"So you're not freeing me, then?"

"You can continue your semblance of a life. I only need to know when you're in trouble. It won't be long. Word is she's already left her private island and is traveling to the States. You will find anything you can about Dellon and report back to me. But really, you don't have to do a thing. Athena will do everything due to her hatred for you."

"I don't have a choice," I say with a shrug.

"No, you don't." He got up. Then he gave me a fake smile. "As usual, you understand everything. Intelligent. Captivating. The consummate poisonous Siren. And now, my lovely, you're free. When you get your phone back, my number is already under contacts. The code name is *Aner*. I need not hear your voice, since we mutually hate one another, as you say. A nightly text will suffice."

6

THE ALCOVE

"THANKS FOR TALKING TO THE AUTHORITIES, GORGIANA," reads a note from my boss on my cart of books. Obviously, Orcus had his fingers in it. It makes me feel good. Really, it does. If it didn't remind me of the jerk who helped me. Well, I'm happy to have my life back. You might look at me as just a simple librarian, but I worked hard to be that. I like my ordinary life.

Anyway, an hour into my shift, that guy named Asher appears, riding up the escalator. He waves at me. Can you believe it? And it's like ten o'clock. I readjust my glasses and thumb through a calculus textbook, pretending I didn't notice him. But he keeps waving. Under his arm he's carrying a book. It's that silly mass market paperback I let him borrow.

"Finished it," he says, walking right up to me. He hands me the book. "You were right. It's awful. Don't bother reading it."

"Maybe it's just not your genre?" I say with a laugh, taking the old book in my hand.

"What are you doing tomorrow night, Gorgiana? Tomorrow's Friday. I thought we could go to the Alcove. You want to? I owe you for all your help with my research. Unless you're still working after closing?"

"You don't owe me a thing. I barely did anything."

"Are you working here after ten?"

"Yes, but I can get off early."

"Are you allowed to fraternize with students?"

"Yes," I reply with a laugh.

"Great! I'll pick you up after ten."

Wait... Uh... Well... Why not? I don't have to lay low anymore. Right?

So here I am sucking on my third bottle of beer, sitting on a stool at a table in the Alcove. Asher has gone through the usual mating rituals, having picked me up at my house in his pickup truck, opened doors for me all chivalrous-like, and sat beside me at a tall table by the bar asking me general questions about work, friends, and why I'm such a homebody. I play the part, nodding or shaking my head, acting coy as hell. Then I spew the usual lies about things like who my parents are and where I grew up. He's cute and I'm content just talking to him. Really, I am. He's underage, so I don't ask him how he's getting our beer. I keep seeing him talking to some bartender he knows behind the counter.

The Alcove is a fun place. Cora would love it. It's right off the beach and you could hear the waves if it weren't for so many tables being packed with yapping students. A large maple bar faces the outdoors and the beach. It's lovely outside and I can see the full moon. Right now, after eleven, the place is packed. There are tall wooden tables with stools everywhere, and nearly every seat is taken.

I didn't change after work. Yeah, I'm still wearing my

usual ugly thick brown sweater and spectacles. Look, I don't care if it's a date or not, I'm not about to look myself, okay? Ash can't handle that yet. Well, Ash is cute as hell. His long blond hair is perfectly combed to one side. He's wearing a nice preppy button-down and jeans. And I'm having fun talking to him.

But then, just when I'm content, everything falls apart. He waves at a group of four people to come over. If I had known there'd be company, I would have said no. I can handle a stray glance from Ash, *but five!* No way. That's problem one. Problem number two is I'm on my way to finishing my third beer and getting buzzed. I'm a lightweight when it comes to drinking and, as routine as it's become, acting out my alter ego things get muddled when I drink.

"Guys this is Gorgiana. Gorgiana, this is Keith, Ravi, and Ted. And over there is Sandra."

Sandra comes right over to me, all smiley. She touches my thick brown sweater and looks deep into my eyes. That's okay because my Fugu doesn't affect women—unless she's gay or she stares for a very long time. Sandra isn't gay. She looks right into my golden gems. Then she gazes down disapprovingly at my furry sweater and old grandma pants. She has long brown hair with blond highlights, a super cute tight red dress, and long earrings. Her face is totally made up with mascara and blush—the whole nine yards. She's got a big grin, probably because she looks pretty and I don't. The other boys are completely oblivious to me, already talking to each other about school and sports.

"Sandra," she says, reaching out. I shake her hand and gaze at the floor.

"Gorgiana," I mutter.

"Georgina?" she asks.

"No, Gorg-iana. Like—"

"Gorgeous," Ash says, smiling sweetly at me and handing Sandra a beer. "Like gorgeous, Sandra."

"What an unusual name. Is it Russian?"

I shake my head. "Greek."

"I've never heard it before. What a fascinating name."

I just nod.

Ash hands me another beer. That'd make four. I lift a hand to object, but it's too late.

"Are you in one of Ash's classes?"

I shake my head.

"What unusual eyes you have," Sandra says, leaning down to get a better look. "They're so pretty, like pure gold."

Got that right.

And that's it. She turns to her friends and ignores me. Well, it's taken her about thirty seconds to write me off as a freak. That's predictable. I suppose the oddest thing is Ash. He smiles at me even though his friends obviously don't like me. The other guys didn't even bother saying hi.

Ash stops talking to one of them midsentence and leans close to my ear, "You doing okay, Gorgi?"

I nod. I lean back and whisper, "You didn't tell me your friends would be here."

He furrows his brow for a moment. Drinks from his bottle, then says, "I hope it's okay. I wanted us all to have fun tonight."

Oh, of course. Sure... No, it's not okay! No, it isn't!

I look at the bottles neatly stacked along a mirrored wall behind the bar across the room. They look blurry. I feel like I'm leaning over the table because I'm ready to tip over.

"I see you have a white blouse under your sweater," Sandra says to me. I'm surprised she's talking to me again. "It's hot outside. Have you lived here in Florida for long?"

"Yes." Twenty-five years.

"Well, it gets hot even inside, doesn't it? Maybe you should take your sweater off."

Why you fucking bitch. But I say sweetly, "Yes, perhaps you're right." I turn from her scrutiny and leave my sweater on.

"Where'd you meet Ash?" Sandra asks. Boy, she's real persistent, isn't she?

"The library."

Sandra laughs. Then she quickly covers her mouth.

"It's her job, Sandra," says Ash, frowning at her.

"You're not a student at Sunland?" Sandra asks. "I'm surprised. You look about our age. Are you going to a community college?"

"No. I'm working at the library."

And the bitch slowly nods.

I turn to the stage across the room for a break from her scrutiny. Nobody ever pays attention to me like this. It's weird.

Up on stage, one guy is working with wires by an amplifier on the floor, and a girl is setting up a microphone near a stool. Another two guys are setting up a monitor close to the stage. I'm thinking someone's gonna do improv or something. Last time I was here, three years ago, two girls sang and played acoustic guitars.

"Why do you like the library?"

Really? The girl's still interrogating me?

"I like books."

She laughs again. Something funny? As Sandra puts up a hand, making me think she's ready to apologize to me, we hear someone tap on the microphone. Everybody in the bar turns. Walking onto the stage is a lady in a red and yellow swimsuit cover-up, a bathing suit underneath. A guy hands her the microphone and she sits down on a stool. "'Billie Jean,' Michael Jackson," she says. Then she bursts into laughter. That's accompanied by the whole bar cheering and going nuts. After hearing her slurred voice, it's quite clear she's been drinking.

"Well, Ash likes reading too," Sandra says, sitting next to me, amid the ruckus. "He's always been a good student. A bit of a nerd."

Ash rolls his eyes and drinks from his beer bottle. Then one of his other friends distracts him before he can say something to me.

I just nod to Sandra. Sandra laughs again and, fortunately for my temper and my eyes, she turns her back on me and looks back at the stage, because the music's starting.

The drunken lady up there sings her words in a jumbled, intoxicated mess. And everyone loves it. Some of the people by the stage are jumping up and down, dancing as if it's a concert.

Pretty soon we're all laughing. Even me. I might be laughing a bit too hard, because Sandra looks over with her brow furrowed. But it's funny as hell.

Tone it down, Gorge. You might be having too good a time.

Well, you know what? Screw it. Bottoms up.

Ash looks over at me and smirks. I mean, what can I say? The sloshed girl is funny as shit swaying on stage. Now she's attempting to dance. Look at that! She nearly falls into the crowd.

I swig down the rest of my beer and raise the next bottle to Ash. He raises his bottle back. I think he's happy to see my smile.

But I'm not happy, really. I'm getting worried. I... I feel too good, you know? It's like gonna make me *me*, but not really me. Do you understand?

Fuck, I don't really care if you do right now, to be honest.

The song ends. I sit there clapping, but I'm not talking to

anybody. I'm a little miffed with Ash, to be honest. I wanted to enjoy the night with him alone.

Ash hands me another beer. I didn't realize I'd finished mine. Wait, that would be...five?

Sandra walks around the table to Ash and says something close to his ear with a big grimace while glancing back at me. I'd hear it if it weren't for everyone shouting. Does she like him? I mean, she's cute.

I take my sweater off because it is a little warm (not because Sandra suggested it). I'm wearing just my white silk button-down. It's really formal. But the bitch is right, it's hot tonight. It's like eighty degrees even in this open bar.

"Why doesn't Gorgiana sing?" suggests Sandra, followed by a guffaw. A few of Ash's friends laugh too, finally noticing I exist. Ash doesn't. He loses his smile.

Sandra runs her hand along Ash's back. I don't like that. Then she laughs again and says something else into his ear while looking over at me. I really don't like her. No, I really don't.

So I look straight into her eyes and say, "Okay."

I'm completely fucked up, you know. I don't drink often. I think this is...the fourth? There's a reason for sobriety which, if things continue to go the way I didn't want them to, you'll be reminded of soon enough.

"What would you like me to sing?" I ask with a laugh.

"Hey, over here!" Sandra raises her hand. "We've got another one!"

"No, Sandra," says Asher, pulling her hand down. "Stop it. Leave her alone."

Sandra looks at me. "But she wants to, Ash. Come on. This is gonna be so much fun."

Ash looks at me, serious as hell. "You really want to, Gorgi?"

I laugh and nod. Ash shrugs.

I'm on stage. I don't know how I got here. I remember maneuvering around a bunch of bodies that kind of swirled by. I fumble my way onto a stool and almost keel over. That sends the room roaring with laughter again. Then I tap on a mic. "Justin Bieber, 'Anyone,'" I say. And I remove my thick glasses.

Everyone in the bar stops talking. No more laughter. All the eyes in the room become focused on me. And it's a bit weird. I'm serious as hell too. Of course the song is by a male, but hey, so was "Billie Jean." And I love this song. It's my favorite song in the whole world.

The music plays, so I sing.

As I sing, I'll... I'll try to pay attention to you. I have to read my lines on the screen. I mean, I know them by heart, but I still have to read a few of them, because I'm fucked up. I almost feel like my voice is coming from someone else. Let me share with you a little secret: I'm a really, really good singer. Too good. Even drunk. My eyes help, of course.

Asher's watching. Look at him. He's moved far from Sandra and folded his arms, and he's fixated on me. Sandra's staring too, looking shocked. Everyone's staring. Boys and girls. All these kids are staring at Grandma singing. They're not just hypnotized by my eyes—they're mesmerized by me.

The music gets a bit heavier, and everyone in the bar stands up and starts jumping up and down like crazy. It's as if I'm in a concert. I stand too. My voice has range and everyone loves it. Not to mention my eyes. But my gaze isn't focused on anyone except Ash—not directly at his eyes of course. I'm focused solely on my date. My night is for him because this is our evening; so is this song. But it's not just the magic of my eyes. I think, maybe, you know, I think, maybe I could like him?

He's cute. Let me win him over for you.

Well, right now, they like your voice, Medusa. Or maybe

it's your eyes because I'm standing on stage with my head held high. Yeah, Medusa's in full bloom for these kids, and they're loving it. It's your time to be in the spotlight. A moment of fame. Show the kids how it's done. Take a taste of bittersweet happiness. It'll all soon be over. Yeah. Do it. Sing it for the kids. Sing it for Asher.

But then the music stops. There's applause. And I... I feel sad. Sadder than I have in years. Tears stream down my face. No one cares. They're all cheering like crazy.

I drop the mic on the stage and run. I nearly trip down the steps into the crowd. I maneuver around a ton of bodies, who pat my shoulder and back. Some are stupidly congratulating me as I rush outside. It feels stuffy. I have to get out. And whereas before the buzz was fun, now the alcohol hinders me and makes me bump into tables, chairs, and people as I try to push my way out. I just want to leave. I don't want this. I want to go home.

I don't head back to Ash's table. I'm leaving.

I'm outside. The place is so popular that there's a long line toward the entrance now. And it's still warm, even though it's nearly midnight. I'm running back home holding only my small purse.

"Gorgiana!" cries a voice. "Gorgiana!"

I cock my head back. It's fucking Ash.

Leave me alone!

"Go away," I say, wiping my eyes.

"Wait. Where are you going?"

"Just get away from me."

"Gorgiana," he says, trailing me. We're in a parking lot beside an alleyway, away from the lights of the club. It's dark enough that my eyes pose no danger, so I spin around and face him.

"What!"

"Where are you going?" Ash asks with a laugh. "That was amazing."

I shake my head and look down. This time it's not because he can see me; it's too dark. I just don't want to look at him. "Yeah, I can sing. So what?"

"Sing? I've never heard anyone perform like that in my life."

"So?" I ask, challenging him and looking into his eyes. "So what?"

"Where are you going?"

"Home."

And I'm running again.

"Wait." He grabs my arm and I yank it back. No man touches me! *No one!* Ever! Not even a nice guy like Ash. I cover my eyes and struggle to stop them from shining green. I try to control my rage. "Let Sandra at least drive you home. We're five miles from your house."

"I can walk!"

"Gorgi," he says with a laugh. Then he puts his head in his hands. "I'm so messed up. Listen, Gorgi, I've never met anyone like you."

"No, you haven't," I reply with my back turned to him.

Then I'm moving again, now walking, and he's still stupidly following. He glimpsed my eyes of course; caught the glare of Fugu. Well, I'm a good enough singer even without my cursed eyes. But now my date had a taste of Fugu too. That's why he won't leave me alone. "I advise you to stay the fuck away from me, Asher."

"What? Why?"

He catches up to me and hands me my sweater. I left it at our table. I snatch it from him.

"Is your whole librarian thing an act?" he asks. "You weren't shy at all up there on stage."

"Oh, do you like shy girls?" I ask, finally stopping in the

dark alley. Okay, he wants to not respect my distance, I'm ready to be a bitch.

Remember, I'm drunk. Okay? Deal with it.

"What? What do you mean?" He nervously laughs. He shakes his head and looks serious again. "Gorgi, we came to have fun. I... I like being with you."

"You don't like being with me. You like that librarian. Shy, quiet Gorgiana. And, anyway, inside it seemed you like Sandra a whole lot more."

He furrows his brow. Then he shakes his head. "Sandra's my sister."

Oh... Oops.

"I like *you*, Gorgiana."

I search his face in the darkness.

I think I like you too, Ash.

I grab him. He freezes in reaction to my sudden move. He's probably shocked by my strength. I embrace him while plopping my lips onto his. Hard. I stroke the back of his hair, touch that little blond wave I adore, and then run my hand down his back. I've been wanting to do this since I met him. I press him real close. And I keep kissing his lips. Then I enter his mouth and dance with his tongue. He hardly objects.

I'm, like, totally making out with him. He doesn't move, but my eyes haven't hypnotized him. No, now he's hypnotized by my body.

I could make love to him. Should I? Even after running out on him?

I walk him backward until he runs right up against the brick wall separating us from the dark alley.

"God," he says, panting. "Who? What are you?"

"I'm the devil."

I grab his hand, pull up my shirt, and help his fingers probe under my blouse, while my tongue continues dancing with his. My tongue turns a little pointy, but it's not fully forked yet. My hair is moving too, but I haven't let the bun out. I just want to taste him. I want to enjoy him. I deserve that, don't I? For all my misery? Don't we deserve a moment of pleasure?

Pleasure him.

His hand runs over my silk bra. I always wear sexy lingerie, you know. The students can't see it. I think it's a way to rebel against my mundane library uniform. I help him slip his fingers inside the lace. I feel him touching the curves of my boobs. He runs a finger along my hard nipple. I'm really excited. I mean...he said he likes me, right?

Should I fuck him? He's certainly attractive enough. And I'm getting excited enough.

Yes. Fuck him. You deserve the pleasure.

"Why?" he asks between kisses. "Why did you pick that song?"

"What song?" I ask with a giggle between kisses. "Just shush and kiss me."

He's pinned against the brick wall. My hand runs down his pants and over the bulge of his cock. He squirms, but he can't back up. There's a brick wall behind him, after all.

I can hear the people in line around the corner. But with my hearing, particularly piqued now that I'm making out with Ash, I'd know if a stranger were approaching. We're alone.

"The song you sang?" he asks. "Why did you choose that song?"

I'm under his belt and inside his pants. I think it hurts his skin a little at first, I pressed so hard to get access. And my fingernails are getting sharp and might have chafed his skin. But I didn't want to unzip him. The zipper can break the spell. It's happened before.

As I touch his cock and give him some pleasure, my eyes shine green over his whole body.

"God, Gorgi," he groans. He hardly cares about green light at the moment. And we're back to making out. And he's back to touching my tits. "Why'd you pick that song? Huh?"

"I love that song," I whisper, rubbing his cock up and down. "I always liked it. Just like I like this. Now stop talking and kiss me."

"I liked it too. Mainly when you sang it. It was as if..." He's trying to speak, but I'm tasting him again. "Gorge, it was as if you were singing it for me."

No... I mean yes, I was. I mean, was I? I was singing it for him, wasn't I? But no, I can't. Because it will never be. So who cares?

It was as if you were singing it for me.

Shit. Ash will never be someone I can love eternally. Because I'm cursed to live a wretched life on this earth forever alone.

I should never have met him. Meeting men never ends well with me. I should have declined the date. I'm a complete idiot.

My fangs recede. My tongue thickens. My hair simmers down. My heat leaves my body. And my body shakes in the darkness.

He's quiet. I think it's because I stopped moving. His lips lightly touch mine, but we're not kissing anymore.

I lose complete control. I step back and wrap my arms around myself, crying. You already know I'm a total nutjob. Are you surprised? I'm...shit...

It was as if you were singing it for me.
I WAS! I WAS!

He has his arms around me, holding me as if I were a baby. But he's young enough to be a few cells in the life of an embryo in Medusa years.

"Shh…" he whispers.

I feel so sick. I drank too much.

I lean over. Now I'm throwing up all over the pavement.

"Are you okay?" he asks, touching my back.

No. I'm sick…but not from drinking. After I wipe my mouth with the back of my hand, I'm back to crying.

"Oh Gorgiana, what's the matter?"

Love. I'll never have it. Not from you. Not from anyone. Let's face it, I'm damned. I keep hearing that Justin Bieber song in my head. Eternal love will never be something I hold. When Athena cast a curse on a young girl in her temple, she didn't just turn her into a snake. She left a gorgon, for time immemorial, to live the rest of her days wandering this earth alone.

"Stay away from me!"

I throw him out of my arms against the brick wall. But then I reach out to him, worried that I hurt him.

"What!" he asks, shaking his head. "What the hell's the matter with you!"

I'm tucking my shirt back into my pants. Then I grab my sweater, which fell on the ground, and throw it over my arm. And then I run.

"Gorgiana!"

Go away!

What kind of fucking name is Gorgiana, anyway? Medusa never would do. Everyone knows Medusa. The name's hardly clandestine. I'm famous. I came up with Gorgiana a few hundred years ago when I felt like my Greek name, Gorgo, was too masculine. Gorgiana is a terrible name, isn't it? A terrible, terrible name. Just like terrible me.

I'm going home to do ice cream and a movie. Maybe I'll down a whole carton. And Asher and his friends can go fuck off. And…you know what? You know what? Why don't you fuck off too?

You're not invited! I'm done with everyone!

7

THE GUEST

I CAN'T GET MY FUCKING KEY IN THE FUCKING KEYHOLE OF MY fucking door. God, I'm so gone. Sorry, by the way. I didn't mean to blow you off. I'm just in a really sour mood. And I've had too many drinks. There I go missing the keyhole again. With two hands this time, slowly, I carefully line the tip of the metal key along the hole until I can slide the doohickey in. Then...let's give this a go.

I fail.

But I turn the knob. Because the door's unlocked. Did I forget to lock it? I never do that. I open the door.

What happened? My house is wrecked. I'm a rather neat person, and clothes from my bedroom are strewn across the entryway mixed with pieces of a broken vase. The light's off and everything's in shadows. My suitcase was thrown open near the door. This is a special duffel bag I have ready for emergencies—in case I have to run. I'm always ready to bolt. But the thing is, usually it's lying against the wall of my bedroom.

I walk inside looking for intruders. I lift my head and smell. There's a strong citric rosewood smell, like what

Grandma wears. It's oddly mixed with cheese and meat. I hear a growl. It's not an intruder. That's me. My anger moves my hair. It increases my senses, despite my inebriation. My incisors drop down over my lower lip. And a green glow comes from my face. I'm in pure predatory mode. I was already in a crappy mood. This really pisses me off. But there's not a sound in the house. All the lights are off, except my shiny emerald eyes.

I creep in.

Of course, by now, if Grandma's here and I'm not just smelling her lingering odor, she heard me open the front door.

My living room is worse. Some jerk turned the sofa completely over near the fireplace. Why? Why would someone do that? If you're going to ransack a house, why turn over the furniture? Why do they always do that? What a useless, shitty thing to do. Of course feathers from torn couch cushions are all over the room too. I can see the adjoining kitchen because someone left the fridge door cracked open. Ah, there's the source of the cheddar and salami smell.

As I go down the hall to the only other room in my house, I hear the sound of a match being struck. Then I see light and smoke from the recliner beside my bed. I smell a cigarette. And Grandma.

"How's my pet?"

Now, I have heard thousands of voices over the thousands of years of my existence, but there is only one that petrifies me and makes me tremble. No, it's not that sick bastard Hades. Or even Poseidon. It's a female voice.

"We're alone, Medusa. I did not bring my guards."

I catch my shadow against the wall, lit by her cigarette. I'm in total gorgon form, a complete killer monster with the snakes on my head moving wildly and hissing. But my shadow is shaking.

"You don't know how hard it's been over the decades searching for you," says the bitch. "You even evaded Hades. I sent agents from all over the world. Never would I have dreamed you were in Florida. I thought for sure you were in Europe. Before I bind you," she says, taking a big drag from her long cigarette, "tell me: why Florida?"

"I like the sun."

"You don't go out during daylight."

"It's warm at night."

"Well, liking warm climates is something the two of us have in common."

I look at her long, dark, curly hair. It's beautiful like my hair, sans the snakes. And I hear the click and clang of her numerous bracelets as she shakes the cigarette butt over my carpet. She always loved wearing too much jewelry.

She takes another drag.

What do I do? I can't fight Athena. I don't stand a chance.

"You can't run," Athena says, reading my mind. "Don't try. Even if you escape, I have twenty agents outside your silly excuse for a backyard. And twenty more up front. And they're quite aware of your eyes."

I have to distract her. Somehow...

"He knows you're here," I say.

"Who?" She takes another drag from her cigarette.

"Hades. He and Persephone know you left Spain. You might be hunting me, but they're hunting you. You won't get far, even if you capture me. They'll get you."

"I'm well aware they're after me. I don't care. The subversives underestimate me. We are far too powerful. And snatching you up is well worth the risk."

"What are you going to do to me?" I hate myself for sounding meek.

"I'd kill you, if I could," she says, leaning forward. "Oh, yes." And I see her painted face with overdone makeup. Athena likes to try to look middle aged, even though her goddess baby-face looks like that of a twenty-something-year-old, like Cora and me. And she has those same bright blue eyes, which I detested until the day Cora saved me. Athena is very beautiful. That sickens me because of how much of a vile, grotesque witch she truly is. "But you and I know..." She leans back in the recliner. "That I can't. My curse cursed me by making you live forever."

"I was raped by your uncle!"

"You never understood. Do you think he came of his own accord? You had a gift even before your change. You drew men with your mutation. You hypnotized them, even before our spell. And then you dared flaunt your looks, your hair, with hubris, more than any other mortal. Just like you did tonight at the club. You deserve your fate, Medusa. You are full of more hubris than any mortal. Few match your arrogance—few, perhaps, except Arachne. You weren't changed because Poseidon deflowered you. That was an excuse. You were transformed because you arrogantly proclaimed yourself to be prettier than Aphrodite. Better than any goddess." She takes another deep inhalation of smoke. I hate that. I don't even like it when Cora smokes weed. "If we can't bind you, we'll see about taking your power. Perhaps, if we can reverse your transformation, we can kill you afterward? Eh? We have lots of scientists who can—"

I'm running. I don't want to hear another fucking word from the bitch.

Then I freeze. The front door creaks open. I crouch, ready to attack. But then I see a trail of ten more agents wearing black behind the guy on the threshold. They're all wearing shades in the dark—they can probably barely see with the lights off. I could mutilate them all easily, only it would give Athena just enough time to snatch me from behind.

So I sprint into my living room. Then, without any hesitation, I burst through my living room window.

It doesn't feel like glass. It feels like I hit a brick wall. *It... really, really...hurts.*

After stumbling, I break out into a sprint along my neighborhood sidewalk. A student walking across the street sees me—or I should say, sees my hair. Yeah, my hair is slithering serpents.

The bitch is right on my tail. I can smell her awful grandma scent tailing me.

I make it across the block in no time. I'm running so fast more kids are staring. That's when I hear a car engine roar. Headlights approach on my left; then the car drifts across the intersection, nearly colliding with me. It's a sleek dark sports car. A woman throws the passenger door open. It's Cora! As usual, even now, she's pretty—wearing a tight black jumpsuit with her blond hair in a ponytail. Her eyes are fiery red.

"Get in."

"Cora?"

"Yeah. Hi. Get the fuck in the car."

I look over my shoulder. I shouldn't. Athena is sprinting faster than any human, about four houses down and closing in.

I'm in the car before I know it. I lower the door down. I'm thrown back against my seat. I'm panting like an animal. Saliva's dripping on my bloody, shredded sweater. My whole body's still suffering from the pain of going through the window.

I'm too worked up to speak. A few of my snakes brush against the car window and some even reach the dashboard.

Cora annoyingly brushes one of my cobras off the armrest between us.

"Calm down," Cora says, gazing through the rearview mirror.

How can I, being driven like a hundred miles an hour through my suburban neighborhood? I hate cars. Not to mention, I was nauseated from all the beer before I stepped foot in her car. Now, with the way she drives, how am I not going to hurl?

She makes it worse, sliding through another intersection, turning right. She tears her eyes from the road for a moment and looks at me.

"Hi," she says, this time with a smile.

"No bike?" I grunt.

"Somehow I just knew we'd need more room. I told you to lay low, Gorge. That performance in the club was really, really not laying low."

"You were there?"

She shakes her head.

"Put your seatbelt on," she says, glancing at her side mirror.

My snakes are back in my hair. I brush my hair back. It's wet. Blood? No, I think it's sweat. My heart is beating like crazy. I was scared, so scared. Athena terrifies me.

"Nice car," I mutter. "It's very black. Red would have gone well for you too."

"Like it? Actually, its Gabe's. I got it for him when we first met. Remember? I told you."

"The McLaren."

"I guess," she says with a laugh.

She drifts and peels through another turn. Headlights flash by on an adjoining street and merge behind us. It's another car driving like us—as if the road were a highway.

Worse, following it is a police car with red and blue lights flashing and its siren blaring.

"We have company," I say.

"No, we don't," Cora says, looking at the rearview mirror again.

She turns the wheel far left at the next intersection, throwing me against the passenger door. The wheels squeal and it feels like the car is about to roll as we turn at practically a ninety-degree angle onto an adjoining street. Then she spins the steering wheel back, the car shimmies, and I'm thrown back into my seat as we rush down a straightaway.

It doesn't take long for her to drift across yet another intersection.

"You certainly know how to drive it."

"Yeah?" she says with a laugh. "I never could pull one over on you, Gorgi, could I? I love this car."

"You can slow down," I say, looking at the side mirror. "I think we lost them."

"There are hundreds of cops all over Sunland right now, Gorgi, looking for you. That's how she found you. Believe me, it'd be my pleasure to go back and pulverize her, but now we have to move. Imada wants to capture you or make you public. Now that you're with me, they won't jail you, but they can still bring your hair out into the light, if you get what I mean."

"Where are we going?"

Cora doesn't answer. She keeps glancing at the rearview mirror. But I don't see any police chasing us anymore.

"Thank you, Cora." I lean back and sigh. "Wherever you're taking me. Thank you."

She loses her smile. "I'm so worried about you, you don't even know."

"It's quite a trip for you to come all the way down here."

"I never left."

We race onto a highway on-ramp.

Now Cora's dodging around cars as if they're obstacles. I see red and blue lights flash in my side mirror. It seems to only make Cora drive faster. I'm thrown back and forth in my seat as she swerves around cars losing the police.

Soon I see a plane take off to my right. Then we're speeding off the freeway off-ramp. Another two turns and we enter what looks like a private road.

An open fence rushes by my window. Then another turn throws me back in my seat. I see another plane taking off. This private road is in the airport.

"Cora," I say, turning to her. "I don't want to leave Florida."

It looks like we're driving on an old, abandoned runway. The speedometer reads one hundred and thirty-five and climbing. There's a small white jet parked on a runway at the end of the road. Cora presses a button on the dash. The phone rings.

"Yes, madam?" asks a dry voice.

"Hashan, we need to go."

"We're ready to take off now, madam."

"We don't have time to taxi on the runway."

"Taxiing down a runway ensures we don't collide with other planes," Hashan says.

I laugh. Cora doesn't.

"Hi, Hashan," I say.

"Is that you, Gorgiana? I haven't heard your voice in so long. So wonderful to hear you again."

"It's good to hear you too, Hashan."

"Chat later, guys," Cora snaps. "Get the plane ready for takeoff now, Hashan."

I jerk forward and hear the squeal of brakes. Then, in the beams of our headlights, a thin man in a black suit digs his cellphone from his pocket and runs up the steps into the plane. That's Hashan. Cora runs around her car and throws open the passenger door. I get out and head to the plane, but she stops me and throws her arms around me.

"Gorge, you don't know how much trouble you're in. If you don't want to end up on this evening's news, get in the plane."

"Where are we going?"

She flicks a couple of pieces of glass from my shoulder. "Toronto. It's safe there."

"What's the hurry? We left Athena long ago."

But I don't need to ask. We both turn toward the sound of sirens. By the entrance to the private road, a group of red and blue lights are approaching fast.

The jet engine rumbles. Cora grabs my hand and yanks me toward her private jet. We run up the stairs, and she closes the door behind her.

"How will we escape them?" I ask. "How will the tower permit us to take off?"

"The police in this city are being controlled by Minerva. The airport is controlled by Orcus."

"What about your car?"

"All goes well, you can have it," she says with a laugh.

"I don't drive, Cora."

"I know."

She gestures for me to sit. The minute I fall down, the plane is already moving down the runway. We're taking off.

This morning I thought I'd be back to my everyday routine. I looked forward to shelving the students' books and borrowing a new one late at night, if I had spare time to read. Then maybe cuddling up by myself to watch a movie. Now I'm watching red and blue flashing lights, through my airplane window, rushing under us. I've learned over many millennia that you never know where life takes you. At least one thing is better. I think all the excitement has absorbed most of the alcohol I drank. I shouldn't have too much of a hangover tomorrow.

A trail of police cars stops under us, but they're about two hundred feet below. I look across the plane. Cora winks.

"You've been so nice to me," I say. "Thank you, Cora."

"Not this time," she says, losing her smile. She reaches for my hand and holds it. Then she turns from me and looks out her window, serious as hell. "This is all my fault."

8

TORONTO

REMEMBER THAT THING ABOUT GETTING ALL RILED UP AND full of adrenaline and the beast inside me burning off my hangover? Yeah? Well, that was complete bullshit. My head feels like it could explode. I mean, it's not as bad as when it had a bullet hole in it, but it's still really bad.

I threw up when I woke up. But, boy, did you see the bathroom I was barfing in? Everything is gilded! *Everything.* There are wall-to-wall mirrors, marble floors, and this really cute vanity chair. And this isn't even Cora's master bathroom. It was the guest bathroom. And the guest room has a giant floor-to-ceiling window looking out on the gorgeous lake, columns built into the walls, and these huge colorful flowered vases, and, well...her house is amazing.

I slide off the most comfortable mattress in the world and grab a pair of opaque shades Cora left on the nightstand and insisted I wear around the house. I feel rested—maybe it's the bed or the tranquility of her home—even though the clock on the nightstand says only eleven-thirty. The floors are a little cold, being made of polished travertine.

I walk to the window. The view is breathtaking. I stretch.

I'm wearing a teal nightgown. I was so messed up last night, or early this morning, that I don't even remember getting into it. I didn't shower, but now I kind of want to. And my hair's a mess—more so than usual.

As you stand with me by the bright sunny window looking out at this, like, amazing vista, do you see my wigglies? Go ahead. Look. I'll run my hand along my hair. See, the snakes move a little in the sunlight. They're small, narrow, and black, but they're still there, getting all excited from the light. That's why I never go out during the day. The bright light shines on my hair, and you can see them. It doesn't look that terrifying. At least not to me. I've been told that to people around me, it just looks like my hair's moving. That's why I always have it in a bun at work. I know what you're thinking. Why not a wig? The snakes eat it (sorry, gross, but true). And they don't put up with hats. Like never.

I yawn. Then I touch the glass. Then I shake my head. Boy, this vista is incredible. In the far background, I catch a ship sailing. And a flock of birds. The clouds are just wisps of white. Far below my bare feet, through the window, I see trees everywhere.

"Excuse me?" squeaks a quiet little voice.

I whirl around and quickly move from the light of the window.

"Who are you?" a little girl asks.

This little tyke is standing by the door in a matching nightgown. Hers, like mine, is a light blueish-green silk one. She looks adorable.

"My name is Gorgiana."

"You're mommy's guest?"

Mommy? Cora?

"What's your name, sweetheart?"

"Moros."

She has bright blue eyes—brighter than any human's. It

reminds me of Cora. It's *literally* as if Cora had a child but, of course, it couldn't be. She's infertile. That's what Cora told me anyway.

"Like my doll?" Moros asks, walking to me and presenting it with extended arms. As she passes it to me, I notice her hands. There's an ever-so-slight blue tinge to her palms. The doll is old and ragged. It has a few yarns for blond hair and bright blue eyes. I take it in my hands. It's a simple thing. But for Moros, it's precious, like a relic. I get her love for that. But it looks old enough for the child to have been born with it.

"She's very pretty."

"Yeah. Mommy says we might go fishing on the lake later with Daddy," the kid says with a shrug. "You wanna come?"

"Sure." She smiles. Then Moros reaches up to touch the ends of my hair. I let her.

"Your hair moves." She giggles. "It's funny." I jerk away from her small fingers.

Oops, get away from the window, Gorgi.

Hashan walks through the door. The olive-skinned butler hasn't changed in twenty years. He's wearing the same black suit and shades as last night. But he's doing something I've rarely ever seen him do. Smiling. He reaches out his arms and I hug him.

"You saw our guest, Hashan?" asks Moros, formal and cute as hell.

"I've been so worried, Gorgiana," Hashan says quietly in my ear. "Cora made me think something terrible was happening to you."

"I'm fine." I turn to the window again. "More than fine. This is the most incredible place I've ever been in."

"Cora knows how to live. But what of you? I've heard from her that you've been in Florida all these years?"

"Hashan?" says the girl, tugging at his pants. "Hashan? Are we going to the lake today or not?"

"It's up to your dad, Moros. Or mom."

"Mom won't want to go." She stomps her bare foot on the floor. "Dad won't either. Maybe Auntie Grace? Or...maybe she can?" The girl points at me. "Can you?"

"Your dad might," Hashan answers. "We'll see."

"Is she Napean?" I ask Hashan, staring at Moros's blue palms again.

Hashan hesitates. "Make yourself at home, Gorgi. Anything you desire. Cora said the house is yours. We're here to help."

"Thanks, Hashan."

"It's so good seeing you again."

They leave and I make my way back to that amazing bathroom. I take off the nightgown, then my bra and panties, and get into this three-person shower. See, unlike at home, I don't have to stink here. (Don't be so grossed out about that. You know, I was fibbing a little. I just don't use perfume or nice smelly stuff, but I shower).

Glass surrounds me and the jets are simply blissful. I turn up the heat and just rest my body under the water. The water stings a little along my legs. I notice two cuts that haven't healed. No, my skin's healed, but there's glass embedded there. I pull it out, each one fast. It bleeds a little. It'll be all right. My skin will heal in a few minutes.

But then I think of that witch in my house again and shudder. It all comes back to me. Even her distinguished 1920s cigarette and grandma smell. I stand there under the water, lathering my body with soap, while trying to forget her. The water helps. It's like a soothing, hot waterfall.

Afterward, there are clothes for me on a chair by the bed. It's not the sort of clothing I'm used to. It's far too elegant. But I'm Cora's guest, so why not? I choose the simplest: a red poncho and sandals. Of course she, or Hashan, thought of everything. Even the sandals fit. Then I meander down the hall and down the wide stairs, trailing my fingers along the shiny gold rail. I hear little Moros giggling down the hall. And I smell eggs.

Sitting at a small table downstairs, with a laptop in front of him, is a tall man with thin, dark hair and stubble along his face. He's cute as hell—like he could fit into a fashion magazine. He gazes up from his screen and jumps up.

"Daddy, Daddy," says Moro, running in. "Did you meet Gorgiana?"

"No, I can't say I have." He puts his hand out to me and gives me a genuine smile. "Name's Gabriel. You must be Cora's close friend. Any close friend of Cora's is a close friend of mine. Call me Gabe."

"You can call me Gorgi." Out of habit, I look down. "Is Cora here?"

"She stepped out to go shopping. She'll probably be back in an hour. You probably noticed we're pretty far from the city."

"You have a stunning home." I walk over to a window. Of course it's another window facing the water. Cora loves daylight and there are windows everywhere around this place. This is not good for me. I quickly step back remembering the girl will see my hair. And wouldn't you know it, the little sneak is looking over with a big grimace.

"It's home," Gabe says with a nod.

"Can we go or not, Daddy!" cries Moros, stomping her feet.

"Go where?"

"To the lake!"

"You be a good girl and we can," says Gabe, wagging a finger. "If we go, it'll be *after* Hashan or I makes you lunch. And that's if you don't act like a spoiled princess."

"We were going to have a picnic," Moros says in a huff with her arms folded.

"I can't picnic," Gabe says. "But that doesn't mean we can't fish."

"Fish?" She smiles and runs out of the kitchen. "We can fish!"

"She's adorable," I say with a chuckle.

He nods. "Cora told me last night you live near Daytona Beach? She envies that. She really misses sunshine up here."

"I live closer to Jacksonville. It's a small beach town called Sunland. But she's got nothing to be envious of. I don't have anything like this. I work in a library at the university."

"What was she doing there for so long?"

I don't say. I'm not so sure I'm supposed to.

"Never mind," he says, turning back to his work. "As long as she wasn't having too much fun."

"She was just visiting," I say. That's sort of the truth.

"Did she bring my car back?" Gabe asks.

At first I think he's asking me, but Hashan just walked in. The butler goes over to the sink to rinse dishes by the dishwasher.

"She left your car in Orlando Airport, sir," Hashan says. Well, that's true, sort of. Surrounded by squad cars. "The car is in perfect condition," Hashan adds, pouring coffee into a cup. "We'll have it shipped back in a few days. If you are in need of it now, I can rush the delivery?"

Hashan winks at me and hands me the cup of coffee. Then he scoots a chair to the table for me to sit in.

"Funny," Gabe says, "she never mentioned you, Gorgi. Hashan lit up more than ever since you've arrived. I've never seen him so happy. There's something about you. And those shades."

"I have migraines," I lie.

He nods and turns back to his computer. "Where'd you meet Gorgi, Hashan?"

"Hollywood. Cora and Gorgiana met at a club about twenty years ago."

"Twenty years ago," he says looking up from his screen.

Fucking Hashan!

"I meant," Hashan says, coughing, "five years ago, sir."

"She has funny hair, Daddy," Moros says with a nod.

9
____

PROPHECY

CORA HAS THESE AMAZING WOODEN DECKS, ONE BESIDE THE house and another a couple of flights of stairs down. They face the lake and it's absolutely to die for. I'm standing on the lower deck, leaning over a metal rail and breathing in this rare moment where I can be outside in daylight without fear and enjoy the view. The rail is sleek and modern and sits on a long granite base. It's elegant like the white marble columns that surround her mansion...or her palace. The house reminds me of a palace. Behind me, her house is painted white with marble columns and sporadic stone statues (statues of forgotten nymph heroes, never gods or goddesses, of course; Cora hates her immortal family). Yet the walls are covered with windows. It's a weird mix of Greek and modern—like my friend.

The birds are singing, the sun's warming my face, and a breeze is running over my cheek and over my small slithery friends. And it feels like what I imagine heaven to be. Maybe this is the closest I'll ever get.

I'm wearing this white Greek dress that's sleeveless and open at the back. There's a golden brooch at the shoulder.

I've got long gold earrings. It looks like I'm all dressed up. And my hair is hanging down. (Gabe's not home this morning.) It's kind of funny that I dress like a total homebody in the library, but here at Cora's place, she wants me to look like a goddess.

You see my hair moving? Feel them? See, out here in sunlight, especially with so few clouds, they wiggle. They love it. That strange little girl Moros loves them too.

I hear footsteps gliding along the wooden deck. It's the gait of a goddess.

I cock my head and smile. Cora's walking with her arms folded. She smiles too. She's wearing the same lovely white dress with long gold earrings that she laid out for me. We look like twins, only her hair is blond. I turn back and enjoy the view, but I look forward to her company.

When she's closer, she says, "How are you holding up, Gorgi?"

I nod toward the lake. "I could stand here forever, Cora. Your grounds are stunning. Thank you."

"Gabe likes it too," she says with a nod.

"I like him," I say, smiling at her.

Cora does what I'm doing. She drapes her arms—far paler than mine—over the silver rail and looks out with me. There are two ships in the far distance. Children are playing down below us, under the trees by the shore. I can't see them, but I hear them.

"Why the white peplos?" I ask, touching her dress. "Why so...*Greek*?"

"For you," she says, turning her gaze from the lake to me. "Hashan's picking up something special from the olden days for supper. I thought we'd dress the part. Wait till you see what little Moros is wearing. It's adorable."

"I like that you and I match, Cora."

"Me too," she says with a chuckle. "We're going to have fun before we send you off."

"I love it here, but I really want to go home."

"Well, you can. Florida's safe now. Athena's on the run. But there'll be more dangers for you. You'll have to be ready to come back at a moment's notice."

"My life is simple, Cora," I say with a shrug. "There's no problem returning."

She shakes her head. "I want you to have that simple life back."

Then we're silent. Is that it? Is that what she wanted to talk about? No way. She's hiding something.

"So, what's up?"

"I'm just sorry," Cora says with a nod. "I'm sorry, Gorgiana. But I don't even know how to start to explain."

"You already apologized."

"I owe you the reason why." She turns back to the water and then, while staring out at the view, she says, "You know the murder of my husband, Danny, by Imada made me fall apart. It made me crazy—crazier than normal." She smirks. "Danny left too early. I loved him so much. But my love for him blinded me to the world. It nearly blinded me to the dangers to Gabriel. And it cost little Moros's mom's life." She takes a deep breath again. Then she shakes her head as her eyes turn red. "Of course, Hades avenged them. You heard the story. He raided a base on Crete. When he got to Apollo's hideout, he found that Imada had sacrificed Hermes by pinning him with Poseidon's trident."

"I know all this, Cora.".

"Well, Hades was given a choice. He could release the trident and chain Hermes, like he did to Zeus and Poseidon. But the risk was that access to the Underworld would be treacherous and uncertain. The other choice was he could free Hermes. But that would let him loose to attack me again. Or he could do what he did. Leave him and bury him. Leaving him was the worst choice of all. It left him choking on his own blood for an eternity."

"But Imada did that to him. It was their fault, not Hades's."

Cora shakes her head. "Hermes had turned mad. Sure. But Hades's act was beyond brutal. The thing is, Hades didn't bury Hermes for me. He did it for order."

"Hades is more of a monster than we are."

"No, that's where you're wrong." She shakes her head, spinning back to me with her red eyes. "Hades never acts out of revenge. He moves pieces on a chessboard. Imada killed Hermes. You're right. They planted the trident. They killed their own. But they knew Hades was coming and could decide whether to free him. Hades made the final decision, and it was tactical. It had nothing to do with Hermes, it had to do with Imada. See, he's not like me. My actions come from the heart." She looks back at the lake, leans on the rail, and puts her head in her hands. "That's why I apologize, Gorgi. Everything happening to you is my fault. Since Danny left, I've acted only on revenge. I ruined Hades's détente. I went to Europe and hunted our enemy, ruining any chance of maintaining peace, particularly with that goddess in Spain."

"Athena."

"Yeah." Cora nods. "See, Athena went after you to get back at me. I knew I'd gotten myself into trouble after Danny died. So I moved here. But what I didn't think about was my friends."

"I don't blame you, Cora. She's always been after me."

"Even now, you comfort me." Then she shakes her head violently. "You don't understand. Your defense of that girl at the college was protected. Orcus absolved you. You would have been free, had it not been for me. I couldn't stop Athena from hunting you after your location became known. Had the war not been declared again, she wouldn't have risked the journey here to get you. You've spent over twenty years in Sunland giving yourself a tranquil life. And I ruined it!"

"Cora, you can't—"

"I can." She raises a single finger. "Five years ago, after meeting Hades in this same spot, I got the information I needed. Then I went alone to Europe to hunt. I murdered up to fifty Imada agents in my search for information on Apollo. I was going to try to chain Apollo myself for what he had done to my husband. We got Hermes, sure, but Apollo was the leader. He wasn't innocent, as they had claimed. Well, Apollo had escaped. Again, my fault. He knew I was hunting him.

"Hades told me about Athena's private island. After a successful raid by me, her goons came here while I was still, moronically, in Spain." She runs her hands through her hair and heaves a big sigh. "Gabe had to hide Moros in a fucking closet." Cora violently shakes her head. "Can you believe that? They almost killed my little girl! If it wasn't for Hashan saving them. Hashan was injured in the raid. But far worse... the invasion messed Moros up real bad. She wasn't hurt physically, but she was only two years old, Gorge. She was back to crying every night like a baby after the attack. Even now, she still has nightmares."

"I'm sorry, Cora."

"I deserved it. I killed many people Athena loved— mortals, of course, people that she considered family. She simply returned the favor."

"Cora, they started it."

"Will you stop trying to comfort me for just a second! Don't you see how it's affecting you! It was because of my actions that Athena went after you. Unlike my family, which now has protection, you don't. You should, by all rights, hate me." She searches my face with her flashlight-red eyes as if she doesn't get me. People do that a lot—'cause they don't. "Imada is destroying your life because of me! This is my doing. That's why I didn't leave town after we met. I stayed to protect you. She came to arrest you and record your transformation. Act like you were some sort of alien creature and imprison you as a freak. Destroy your life. Not because of you. Because it would hurt me." She turns from me and puts her head in her hands again. "I'm sorry. I'm so sorry. She knew she couldn't get to me, so she went after you. Don't you get it?"

"Yes, Kore. I get it."

"Then why are you even still talking to me?"

"Because you're my friend." I put my hand on her back. She shakes her head, still in her hands. "And you're wrong. Athena would have hunted me anyway."

"Oh, Gorgiana," she says, looking up with her bright red eyes. "They should never have done what they did to you. You should hate all of my family, including me."

Then she dips her head in her hands and shakes.

Is Persephone crying? Shit. I run my hand along her back again. I cry a lot too. You know that. Look, my life was ruined thousands of years ago. I'm used to misery. But Cora? She's just confused. I mean Athena's the one who cursed me. My life was in ruins after she transformed me, until Cora saved me from my island.

"You're the only one who's ever cared about me, Cora. I'm a monster."

"You're not a monster, Medusa." She shakes her head

and takes a deep breath. "I am. I'm the greatest gorgon to have ever walked this earth. Your sin is an island full of a hundred statues. Mine is a thousand-fold worse, with the destruction of my beloved home."

"If only they knew you saved a monster from Sarpedon."

"I owe you so much more," Cora says, shaking her head. She runs her wrist across her eyes to wipe the tears. "So much more. Shit." She straightens up. "I still have to tell you something."

"There's more?" I actually chuckle. I mean, what else could be wrong?

"I can't discuss this in front of Gabe or my little girl. You can't ever tell them. Promise?"

"Sure, I promise, Cora."

"After the attack," she says with a nod, "Hashan demanded that I give my daughter a name. I was just calling her 'baby.' He wanted me to name her something. I told him, I don't care about names. I saved her and I will protect her because she's the last surviving nymph. But that was all. I'm not her mother. I mean, me? Come on.

"Well, one morning, when I was really messed up—I was back to falling apart after Imada's break-in, you see—I shouted at Hashan to name her whatever the fuck he wanted. I said, "call her Moro for all I care!" I thought no one in Canada would ever recognize the Greek name for 'baby.' Moro just sounded like a cute name. And, you know, Greek was always the closest dialect to Atlantean. So Hashan started calling her *Moros*. Gorgiana, do you recall the ancient meaning of *Moros* from your dialect in Sarpedon? Not *Moro*, *Moro* with an *s*? *Moros*?"

I think for a moment. Then I say, "Doom"?

"Doom," Cora says, slapping her leg. "That's right! Doom. Without thinking, I christened my kid the personification of destruction. And you know I hold prophecy."

"Oh, come on, that's just a coincidence."

"No," she says, shaking her head. "It isn't. How can it be? It came from my lips. I went crazy on Hashan, of course, but he's sure I said *Moros* with an *s*. After a couple weeks of not speaking to him, I believed him. It's my stupid prophecy. I paid for my sins—my binges—by uttering that awful name. See, I was fed up. I had given up and gotten drugged every night for weeks after that break-in. I couldn't take it anymore, Gorgi. I couldn't handle it that Imada was going after those I loved again. Athena knew how to upset me, and she screwed me up good. Well, when I returned sober, and Gabe and I, of course, made up—because, for some reason, he loves me, don't ask me why—I found Gabe calling her Moros every day. To me it still only means one thing: 'doom.'"

"Then why didn't you just tell Gabe to change the name?"

"I did. I did. I started calling her *Moro*. I told Hashan to use *Moro*. I even told little *Moros* that her name was Moro. Well, you met my girl. You think the kid wanted to change it? She's a little devil. She wasn't about to change it—especially when the little monster realized it upset me so much. And Gabe was never told the true translation."

"I won't tell him."

"I know you won't. My point is, we're heading into dark times, and that's my fault too. It's all terrible. And I don't want Gabe, or even that adorable little witch, to ever know about it."

"Dark times?"

"Doom," Cora says with a shrug. She throws her blond hair back and nods then drapes herself over the rail again. Her eyes become even redder. "The end of everything. I dream the same thing almost every night. I finally see my long-lost mother, Nephrea, her light-blue-tinged skin shining under the green sun, staring out to sea. At first, just seeing Nephree is pure heaven. Then I see my home. Seeing Napea, Azure Blue, and the blue-green forests and purple sands is wonderful too.

"Gabe and Moros are playing in the sand, making sand castles. Hashan does his usual sentry stuff, just standing over them. But then comes a wave—not just any wave—a wall of water, washing up and drowning everyone and everything I love."

"It's just a dream, Cora."

"I shall be the instrument of the world's destruction," she says, shaking her head.

"I don't think you're going to hurt us."

"I will," she cries, glaring at me. "I will. I already destroyed my beloved home. What makes you think I won't do it again?"

"You did what you had to do to stop Imada. You destroyed Mount Olympus."

"I murdered scores of people, Gorgi. Thousands. I destroyed the race of my mother. My true family. You were turned after the flood, Medusa. You don't know what I unleashed onto this world. The bloody gods, in the end, won. I lost more than they did. And I was left alone."

And then she has her head in her hands again, shaking. But she won't sob aloud. It's like she doesn't want me to know she's crying.

"If it happens," I say, rubbing her back again, "do you know how? Or when?"

She shakes her head.

"Your prophecies don't always come to pass."

"They always do. They're just sometimes not read accurately."

"Is Moros a nymph?"

"Of course she is," Cora says with a shrug, throwing her

hair back and standing straighter. "Gabe is related to Nephrea. Moros is his niece. Imada's managed to exterminate every remnant of Napean nymph blood, except them. Now I protect them. They are the last nymphs left in the world."

"Extermination is all Imada does, Cora."

Cora shakes her head. "I found out why Hermes killed Danny. He was sent to prick me, do something that would force me to retaliate and convince Hades to jail me. But Danny's death was a blunder. It went too far. Aside from Hermes blundering up as usual, I learned Athena and Apollo were stirring the pot again because of an ancient prophecy. I had forgotten it. It says that the world will quake once more from the rage of the grain goddess upon the birth of the first and last male nymph. Demeter and I are grain goddesses. And you've met Gabriel. I've never known a nymph to be born male. Think of his name—Gabriel, the archangel heralding revelations. I asked his mother to give him that Christian name, again without thought, when he was born. Hades knows the prophecy. This house is a fortress. Hades protects us from above, and there's a secret military base next door. A local army reports to him. And don't think Hades is watching because that motherfucker loves me."

"If you have so much protection, why worry?"

"Because it's foretold that they'll fail!" She shakes her head and says almost in a whisper, "Don't you see the stars? I'm going to destroy everything, Medusa. Doom. Destruction. And why? Gabe and Moros are all I have left. I tell you, if anyone—god, goddess, Imada, anyone—touches a hair on their heads, it's over. The end. The genocide of the Ambrosia family means the death of Nephrea. I won't let that be. Even if it means destroying this whole fucking world!"

"You won't destroy the world, Cora." I even laugh because it seems like such a ridiculous thing to say.

"I've done it before," she says, shaking her head, leaning over the rail. Then she stares over the lake with her red eyes shining like flashlights.

O-k-a-y. Well...now. Let's...go have dinner?

10

MY RELICS

I am so happy to be home. After Hashan flew me by private plane and chauffeured me back to my neighborhood, I rushed to my front door. I try the key and forget that the door's never been locked. Then I enter my home.

But joy changes to unease as I walk across the threshold. My last memory is of my archenemy lamely smoking her long cigarette in my bedroom. And seeing stuff still strewn all over the floor reminds me of her. In fact, there's still an ever-so-faint remnant of her stench. And there's another smell... it smells like something's burning.

I enter charred remnants of my living room. Well, my house wasn't completely burned down, only a section near the fireplace, charring one of my lovely brown maple walls. My house is simple, you know, but I take pride in every square inch. I'm not happy about this fire damage. I can't see how bad the damage in the room is because I can't turn the light on. The switch isn't working. It's also evening and with the drapes closed, it's super dark—except the light from my eyes. My green is glowing brighter because I'm getting angry again. And—

Oh no.

My green eyes turn moist. I hear crying.

No.

Is that you? Fuck!

I'm on my knees by the fireplace. I'm holding pieces of a charred figurine—the cold manifestation of my archenemy's cruelty. My relics. They're small, portable. Now they're lying broken, strewn all about my living room floor.

Let me...let me tell you about them.

I hold a broken, charred frame containing an image of Sir Lexington Hesley, known to me as Lex. It is now warped, full of swirling rainbow colors and an image of half a body. Part of the frame was burned off. Lex was my husband, a rarity in this eternal hell. The burned part was me. I had on a long late–nineteenth century dress. You'd never recognize me in that picture. Well, you'll never see it anymore. It's ashes.

By my knee is a black, charred slab. I recognize it from its size. It was once a lovely small wooden figurine of Aphrodite. Well, it was named Aphrodite by the artist, but he told me secretly it was really me. He was Felix, and I loved him to death somewhere around 300 AD. God, that was so long ago. I couldn't tell you the exact year. We were so in love. We... I pick up the charred carving. It's trash, barely recognizable. I... I got married to him in secret. He was one of the first men that was crazy enough to wed me.

Beside this ashen rock is a mound of ashes. From its shape, this was my conch shell, given to me by a young boy who fell in love with me a hundred years ago by the shore. Mixed with that is a small wooden statue of two cherubs in an embrace now turned to ash. Another relic survived the fire, but not Imada's wrath. A golden Claddagh ring with a crown and heart, now in two pieces. Perhaps it's worth the most since it's gold? Not priceless, but actual gold. None of this stuff is worth any money, really. But it's priceless to me.

I'm crying and crying. It's complete shit, you know. What did I do to deserve such a thing?

It's not just Cora. Cora blames herself, but I know it's that bitch's cruelty. Cora calls herself the greatest monster to walk the earth. Bullshit. Minerva is. I hate Athena so much! *I'm going to tear her to pieces!*

Thick, sticky fluid drips from my right hand as I dig my sharp nails into my palm. And as I lean down, my snakes are in full bloom, striking at the carpet. I need to, I have to, strike at something.

I've gotten careless. I always protected my relics. Perhaps worthless to some, they meant everything to me. Two decades of peace made me vulnerable. I left these things out in the open for her to destroy. My relics were always small and easy to carry. But now, *they're gone!*

Stop crying, Gorgiana. You're being a crybaby.

But they're all gone!

There's a knock. My head snaps toward the front door. Normally, I would have smelled the approach of this human, but I'm too upset. Of course I can't show myself. I'm so riled up I'm in full snake mode. My vipers are practically jumping off my head. And my tongue is running over sharp fangs. There's another knock. If Orcus hadn't taped and boarded the living room window, the intruder could just walk in.

I rush by a crack in the wall. It's Ash! And I think he saw my shadow.

Shit!

"Gorgiana?"

"Just a minute."

I run to the bathroom and turn on the light switch. The switch works! It's the only light in the place that works. See me in the mirror? I'm crouched over. My hair's undulating so violently it looks as if it's going to slither away. My face is wrinkled like a prune. My eyes are a bright, shining unnatural green. My fangs are showing. My fingernails are sharp as knives, and my palms are bleeding. I mean, I could scare the shit out of Frankenstein.

Calm down. Just calm down, Gorgi.

But it's all gone! It's all fucking gone!

There's a knock again. This guy sure is tenacious.

"Gorgi, I have to talk to you."

I thought it was over after I shoved you against a brick wall?

"I can't right now," I holler. "Sorry."

There's silence. I hear my heart thumping in my chest. Or is that his? I get confused when I'm in predator mode.

Is he gone? It's quiet. He must have left.

I sigh, walk out of the bathroom, and head back to my bedroom. Who knows how many relics she found in my closet—

"Your door was unlocked and—"

Oh, shit!

He's standing by the front door.

"Are you barging in?" I cry with far more venom than intended. A green light flashes in the room, before I cover my eyes. He doesn't see my form in the shadows. I'm guessing it's too dark. Yes, it must be. He hasn't bolted yet.

"Gorgiana," he says, standing by the threshold, "I came to apologize. I invited you to the Alcove for fun. All it did was upset you."

Apologize? To me?

"It wasn't your fault," I say.

"It was," he says, walking forward. "Or maybe—"

"Don't step any closer."

"Why?" he asks with a chuckle.

"I'm not decent... I...haven't combed my hair." He walks closer. "I mean it, Ash!"

"Okay. You—" He looks at the fireplace. There's just enough light from the bathroom to illuminate the charred wall. "What the hell happened here? It looks like there was a fire."

"Nothing. Just a break-in. Can you just go?"

"Sure," he says, putting a hand up. "I guess. Sorry. I just wanted to apologize. And... I wanted to give you this." He reaches into his pants pocket and takes out something metallic. For a moment, it reflects green. I quickly avert my eyes. "It's a little keepsake from my grandmother. Or great-grandmother. I thought you'd like it."

He turns the object in his palm, and it shines silver in the bathroom light. It's metal and looks sharp, but too tiny to be a knife. He hesitates. He slowly walks forward. I touch my hair. It's behaving. And he's not lit green.

I let him get closer.

He's a little taken aback by my appearance as he steps closer. Being that my wigglies are all in check on my head, I don't know what's wrong. But then I realize my hair is still probably a complete mess. He lays the silver thing on my palm. It must be too dark for him to see all the cuts and blood on my right hand. The object isn't green anymore—it's silver. It's a silver cross.

"It's a—"

"Bookmark," I interrupt him.

"I should have guessed you'd know. It's been passed through generation after generation in my family. My grandmother gave it to me last year when I started here at Sundale. I thought after what happened, and having to weather the scrutiny of my sister—"

"She's not that bad."

"Don't lie. Well, you get used to her. Anyway, I didn't tell you my friends would be there. It seemed you didn't like that." He looks down in the shadows. He shakes his head as if debating whether to continue. "I guess, I didn't respect you. I think it's the way you act. You act...simple. I mean, not simple. Modest. Not stuck up, you know? I thought you just wouldn't care. But, I mean..." He looks up at me. And I love that I can look at him too, because it's dark. "That's silly, because you're the most beautiful girl I've ever seen. My sister said so too. And you're so cool, I mean, man, you're an incredible singer. You deserve all the respect in the world. When you got up on stage, you were amazing."

"Thanks."

"I loved it."

He gets quiet. I'm feeling his cold keepsake in my hand. I'm running my fingers along it. And I want to cry. If I wasn't sure he'd run, thinking I'm a full-on nutso, I'd do that. I'd cry. But, God, this gift in my hand is so sweet! In my deepest doldrums, it's probably the only thing that anyone could have given me to pull me up. Because it's another relic!

My heart's beating fast, not in rage or a desire for revenge, but for Ash.

"Thank you, Asher. It's really nice."

"Really? Oh, good." He heaves a big sigh. "I didn't know how you'd take it. I think it's real silver. It's meant a lot in my family. I was hoping it'd mean something to my favorite librarian. I think it's valuable because of its age. But I hope you don't think it's dumb."

"I love it, Asher. I absolutely love it."

"I'm so glad," he says with another sigh. He puts his hands in his pockets and looks around the house. "Man...so, what happened? And why don't you have your lights on?"

"The electricity got damaged in the fire."

"Oh." He nods, looking around the dark room. Then he walks to the door. "I should go. I kept stopping by. Glad you were finally here. And I'm so happy I brought you something that—"

I grab his wrist and tug him close. Then I gather him up tightly and kiss him on the lips. Our tongues dance and, in the darkness of my home, I hold him so tight. At first, he just exhales in surprise. It's probably another oddball, freaky thing for me to do. Yeah. But my heart is raging. I... I'm trying to keep my hair in check too. But unlike at the club, I'm not drunk and I know them wigglies are getting jumpy with my arousal. Attraction makes them excited too.

I slowly pull away. But I don't want to.

"Oookay," he says with a laugh. "That was weird and unexpected. You're the strangest girl I've ever met. Guess you like my gift?"

"Aha." I laugh and nod.

"Can I," he says with a cough. "I mean, can we meet again? Soon?"

"Of course."

"How about in a few days. I'd ask for Saturday, but I'm helping my roommate move something in Orlando. I was thinking Sunday? You don't work in the library on the weekend, right?"

"Sometimes I do, particularly during finals, but they're over. Aren't you going home for the summer?"

"No. I'm rooming with a friend. I'm actually about a block from here. We're renting a house and I'm staying on campus. I'm taking a couple summer classes too."

"So we're neighbors?"

"Yeah." He chuckles.

I stare into his eyes. I can't determine the color, but I can see the contour. And because I can't see the color, I know I'm safe for him. It's my gold or, good heavens, green eyes that drop men into a trance. And then I realize that, although we're not kissing, he's still holding my hand and rubbing the fingers of my left hand (luckily not my cut-up right one).

He looks to the side for a moment. Then he says, "How about a movie? You like movies, Gorgi?"

"I love movies."

"I'll pick you up at six on Sunday. We'll catch whatever you want. Okay?"

I nod.

Then he's gone.

I'm holding his gift in my bloody hand. I walk to the only light working in my home—the light in the bathroom—and I gaze at the shiny thing. I take some wet tissue paper and clean off my blood. There's not too much. My hand is already healing. The polished silver of God's cross shines over my cut-up palm. Then I look at myself in the mirror. Frankenstein wouldn't be scared now. I look like a normal human girl. Don't I? A very beautiful girl, right, Medusa? But my hair's a mess. I hold the cross to my chest. I shall cherish this forever. See, it's one of the rarest of rare things in my miserable life when I receive a relic. It doesn't matter what it is. It doesn't matter how much it's worth. They're priceless. And I always recognize them the moment they're handed to me. And best of all, this relic is silver. Metal and jewelry usually survive fires, you know.

11

THE GUARDIAN

I can't sleep. I keep thinking of Ash. Sorry. You didn't know that the famed terrible, fearsome Medusa is a romantic, did you? Well, I know a good man when I see one. I've been around. But the problem is that when I get hooked, I really get hooked. I like fall in complete, stupid love, and the crush overwhelms me. I like Asher. I really do. That's why I got up early in the afternoon and acted weird, like a normal girl, applying makeup and trying on a dozen or so blouses and pants to see what he'd like to see me in. Something not too fancy but not too boring. Pretty, but not too pretty. How do I entice a man but keep everybody else's eyes off me? Sounds pompous, I know—but, look, I'm Medusa. Sexy but not slutty. Well, I don't want this boy in bed. I want him in my arms. Or holding me while watching a midnight movie with a bag of popcorn. You know, love. And he's a good enough man to give me that. I just know it.

Isn't he? Remember his smile. His perfect white teeth and that extra wave of golden blond hair.

I'm applying a different stick of lipstick and humming.

I'm in such a good mood. Doesn't life work in funny ways? My life was almost over and now this. It's so rare that I meet a man that doesn't run away thinking I'm a freak. Because I am.

This lipstick is black. See? No, that's too weird, isn't it, Medusa? I'll give him red. That's sexy.

Giggles.

Maybe I'll even risk perfume. It will be dark in the movie theater. Right?

No! Medusa. You crazy?

Fine.

I'm carrying his silver cross in my pants pocket. When I fix the fireplace mantle, I'll put it up there. For now, I like running my fingers over the cold, sharp metal. I take it out and lay it on the sink to look at as I continue to make myself pretty.

I look down at my black blouse. It has lace around the arms. I brush back my hair, and a stray snake waves by my forehead.

"Now you behave, little wiggly," I say, pointing at my hair. "Behave. I really like this guy. Don't scare him."

I tuck it back in my curls and giggle. Am I grossing you out? Nah, I already enchanted you a long time ago.

The shirt looks hot and sexy. *Too* hot and sexy. That and, after a spritz of perfume... I want him to feel the way I felt when he handed me my new relic.

I open a perfume bottle. It smells real bad. Oh well, forget perfume. And, hmm, this shirt looks a bit too vampiress-esque.

"Ugh!" I pull off another blouse in a huff and walk back to my dresser. I have to find something better.

I grab a navy-blue blouse from my dresser. It will go well with my long black hair. Of course, just in case, the hair will have to be tied in a bun for my little wigglies. Or perhaps a ponytail? I suppose I can wear my bushy grandma sweater over any shirt I wear. And then I'm thinking, why does it matter what I wear under the sweater? He's not going to see it. Unless it gets hot in the movie theater. It could? No, it never gets hot in movie theaters. They seem to run air-conditioning even during the winter. Hot in movie theaters—wait, what were you thinking?

Giggles.

He takes me in his yellow jalopy. He tells me he loves the truck because he can fit his surfboard in the back. He asked me if I surf. Uh... Yeah. Right. Actually, I have, sort of, before it was called "surfing." But no. No, I haven't.

The movie theater is not too crowded. Even though Sundale is a beach town, the theater is practically inside the university, and everybody's heading out for the summer. Fewer people helps me relax.

"You want popcorn, Gorgi?"

Of course I do.

Before I know it, I'm sitting beside him in the front and center of the theater. We have an aisle all to ourselves. The movie I chose is titled *Magnus*. It's a total guy film that I know he's going to love, because it's got lots of sword fighting and killing. It's about the emperor Charlemagne. But it also has a love story about his wife. The thing is, I knew Charles the Great. He was a total womanizer. Of course he even courted me for a while until I showed him my wigglies. I mean, he had ten wives! I've had more husbands than that, but not during the same decade!

Ash is already into the movie. He's leaning forward. I can

tell it's going to be good. It started right off the bat with fire and dueling.

Let me tell you something funny. You know the last time I saw a vampire movie in a movie theater? It was Francis Ford Coppola's *Dracula*. Well, there's this memorable scene in the movie where Dracula is watching Superman fly off into the sunset on a movie screen. It's touching to Dracula because he can't go outside in daytime. It's a real short clip, but that scene meant the world to me. And guess what I did? Yep, I bawled my eyes out. I cried and cried during that scene like a baby because I can't go outside in daytime either —just like good ole Dracula. So there I was laughing and crying at the irony, and the whole theater thought I was a complete loon. You get all the twisted connections in my head? They're not just snakes. I lost complete control of myself in the dark theater laugh-crying. Movies can really touch you in weird ways like that. I have to make sure I don't do something stupid like that tonight.

Ash slowly takes my hand. I *love* that. Meanwhile his other hand keeps rummaging through the popcorn box. He moved real slowly to touch me, which is cute as hell. I run my fingers along his to tell him I like it. The cuts from my temper tantrum that night have, of course, completely disappeared.

He reaches over and whispers, "Liking it so far, Gorgi?"

"Aha," I reply.

Who cares? But I nod and lean over to whisper, "Yeah," and I peck him on the cheek. He squeezes my hand more tightly.

The first girl comes on the screen. She's wearing this heavy draping violet dress that looks totally uncomfortable and impossible to walk in. It's about twenty minutes into the movie. I laugh. Oops. I don't know what the hell she's wearing, but it ain't ninth century, I can tell you that. I think it's stuff like this that makes me enjoy Persephone's company so much.

Ash looks over but then turns back to the screen. He's still holding my hand. It's getting a little sweaty. I totally love that too.

That's when I feel my wigglies get jumpy. And it's not from my attraction to Ash. The snakes on my head are still caged in my bun, but they're getting pissed off over something. Danger? Beyond the scent of buttered popcorn, do you smell it? Yep, I smell it too.

Four guys wearing dark suits walk down the aisle to my left. They go close to the screen and just stand there. But the weirdest thing isn't their pitch-black suits. It's their glasses. They're wearing sunglasses in the dark. And they're staring right in our direction. I'm trying to enjoy this epic movie, and they're staring at us. They could be part of Project Orcus, or they could be Imada. I don't know. All I know is that their shades are obviously to protect them from my glare.

I let go of my now-wet palm and lean over to Ash. "I have to use the girls' room. I'll be right back."

He nods.

I walk up the aisle and feel their footsteps behind me. My incisors are tingling. So are my fingernails.

Civilization has made things different these days. Long ago, I'd turn around, jump them, hurl their bodies against the wall, then question them later. If they were there to harm me, I'd tear them to shreds and spew their body parts all over the theater. Things are more civilized now.

I walk gingerly, acting like I don't know four guys in black suits wearing shades are trailing me. Will they go into the ladies' bathroom? Probably.

I cock my head over my shoulder. All four of them quickly turn. What's the matter? Don't trust your sunglasses, boys?

I walk into the bathroom and turn to the mirror. Then, as I pretend to fix my bun, I pull out my phone and text my guardian angel—that asshole Orcus I can't stand. I message the contact "Aner." *Aner*, by the way, means *man* in ancient Greek. Yeah, Hades is a man. Everything bad about one.

I type:

Are your goons following me? Or is this the trouble you wanted me to report?

Then I wait. I touch my hair again. My vipers are pushing and pulling, hurting my scalp.

A human walks in, but it's a dark-skinned girl. She's got on a skirt and looks like she's probably a student on a date too. She washes her hands beside me and smiles. Then she looks at my eyes. I can mesmerize women, but the effect is far weaker—unless they're gay.

"You have beautiful eyes," she comments.

"Thank you." Got that right.

She nods and exits through the door.

The goons don't come in yet.

Finally, I feel a vibration from my phone and read the following text:

Those aren't ours, Medusa. I'm sending backup.

· · ·

I shove the phone back in my pocket, roll my eyes, and lean over the sink with my head in my hands. My hair is getting restless. I squeeze my hand, careful not to squeeze too hard and cut myself with my fingernails, because I yearn for that boy's touch again. Cut-up hands will ruin the mood tonight, right?

Wait. Who am I kidding? I have an army of Imada waiting for me outside the door. Movie's over.

Gorgi! What about Ash! Shit, what about Ash! Wake the hell up. Why would you leave him alone in the theater? He needs protection.

I throw the door open. They're gone. But I still smell them. They've run back into our movie theater.

I rush faster than human speed. A little girl nearly drops her box of popcorn seeing how fast I'm moving. I throw open the door and half the people in the theater turn.

But nothing's wrong. Ash is still sitting, alone now, at the front of the theater munching on popcorn and watching the movie. I sit back down beside him. My heart is thumping. My body is shaking. I'm struggling to keep calm.

"You okay?" he asks.

"Yeah. Fine."

He offers me the popcorn box. I shake my head.

Where are they? It's dark but not too dark for my predator eyes. But I don't see them. There are too many people behind us in the theater mixing with the smell. All I have to do is look for freaks with sunglasses.

What do I do?

My gaze turns green, and I quickly cover my eyes. That's okay. I can still see the whole theater with my eyes closed. I can smell it.

I'm not worried about me. I'm worried about Ash. All it will take is one bullet hitting his head and he's gone.

Are you crazy? Don't think of stuff like that!

He reaches for my hand again. Fuck, I so want it, but I can't let go of my eyes. But that makes him suspicious, and I sense him turning toward me. I quickly use only one hand to cover my eyes and hold his hand with my other.

"Are you okay?" he whispers again.

"Sure. Yeah. Fine."

"What's wrong with your eyes?"

"Nothing. Sometimes they get dry."

What would Cora do? She'd probably stand up in the theater and shout at the cowards to show themselves. Then she'd tear them apart. I can't do that. I sense Ash looking at me funny.

"The movie's good," I say quietly in his ear, squeezing his hand. I peck his cheek again. But I don't move my hand from my eyes. And my lips quiver a little.

He nods and leans closer to my side. That's so cute.

I hear a gun cock. A few people in the theater stir.

That's it.

"We have to go, Ash."

"What?"

"We have to go," I hiss.

"All right," he says.

Wait a minute. They're cocking a gun? Why the hell would they do that?

They want to scare you. They want to get you out of the theater.

Check. I'm scared. All it takes is one of these goons to fire a hole through my date's chest.

Stop thinking of that!

Ash is standing up. That's worse because now he's a sitting duck. I grab his hand and yank him outside. Then I feel them. They're following us. Of course it's a trap. They want me outside. But I don't have a choice. I've gotta try to protect Ash.

Where's my backup anyway? The bastard's text came a few minutes ago. Doesn't Orcus have the CIA, NSA, or whatever the hell he uses, crawling around Sundale?

"What's the matter?" Ash snaps.

I ignore him. I'm holding his hand and rushing him out the theater exit.

But he turns me around hard near the exit. "What's wrong, Gorgi!"

"Look, I'm sorry, Ash, we have to—"

Ash's eyes open wide. He freezes. But it's not from my gaze. He cocks his head back and sees three agents wearing shades behind him. Now, Ash is a strong guy, but he doesn't dare struggle. He puts his hands up. That's when I notice the guy behind Ash is holding a revolver against his back.

They have no problem walking in the direction we are heading. The sliding doors open, and we exit into the dark parking lot.

"Follow us or I'll shoot him."

I could turn my snakes on them. They could swing around and choke them to death. But he's endangering my date. They obviously know who I am. They don't even bother pointing the gun at my back.

"Don't hurt him," I say. "I warn you."

Ash glances at me. The look kills me. It's a weird mix of confusion and rage. I feel horrible. This is the kind of thing that happens to me, and it's why it's so rare for me to find a man. Everything is over between us.

Are you an idiot! Who cares. Protect him!

One move. It would take one false move for me to shove them away from Ash and tear them apart. I'm watching and waiting. But these guys are good. They're professionals and aren't giving me a chance.

"Come slow and we won't shoot," says the dickhead behind me.

"You shoot," I grunt, "and you won't live long."

"We know. We need to talk to you. That's all."

"Just leave him alone. I'll tell you anything you want."

"What's going on?" asks Ash.

Three other goons in black arrive and march with us to the back of the theater parking lot. One talks through a walkie-talkie device by his shoulder. They're all, strangely, wearing shades. Ash probably thinks they're hunting aliens, or something. I suppose...in a weird way, they are.

"Why does he have to go with me?" I ask.

"Because you won't follow us otherwise."

Professionals, I told you. Imada.

They take us to this sleek pitch-black semi-truck that looks like a spaceship parked in a secluded space in the back of the parking lot. I don't know what their intentions are, but I know they're not good. As one of them lifts the back door of the truck, a bright white line shines from inside the cabin and makes me squint as the door opens wide. There's a pile of industrial steel chains in the center of the truck. And the truck has super-thick walls, far thicker than usual. Now I get it. They mean to chain and transport me.

One of the goons stands in front of the truck entrance. "If you want me not to shoot him, you'll go inside. Get in or he dies. What will it be?"

Where the hell is my "backup"!

"I'll go if you swear to not hurt him," I say.

"That's the deal. Get in. Then he goes free."

"What are you guys talking about!" cries poor Ash.

I can't turn. They've got two men by my sides and if I turn, he'll see the green coming from my eyes. Maybe he has already? Well, I don't want to turn. I couldn't bear his expression.

I turn. His mouth drops and he stiffens. He freezes. See, he sees *my* shiny green eyes straight on. Can you believe it?

I'm so agitated that I don't hide my gaze. I can't even fucking say goodbye to my date!

They walk me up a ramp and inside the truck.

"How do I know you guys won't hurt him?" I ask again.

"We'll chain you while he's outside. When you're secure, we'll let him go."

"How do I know you'll let him go?"

"Do you really have a choice, Medusa?"

No.

They still have the barrel of a gun pointed to his back, but he's petrified. He's deep in a trance because of me. Perhaps that's best. As they bind me in like a thousand heavy chains, he just stands there with a vacant stare. Of course I continue to look right into his eyes to keep him asleep. Honestly, I think I do it more for me than for him. I don't want him to be aware of any of this.

The assholes hurt my wrists and ankles. They're not gentle. It doesn't bother me. I'm shaking out of fear for Ash. I just know they'll hurt him. Imada is heartless. It'll be their pleasure to shoot him anyway.

Another chain runs over my stomach. Then another over my chest. I'm brought to my knees. I don't let the snakes come out. No. Not while Ash is watching. I could resist, perhaps kill one of the creeps with a viper or two. But I won't. I can't let my new friend see who I really am. I do everything I can, with all my will, to avoid letting him see my snakes.

More chains run along my neck. I'm pinned in the center of the truck.

When they secure all the chains to the inside of the truck bed, one of the guys standing beside me looks at Ash.

"Just let him go," I say, almost in a whimper. "Please."

"Let him go," the guy says.

A few of them jump out of the truck. Two stay inside as

sentries. Then the door closes. The white light turns off and is replaced by a dim red light.

I lose it and cry. I don't care that two guards are still there. It's over now between Asher and me. If he lives—and God willing he does—he'll never see me again. So I cry, and cry, and cry. Have you figured it out yet? Behind all my wigglies, Medusa is just a crybaby.

12

THE SNAKE HOLE

T HE TRUCK STOPS AND I SQUINT AS THE RED LIGHT INSIDE THE truck returns to bright white. We've been driving forever. My knees are throbbing. I don't have a watch but if I had to guess, I'd figure it has been a couple of hours. The door is slid open, and over twenty guards in black with shades walk in. This should be interesting. It's one thing to trick me into getting into the truck, but now, how are they going to keep me from attacking while unlocking my chains?

Easy. They don't undo my restraints. Each guard grabs a thick chain. One guy in the center signals for them to lift me.

"Hey! Take it easy." I try to get the leader's attention, but he turns around and ignores me. "There's a lady behind these chains," I add. They all have their backs turned to me. "*Yoohoo.* I said easy, fuckers."

They were probably told to not say anything to me. I have a slick tongue too, you know.

Now I'm being dragged by these restraints down a very dark corridor. It pulls at my joints and hurts a lot.

This bald bitch in a black T-shirt and pants walks up to me. Her pants are tapered, stopping at large black leather boots. If she had hair, it'd be blond because her eyebrows are blond. Then she might have been attractive. But the bald head doesn't look good on her. It's more of a buzz cut, really. And she's got these black tattoos on the side of her neck. Many of the tattoos are swastikas. She smirks in my face.

"Medusa. He's expecting you." She signals to the guards. "Drag her to him."

They drag me, but then the bitch claps.

They stop. She walks up to me and stares right into my eyes. She examines my face.

"Fascinating. Your eyes don't bother me. But they're green. Why does it only work on males? Why should your power matter depending on the gender?"

One of the snakes in my hair snaps at her eye. It stops about an inch from her eyeball and would have pulled it out if she hadn't moved. Damn. Just a little closer and I would have sucked her eyeball out.

"Why don't you come closer and you can study it some more?"

"Punish it for that," she orders.

They yank the chains so hard that I'm thrown to the floor. My right wrist was pulled so hard that, I think, if I were mortal it would have snapped off. And my head feels like it's going to snap off too. I struggle to breathe. Then I scream in pain.

"Do it again," she says with a smile, looking down at me. "Explain to it who its master is."

Again, they throw me against the ground. Some of them pull my restraints by leaning all their weight against me. I scream again.

"Strike at me like that again," the Nazi bitch says, leaning down and wagging a finger, "I'll have them pull your arms from their sockets."

"*Fuck you!*" I shriek loudly enough for her to cover her ears in pain.

"Do it again," she orders.

Bang. I strike the floor and am pulled in all different directions. My body feels like a marionette directed by a schizophrenic serial killer. Sweat's dripping from my face. I don't say another word. I... I've been tortured over the centuries enough to know when to shut my mouth.

"Do it again," she says. "Make sure it remembers."

Shit!

I'm pulled again in all directions and dragged across the floor. A few more screams and...that bitch is laughing at me. Can you believe her? Some of the guards spit on me. Others kick. "Stand the beast up. Yank it up! Go ahead." They throw me into a standing position and the movement makes me shriek in pain again. "Another word, Medusa?"

"No," I say, panting.

"That's a word," she says. "Do it again."

Fuck!

They're all laughing now. They think my misery is sooo funny.

"Okay, that's enough," Nazi-cunt-bitch says, laughing. "Drag the thing to him. But don't be gentle. Teach it submission."

They drag and slide me along the floor through a few corridors, making sure to have me collide into walls. Then we enter this really creepy large hallway. I feel sick from the pain as I'm pulled mercilessly along the stone floor. A few snakes curled against the walls scatter as I collide a couple of times with a wall. These snakes aren't from my head. I smell the little lovelies all over the hallways. These chambers are full of snakes.

I'm dragged into a huge chamber. Torches are lit on marble pedestals leading to a central dais at the far end. The torchlight flickers brightly around the dais, but the place is dark enough to feel as if it's a cave. And it smells musty and earthy.

"Remove its chains," says a male voice, echoing in the chamber. As all the leftover guards remove my chains—it takes some time, there are a lot of them—I see a figure on the dais. The man wears a white suit without a shirt. He has thin blond hair. He's pale but his muscles are rippled inside the sports jacket.

My eyes are shining green with pain. As I gaze at the dais, my emerald light shines back at me. I notice that the walls closer to his chair are reflective, like mirrors.

"Bring the creature to me, but stand back." Only my wrists are still shackled. He quickly adds, "Don't think of resisting, Medusa. You're close enough now that I can stop you myself."

"Who are you?" I ask. He says nothing. So I move closer to the reflection of my own emerald glow. My legs are burning in pain, but they're free of chains. "Orcus will find me. Whatever you intend, he'll track you, bind you, and kill all your followers."

"Was she tracked, Mavis?" he asks one of the guards behind me. I glance back and all the goons are staying by the entrance. I get that they're avoiding my green glow.

"No. We smashed her cellphone after we bound her in the truck, sire."

"You're not going anywhere," the man on the raised chair says. "And, if you didn't notice, you went blind. Orcus has no idea where you are."

"But you're hiding," I say, squinting my green eyes, trying to make the man out. My own glare is making it hard to see him. He's wearing shades. "It's just a matter of time before Orcus captures you."

"Care for déjeuner?" he asks.

"Déjeuner?"

"Something to eat. Your last meal." And he laughs.

God, my arms and legs ache so much from those chains.

"I know what a déjeuner is. I mean, what the hell are you talking about? And what monster are you? Satan?"

He laughs again. I don't think it's very funny.

"You always had a good sense of humor, Medusa."

The familiarity of those words sends memories stirring, and his voice just changed. He seems to have shifted from a Spanish accent to Greek. Ancient Greek. His thin blond hair and giant musculature make him like a pale version of Hades.

"Apollo?" I ask.

"An old name," the man says. "Primeval. I haven't used that in over a century. Call me Dellon."

"You didn't sound like Apollo."

"Come. Come closer and you'll recognize me. Guards, as she moves closer, her cursed eyes brighten my walls. Leave us."

The guards behind me close the door as they leave. Apollo gestures to a wooden table below him, "I've prepared cheese, wine, bread, olives." His accent is definitely Greek. Was the former disguised? "Your journey took all night. It's breakfast now. Here is food fit for a goddess. All the food you once loved on your island of Sarpedon lies before you, beast. Figs and meat. Enjoy your last civilized meal, Medusa. It's a feast. But it shall be your last."

That doesn't sound good.

"My name is Gorgiana."

"You should have no name at all."

My eyes glow greener from that and turn the whole cave green, even the back of the chamber. Then I feel the wigglies enlarge and move about my head. My fangs come out too.

But that feels stupid. It's almost as if it happened on cue when he said those words, merely proving his point.

He steps down the two marble steps from his dais and stoops over the table, grabbing a fig. The table is low to the ground in the tradition of my homeland. Way back then, we didn't sit on chairs. He pours some wine in a glass. But he's not pouring it for me. He drinks the glass of red wine himself.

"Go on. Eat. Enjoy."

"What are you going to do to me?"

"What should I do?"

"Set me free."

He drinks some of the wine and then wags a finger with a laugh. There's his sadistic sense of humor again. "No." He shakes his head. "No. You know, your allies should be your enemies, Medusa. You should, rightfully, follow Imada. We provide world order and justice. Those you follow run nations, we run the world."

"I don't follow anyone."

"You answer to Cora."

"Cora saved me from my island. I owe her my life. Ever since I was cursed, she's treated me—"

"As her pet?"

"*I'm not her pet!*" And I growl at him, like a lion.

Idiotic, Medusa. Calm down. You're proving his point again.

But why do people keep fucking saying that!

"You are her pet. You're not a woman. You're certainly not a lady. You're more like a dog." He lowers his head and rubs his eyes. "Even now, your cursed eyes affect even me. You are a murdering ophis, created by my own hand to torture and mock my power. Now you shall entertain me, dog. Sit. Sit on the ground and entertain. Drink. Eat if you're hungry. I feed you. Go ahead and eat while we talk."

"Go fuck yourself."

He walks up the two steps of his dais and sits back down. Then he sips wine. He gestures to the food on the ground.

I walk over to the table and spit on it. A nice thick loogie. Then I kick some of the food off the trays.

"*Kyon*," he says, rolling his eyes. *Kyon* is the ancient Greek name for dog.

"Before I do to you what he did to my father and brother," he replies, "I thought I'd be kind enough to tell you why I'm doing it. It is not revenge. Certainly, your fate will be hard on your master, Persephone. But it is not being done out of revenge for what Hades did to my poor little brother. Imada believes Hermes deserved what was dealt to him."

"Because you did it," I blurt out. "Then you ran. Hades simply walked out and didn't release him. It was you and, probably, Athena who gave that horrid sentence."

"No." Dellon raises a finger. "It was Athena." Then he stupidly puts a finger over his lips. "Your holy goddess and benefactor."

I growl again. I hate Apollo, but I hate Athena far more. Normally I'd be shaking before him, but the sharp pains I keep feeling remind me of what he and his guards did to me. I'm spurred on, wanting to charge him.

I hesitate.

Then I just do it. I rush forward. Behind his shades, his eyes flicker from blue to red and make me pause. I break the metal chains from my wrists before him and growl loudly enough to make him turn from my thunderous voice. He squints his red eyes. Then...I charge him anyway.

I'm hit. My hair snaps at him without my control, but my wigglies come right back, touching my cheeks and licking the pain from my face. I find myself hurled twenty feet by a single strike of the back of his hand.

"I am a god!" Apollo cries. "You disrespectful bitch! By all right, you'd be struck down by lightning if my father still reigned! You attack me? God of the sun? This is why you were cursed in the first place. You presided in my sister's temple telling everyone how much more beautiful you were than the gods."

"That's a lie!" I say, gripping my face on the ground. "I never said that! Athena lied out of her own jealousy!" He struck me so hard that there's a cut in my flesh, and I feel movement in my cheekbones. I think he broke my jaw. It... hurts... *so... bad.* "I bowed! I was her model priestess! I didn't recruit new members because I was pretty, I brought people into her temple because I was a model in action through my worship of her. Athena lies. She was jealous. I never blasphemed her! I never did that!"

"You just called a god jealous! *If a god says you blasphemed, then by the gods, you shall admit to blaspheming, Medusa! That is the order of our world!*"

A large snake, feeling bad for me, slithers over my leg as I lie on the ground. It's not mine. It's a garter snake. Apollo's. I notice a ton of them wandering about his temple in the darkness. He has almost as much of an affinity for snakes as I do.

"Even if I did," I say, forcing myself on my feet. But I close my eyes for a moment, sick with agony. "Even if I did, it doesn't excuse what Poseidon did to me. If there is any justice left in this world, your uncle deserves to be bound forever."

"There is only one justice, Medusa. Imada. There is no other."

He runs his hand through his blond hair. Then he hurls his glass of wine at me. It cracks and shatters over my head. I shriek. If it weren't for the excruciating pain in my jaw, in my bones, in my torn flesh, I'd charge him again. But I'm practically holding my cheek together.

I'm scared.

I start crying.

Don't cry now!

"Do you have any idea," Apollo says, laughing, "how perverse it is to watch a terrifying monster cry?"

"*Fuck you!*"

"Imada, Medusa." He walks back up his steps and sits back down. "Imada. Eventually Hades will find me. But he won't find us. Many of the mortals who run our secret society will live on, even if he's able to capture all of my family. We are simply too entrenched to be stopped. No matter what my or my sister's fate shall be."

I'm in too much pain to object. I can't say a word. I don't care. My head feels like it's splitting in half. It's not the glass, it was his arm. His swing was harder than that of twenty men.

The room is blurry. The floor seems to be moving as if I'm on a ship at sea. And I feel nauseated.

I vomit on his dirty floor. A slithery snake nearby skitters away.

"You, my dear, shall be my example for your master," he says. "As you suffer, Cora will suffer. She destroyed my home. My small acts of torture are nothing compared to that. The misguided whore loves her cur. So now, my pet, witness your fate. You will be stripped. That will allow you to be the wild dog you are. Your clothes will wither and decay after a thousand years anyway. But..." He raises a finger. "Our chains won't. You shall remain chained like Uncle, Father, and my brother in a dark crypt until the sun darkens this world. And after millions of eons, after my glorious sun no longer shines over Gaia, even then, if the world is not gone, you will still suffer in darkness, chained, Medusa."

He jumps back down his steps and grabs me. Then he

dips me back in his overbearing arms and forces a blindfold over my eyes.

"Mavis. Take this thing to cell block three. Give it our deepest hole. Let it starve, immortal, forever."

"My pleasure, sire."

"And don't be stupid and let it goad you," Apollo says. "Be careful. Keep the shades on and her blindfold over her eyes until she's buried. And ignore its tongue. It has the most beautiful voice. Don't let it speak. Drag it by its chains and leave it buried to rot."

My face is healing, but it's going to take another hour for it to be whole. So the bones in my skull rock and cause more tears as Apollo's men push and pull me, by my thick chains, yet again. Even the blindfold presses against my fractured bones, hurting my face.

I scream. They're viciously pulling my arms and legs again. I can't take it anymore!

As I'm dragged out of the room, I hear more of Apollo's stupid venom. "I wonder how it will feel, Medusa, to be chained in darkness forever? At least my father has firelight. Unpleasant, I think. I'm betting you'll create a whole world in that sick head of yours to entertain yourself in. If you haven't already?" He laughs. Even as I'm dragged through the chamber, the asshole keeps blabbering and enjoying his own bestial mirth. "I shall play the lyre joyfully over ridding the world of you, viper."

Talk about hypocrites.

13

MY END

WELL, MY FRIEND, NOW COMES THE SADDEST PART OF OUR life. The end.

You've stuck with me up to now, haven't you? Nowhere left to go. I'm kneeling, restrained in thick chains, in pitch blackness. At least I have you. Don't leave me. Please. No, don't you leave me.

I'm shivering. You know the pervert left me naked, right? Why? Aside from being an old loathsome pervert, why would he do that? So I must suffer being cold, of course. The metal chains absorb the stale, frigid prison air, and I find myself shivering almost as much as growling for food. See, he planned to starve me. Boy, he really hates me almost as much as I hate him. Knowing him, he probably poisoned the food I didn't eat.

I can imagine what the cell looks like. I caught a glimpse before they shut off the lights. It's white walled with white flooring, spacious, even though I can't move. They put me in the center and anchored me with metal restraints from the walls and ceiling, just like in the truck. There's nothing else here. It kind of reminds me of the interrogation room where

I met Orcus. Speaking of Orcus, where the hell was my "backup," anyway?

"Fuck."

Occasionally I say a word like that out loud. I don't know why.

"Fuck."

Just like that. Hear that?

"Fuck."

After a while, it feels weird hearing my own voice. Perhaps I should just talk to you out loud? I mean, there's nobody else here.

The snakes on my head are hibernating. It's like they're dead. Drained. You know, I didn't eat any of the gourmet shit that he made out of the kindness of his empty fuck-heart— perhaps I should have. I'm starving. Believe it or not, over thousands of years, I've never starved. This is a first. My stomach hurts. I'm so hungry. And I'm tired. And weak.

I'm crying...shit, here I go again.

Occasionally there's a noise. It's usually a bang, as if someone is banging on the walls. But when they brought me down here, all the other cells were empty.

Perhaps it's snakes? If they're snakes slithering in the dark, I don't mind. Ever since I was transformed, snakes calm me. I could curl up and sleep beside a hundred of them without a care in the world. But rats... God, I hate fluffy, scurrying rats. They're so creepy. They're like bugs. Insects. Oh, God, talk about disgusting. I hate creepy, slimy hard-shelled insects.

Occasionally I smell the room. That gives me a rough schema of the place. I can even see the inner chambers outside. But Apollo's right. Even though it's not completely dark in my mind's eye, the view of empty chambers buried, like, thirty stories underground will eventually turn me totally crazy.

I close my eyes. I try to sleep. Again…

My right arm wakes me with searing pain. They pulled my limbs back with the chains, and it's hella uncomfortable. Occasionally I feel a tug. All it takes is a slight move and my whole body is yanked around.

I breathe hard.

Too hard. I can't breathe.

Wait, are they sealing off the air? That's one way, I suppose, to make me feel like Hermes. Another form of torture? Instead of suffocating in blood, I just suffer from lack of air? Is that any better? Did they cut off the oxygen in the room?

My wigglies wake. They're moving about over my head because I'm scared. I can't breathe. The room lights up green. That's my eyes.

The pain in my arms is unbearable. I yank at the chains so hard. I'm pulling with enough force to move a car. It's… hopeless. The chains won't budge.

I scream.

Why, Gorgiana? Why scream? No one can hear you.

Nobody cares. Nobody ever did.

I feel dizzy.

I'm breathing better. It wasn't lack of air, it was me panicking. Just one breath at a time. And then…

How long is forever?

How long is eternity?

What is life like in perpetual pain? Hell? I suppose I

deserve damnation. If anybody deserves to be damned, it's good ole Medusa.

For now, my arms don't hurt much anymore. But I feel sick. I dry heave. Nothing comes up. I can't even throw up.

Occasionally I light up the room with my rage just to see again. It's only for a moment. Everything turns green around me. I see my chains connected to the walls.

Wait. There's a shadow standing in the corner. But now it's gone. No, there it goes scurrying along the floor again. It's a long brown snake here to keep me company.

"Come here, my lovely. Come to Medusa. Keep your momma happy and warm."

14

UNHINGED

My eyes squint in a sudden bright light. My heart races. I look about me and my prison cell is blindingly white. I have no idea how long it's been since I was chained. Or how long I drifted off. Maybe it was all just a terrible dream?

This big guy in military garb—a green cap and camouflage shirt and pants—enters through the door. He drops a small duffel bag. His eyes are shiny bright red. I know what that means. He's a god. But sweat is dripping from his face. Then I recognize him through my blinking eyes: it's Cora's bastard husband, Hades. Orcus.

"Medusa," he says, "I won't ask how you're doing."

"*Where have you been!*" I scream, lunging at him with chains clanging. I cry out in pain as the chains tear at my body. I growl like a lion. "Some help you were. You left me!"

"Turns out," Hades says with a smile, scratching his stupid bald head. "Your temper tantrum over that college rapist at Sunland has turned into a Godsend—pun intended. I provided you backup. We followed you. But I had to strike at just the right moment. You had to be patient."

"I've been caged for weeks, you shithead!"

"If you had a watch, you'd see it's been only one week, Medusa."

"I fucking hate you!" I cry. My eyes are full-on green flashlights at this point. Hades doesn't stir. Actually, he seems to get calmer. His eyes change from red to blue.

"Let me tell you a story," he says with a smirk.

"Move your eyes away from my body first, pervert."

"But you have stunning curves."

Sick fuck.

"You're very important to Cora," he continues, looking away, "That reminds me of her fabled nymph foster mother and daughter—Queen Nephratee and Queen Cassandra. Thousands of years ago, they once suffered in a dark prison in the Underworld, like you just did. But that was four millennia ago. At the time, Zeus still reigned over the world. I had to pretend to imprison them—"

"Do you have a point with this?"

"Cora doesn't know I pretended," he says with a nod. "I knew she was helping them. I suppose she found out later that I helped Cassandra escape. But she didn't know I was watching when she helped her mother, Nephrea."

"Like I said, what's your point?"

But I really don't care. See, he's yanking at the chains attached to the walls and ceiling as he's stupidly yapping. He's freeing me! He can blabber as much as he likes if he's gonna do that!

"My point is, don't thank me when I'm done," he says, pulling another huge chain from the wall.

"By not coming sooner," I snap, "you probably cost my friend his life!"

"Your male interest is very much alive, Medusa. But I needed enough time to do a successful raid. Unfortunately, you had to suffer in the meantime."

"Well, I'm not thanking you. I can't stand you."

"Impertinent and immaterial." He laughs. Then he tears another chain apart over my stomach. "You are Medusa, not Gorgiana." He meets my gaze. I growl at him loudly enough to make him wince. A few snakes in my hair snap at his face. "Medusa," he repeats with a nod. "Unlike Kore's silly sentimentalities, to me, you will always be titled lovely Medusa. Perhaps I haven't been kind, but you must admit, I've never treated you like a dog. They stripped you, chained you, and dragged you." He walks back to the door and pulls a long red shirt from his bag. I'm still chained by my wrists, but he drapes it over my head. "Only Imada is that low. I've detained Apollo—because of your help. For enabling me to find him, I'm eternally grateful. And now I owe you. You've earned your freedom." He raises a single finger. If I were loose, I think I'd bite it off. "Now here's your reward, viper." He stands close to my face and stares right into my eyes. My green light glows over his short beard and heartless face. "There are a hundred Imada operatives still roaming these crypts. They were involved in chaining, disgracing, and dragging you, and then caging you like a dog. Now I'm freeing you. Go be free, Medusa. And please, do as you will."

He stops working the chains. There are only two left—binding both my wrists. He backs up and bows before me, sweeping an arm in the direction of the door, as if he's some nobleman and I'm a queen. "But don't forget to pay your respects to your jailors, my lovely."

I throw my whole body forward, in fury, against the two chains, lashing out at him again and again until the metal snaps from my wrists. Then I growl again. My snakes have enlarged and are moving like crazy. And my eyes are so bright that Hades is shining green. He doesn't say a thing. He smiles sardonically and gestures once more to the door.

"I'd kill you, if I could!" I grunt.

He nods and gestures one more time to the exit.

I rush by him. I'm free!

15

RAGE

You might want to close your eyes. And your ears.
Sometimes I do when things get like this. Sometimes I do
really gross stuff to people and I can't bear it, so I sink into a
trance. I find that when the beast comes out, it can be too
much. See, that's another thing people don't mention when
talking about Medusa. My prey is not the only thing petrified. Sometimes I petrify myself—to not feel, I mean.

I'm hurdling down the dark hallway at super speed.
Imagine a tiger being let loose. That's me.

I feel a rise in my chest as I run. I feel so good. All the
pain of days of darkness, silence, and terror over being
buried alive forever has left me. But I remember the pain.
My restless sleep in darkness where I'd wake up in intense
pain, from a slight change in position, as my body weight
tore against my wrists, neck, or feet. If I were human, those
moments probably would have sheared my limbs off. I feel
the memory of that pain. Then I think about how I thought
I'd be like that for an eternity.

I close in on my quarry. I can smell the humans.

I burst through another door. Then another. I'm moving fast. There is no patience in beasts.

I stop for a fraction of a moment. My nose and all the snakes on my head rise and sniff. The humans are higher up. When Apollo said he'd bury me, he wasn't kidding.

I burst a door open that leads to stairs. After I climb a floor, there's a dim light ahead.

I move more quietly.

A group of men is standing against the wall of an adjoining hall. I don't see them, I smell them. In my mind, I see two have semi-automatic rifles slung over their shoulders. Another two are further down the hall, sitting against the wall talking quietly and thumbing through papers. One's eating chips. With my heightened sense of smell, the chips stink.

There is no way for me to go around them. My chamber stops here.

I stop breathing so I'm completely silent, though my heart is still exploding in my chest. But as an A+ predator, I can slow that too.

Calm yourself. Don't be too hasty. Their rifles will cover you with bullets and knock you unconscious. Then they'll bury you again without your reward.

I sense a snake slithering ten yards from me in their hallway along the wall. Good. Apollo has vipers everywhere. See, snakes are sacred to him—except good ole Medusa, I suppose.

I call for the big wiggly through telepathy and have him make his way to the sentries closest to me. Then I have it creep up a guard's boot.

The guard jumps.

"Keep quiet, you idiot!" says a female voice in a forced whisper.

"But a snake's slithering up my leg!"

"*Keep quiet!*"

"My god, I can't get it out! It's inside my pants."

She and another guard laugh.

Come to me, lovely. Bring the nice guard to me.

He's close. Around the bend. His friends are laughing as he stumbles right into my hallway.

Just a little closer. Come on. Just a little...

I snatch him. Then I turn him so that he looks deeply into my eyes. He freezes under the green light. I cuddle him and run a hand along his face as my snakes wrap around his neck. He's bearded. He's got scars along his forehead—a real tough-looking guy. Well, he's not tough in my arms. He even purrs.

I yank him under my arm and drag him downstairs so quickly and quietly that his friends are none the wiser.

My poisoned eyes have taken their full effect. He doesn't make a sound. On the stairs, I use my nails, now quite sharp, to cut a hole in his neck and tear out his artery with my fingers. After centuries of murder, I'm quite familiar with human anatomy. With so much pain, he'll shout whether he's under a trance or not. So, quickly, I use my other hand to enter his mouth and rip out his tongue. He can't talk now. See, I'm smart. But I still have to act fast. He's not far from his friends. He could still cry out. So, as his body shakes under me, I thrust my hands through his ribs and cut his lungs to shreds while my snakes tear the flesh from his face. Then I pull off his head. Does my plan make sense?

I think...it does. I close my eyes for a moment. I told you I get a little foggy when I hunt like this.

I open my eyes and look upon my kill. Lifeless. Gone. Dead.

Gross, his sticky juices are all over my face and hands. I

use my wigglies to lick up the blood from my face. Then I rush back to my post.

The other guard is standing and staring into my dark corridor wondering what happened to his friend. But I've been far too quiet for him to know that I just shredded and decapitated him.

One step. Two steps. Three… I do the same fucking thing —all over again—to him. *He, he.*

Another old guy is now in pieces on the floor by the stairs, beside his friend, their pools of blood mixing.

The last two guards are still leaning against the wall at the end of the hall. That's how good I am. See, I was that quiet. I hear a walkie-talkie say something, and one of the guards whispers into it.

"Where's Digger?" one of them finally whispers. It's that lady's voice again. "You see him? Where did he run to?"

"They're probably patrolling."

"We told them to remain at their post."

The lady gets up and walks close to the darkness. Real close to me. My calf and quadriceps are twitching, ready to snap. Damn, she turns back.

"We should go further downstairs and away from—"

"I ain't going anywhere near that thing, chained or not."

Wait a second. I know that woman's voice. It's that sadistic Hitler-bitch that tortured me! She enjoyed stretching and yanking my limbs.

I'm going to fucking kill her!

But that's why she's here. They brought someone on guard that won't be affected by my eyes. Clever.

I run my tongue along sharp teeth and lick my lips. You can't imagine how much pleasure I'm going to get shredding that Hitler-bitch. I'm remembering the searing pain in my arms and legs as she coldly ordered her friends to keep stretching me. I'm going to do that to her. I mean, I'm going to pulverize her.

But I have so many more morsels left. How do I kill discreetly? Well...

Fuck discreet.

I walk right into the hallway. The look of terror on the she-Nazi's face is priceless and really worth it. Blood is dripping from my chin despite my wigglies licking it off.

See her expression? Isn't it funny?

Giggles.

I laugh. Yeah, I laugh out loud. Who's the laughing bitch now? And you have to understand that I don't have some kind of sinister monster voice. I sound like a lovely girl laughing behind my full-on vampiress look. I'm this total serpent from the depths of hell, but my voice is still Gorgiana. And Gorgi's laughing at her.

Because I'm going to FUCKING KILL HER!

The guy right behind her brandishes a pistol. I lose my grin.

I leap across the hall. I haven't laid eyes on the man yet, but I know from experience another way I can freeze him. Terror. Pure and utter terror. Just as she ordered done to me, I yank at her limbs, only I tear her arms right off in front of her friend, pulling them from their sockets in front of his eyes. Then I look at him as he quakes.

BANG.

My arm is thrown back and almost makes me fall against the wall. It hurts so bad! His bullet hit my chest and broke a few bones, I figure. I can hear a gurgle as I take a deep breath. He fires again. Now I'm getting angry. I stare into his eyes. He's mine. But he manages a third shot. The pain is blinding. But I can't black out... I just can't.

I shake my head a few times.

I look down and realize that the guy lost his head. Did I do that? Hmm? I don't remember. I told you, when I get like this, I stop watching.

Those gunshots hurt so bad.

There are more soldiers shouting through the halls.

I run. Not away from them, to them. One turn. Then another. Then another. There's no more stealth, there's speed. But my head is pounding. It's hard to breathe. And my chest hurts with every step. I can smell the next three victims. They're rushing down a deep stairwell right toward me.

I have a soldier in my grasp. I'm breaking his back. His vertebrae are popping as I tear him in half. Blood is everywhere. I hear another gunshot. I bludgeon that one in the stomach with my fist. In the olden days before bullets, as you can see, there was no one except a god that could stop me. Perseus? Come on. Give me a break. Talk about myth. I have no trouble looking at my reflection. Right?

Someone from behind tries to club me. My snakes see him, they grab the rod, and toss it. I spin around. I use my fangs and sharper teeth this time, and real beast-like, vampiress-esque, I bite into his neck, ripping out his veins and arteries and snapping his throat, like crushing a brittle pipe between my teeth.

All the lights on the ceiling shut off.

Do they think they're blinding me? Really? How funny. I can see everything in the dark with my nose.

I hear what sounds like tin cans being thrown down the stairs. The hallway gets smoky. If I were human, this would probably be curtains. But I'm not human.

I rush across the now dark, smoky hall and burst through a stairway door. The soldiers turn in shock. They're wearing gas masks. Is it nerve gas? Mustard? Chlorine? They used to try that when I fought soldiers on the western front.

I hold my breath and grab a soldier who's running up the steps by the leg. He kicks and screams. Then I tear the mask right off his face and throw him down into the hall below. His lungs can go find out for themselves what they unleashed. I use his mask, but I have to move it around my cobras to fit it over my head. It's a bit challenging, but not impossible.

Gunfire flashes along the dark stairway. A stray shot nicks my neck. Stray bullets only piss me off more.

This is a very long stairway. Beside the metal railing, there's a gap and I can see up like twenty floors.

I rush up the steps. Now it's easier than ever to catch them. Many of the soldiers are hiding out, and after I ascend three or four flights catching up to them, I just fling their feeble bodies through the gap in the stairs. Falling four flights surely breaks their necks or cracks their heads open.

More gunshots.

Then, all of a sudden, everything turns dark...

I smell a nutty metallic smell. The detonation is blocking out my schema of the chambers. I force my eyes open. My ears are ringing. I'm coughing and lying on my side, hanging off the side of a blown-open stairwell. They must have thrown a bomb.

I falter. The ringing in my ears won't cease. I force myself up. There's a gap blown open in the center of the stairwell. It's a treacherous leap if I miss—a five-floor drop. I'd survive, of course, but it'd be hella painful.

I leap...and make it. Then I race up the stairs to kill the rest of them.

I grab more legs, hurling them down. I rip the rifle from the strap of a soldier and use the butt of the gun to alter his face. More shots echo. They flash in the darkness. Eventually, I have climbed nearly thirty stories—I've lost count, but the drop between the steps is pitch black. I can't see the smoke at the bottom anymore—I'm too high up.

At the top, at the end of a hallway, I stop by a double door. I stop because the rest of the Imada army, like fifty of them, are lying on the ground with guns pointing, waiting for me to cross the threshold. This could be it. This could be the end for good ole Medusa.

I sniff the chamber through the walls and gaze with my mind's eye at every soldier in the room. There are Doric columns along the chamber and... ah, I remember, I remember this room now. This is Apollo's throne room. This is where I met the jerk when I first arrived.

But this is a side entrance near his dais. From here, I sense his throne to my left behind the door. But he's not there—at least, nobody's sitting on the throne.

I have only one choice—to move as fast as I can. If I retreat, I'm buried anyway.

After a deep breath, I charge through the doors.

A flash of green makes me squint. It's coming from my own eyes. Now I recall the silvery walls by his throne. My eyes, now brighter than ever, flash along the reflective walls of Dellon's chamber. Were they gold or silver? They were something shiny. Now they're glowing from my bright emerald eyes. And I'm so pissed that the green light is blinding. I sense the room, more than see it, with my nose. Only a few soldiers are wearing infrared goggles. They're the only ones who don't become petrified. Everyone else instantly freezes.

Hey, what do you know? It's not my end after all. And, well, being that it's Dellon's court, there are quite a few wigglies moving about the floor too. That's convenient. The snakes can take care of those stray soldiers I can't mesmerize.

Come, lovelies. Come and help mommy, Medusa, stop the mean soldiers.

I shall attack them one by one with the help of my little friends. One at a time. Just as before, I'll go after each and every one. Ready? You remember the chains, don't you? Oh, yeah.

One...

16

THE BEACH

I knock on Ash's front door. He's staying in this cute one-story house, just like mine, probably of the same construction because we live on the same street. I know Ash is here because the first thing I did when I woke up in the middle of a grassy field in Arkansas was beg the first guy I saw, on a nearby highway, to lend me his phone. Then I called that asshole who let me loose on Imada. When Hades got on the line, I didn't let him talk, couldn't stand his voice. I just asked for one thing: Ash's address.

God, I'm frantic. I'm so worried about Ash.

I readjust the bun on my head, straighten my granny sweater and thick glasses, and wait. Yeah, I stopped for, like, five minutes at my house to get dressed in my second librarian outfit. I didn't have my key, but the wall was still boarded up so it wasn't hard to break in.

You want to know what happened to me after I went berserko in Dellon's lair? Beats the hell out of me. It must have been pretty gnarly, because I black out when things start to get gross. I remember coming home on lots of buses though. It took two days to get home. Why, do you ask? I had to ride only at night and hide like a vagrant during the day because of my hair.

This short, chubby brown-haired guy with a black-and-blue tie-dye T-shirt and shorts opens the door, and light floods the darkness outside. He furrows his brow and stares at me as I look down.

"Is Ash here?" I ask quietly.

"You know him?"

I nod.

"Uh…" He's looking me over. He's like examining me, which I really don't like. Finally, he says, "No. He's not." But I smell another human inside. I recognize the scent. I look around the guy who opened the door. The light's bright inside and a TV is blaring.

"He's not here," the creep says again, leaning forward.

I reposition my glasses, stand straighter, and say, "Can you tell him I stopped by? Tell him I can meet him at my place. Tell him—"

"No, I don't think…" He stops midsentence and develops this grimace. "Wait, you're the lady who works in the library, right?"

"Gorgi?" cries a voice behind him.

It's Ash. I literally push the jerk to the side and walk in. Asher runs straight into my arms. We hold each other tight for a moment.

I step out of Ash's arms and look down. "I was meeting your friend."

"Dale, this is Gorgiana," Ash says.

"*That's* Gorgiana?" he asks. "Oops."

"This is my best friend, Dale," Ash says. "Come in. Come in."

"God, Ash," I say, "I was so worried about you."

"Me too. I kept going by your house again." He looks down and sees my shoes. I'm not wearing any. I told you I was in a rush. Worse, my feet are caked in filth.

"Sorry," I say, looking down with a shrug. I probably smell too. I told you I rushed over to make sure he was okay.

"I'm just so happy you're okay, Gorgi. Come in."

I catch Dale shaking his head as I walk over to the adjoining kitchen. It's a simple kitchen separated from the living room by a counter, just like my place. Well, Dale's written me off as a freak. I guess I won't be pals with Ash's best friend.

"I'm so sorry, Ash," I say.

"Why say that? You didn't cause any trouble. We were attacked. I went to the police and filed a missing person's report, but they weren't of any help. Like I told you, I rode by your house every day since Sunday. I knocked on your door a thousand times—"

"You're so cute."

"I was worried."

"I'm fine."

He nods. But he doesn't look like he believes me.

"Ash, what's the last thing you remember after I left?"

"I woke up in the parking lot," he says with a shrug. "I remember guys in black suits bringing us to a truck before that. And I would have rushed them if one of them didn't have a gun stuck in my back."

"I know you would."

"Then I just woke up on the ground."

"But you don't remember seeing me in the truck?"

"No. Should I?"

Oh, thank God. He doesn't know. He doesn't recall being thrown into a trance. He still thinks I'm human.

Now I can just go. But I don't want to go.

"Did they do anything to you, Gorgi?" He leans down and looks in my eyes with such concern. It's sort of safe because I'm wearing my thick library spectacles, but he's looking closely enough that he could freeze. I turn.

"I was rescued by my family," I say.

"What sort of family do you belong to?"

I really don't know how to answer that. But I've dealt with this sort of stuff a million times before. I simply look down and act coy. Then I don't say anything.

"Okay," he says. He buys it, for now. "I'm just glad you're all right."

"I'm fine, Ash."

I look up a smidgeon. He's squinting. I brush the bangs from my eyes.

"What?" I ask with a smile.

"I'm trying to figure you out. You're such a mystery." I hear Dale scoff in the background, like a dick. "You have to be the most mysterious girl I've ever dated."

"I like you, Ash," I say with a nod. And that's a stupid thing to say. Nothing like being forward with a man. I mean, when you're a pathologically shy librarian. But that's what he said to me at the club.

I hold my hands together, playing with my fingers. In my periphery, I see his friend drinking from a milk carton and staring at us. He really doesn't like me.

"You want a drink or something?" Ash asks.

I shake my head. "I'd rather go to the beach. You said you like that. It's not far from here. You'd have to drive, though. I don't drive. You want to, Ash? You want to go to the beach?"

"Gorgiana?" he asks with a big smile.

"Yeah? What?"

"It's one o'clock in the morning."

"Oh," I say with a coy smile. "But you said you like the beach. And there's something I want to talk to you about." Then I look up at him and show him my eyes straight on. Yes, I'm wearing glasses, so a glance doesn't make him freeze, but I can still mesmerize him if I look deeply enough. Okay, using my cursed eyes to get my way is deceitful and wrong. But, hey, I really want to walk with him tonight, even if it's late for him. Selfish? Sneaky? Manipulative? Sure. But hey, I'm a monster.

He freezes for just a second, then—

"Okay," he says. "Sure, why not?" Then he chuckles. "Wait a second. Let me go get my coat."

"Don't forget the sunscreen," says his dickhead roommate.

"I'm different."

He laughs. That hurts a little because I'm trying to confide in him. He quickly loses his smile when he glances at my profile under a streetlight.

We're holding hands walking along a sidewalk. I feel the salty air brush against my face and I hear the waves. We're not far from the water. I love the beach, you know, just like Cora. I just can't go during the day. I meander along this walkway near the sand all the time in the early morning before sunrise. It's just, I usually don't have company. You get it. Now I have to explain this to my new human friend. I mean, I don't have to, but I want to. But telling him I'm different wasn't supposed to be funny.

"Sorry, I don't mean to laugh, but you are different," he says with a shrug. "Is that what you wanted to tell me?"

"No."

"Our first time out, the shyest girl I've ever met got in front of a hundred people and transformed into a rock star," he says. "Then she jumped me."

"Sorry, but you're cute," I say with a shrug.

"The next time I went out with you, I had a gun stuck in my back."

"That wasn't cute."

I stop and look at the waves. See, I don't want to tell him, because I've done this a hundred times before. It's not like I've taken a vow of silence about my identity. That's not it. I know what you're thinking.

You just went to his house, Gorgiana, not only to make sure he was okay, but to make sure he didn't see you transform. Now you're planning on telling him about who you are!

Yeah. Well, I like him. And now I want to risk it.

Or do I?

If a guy's special, and a bit weird, he won't run home when I show him who I am. But if he's normal—and this boy has that long blond surfer hair and looks very normal—Asher will suddenly remember that he has to study tomorrow and will take me home. Then he'll avoid me forever. I'll be lucky if I don't have to talk to the police and get that creep Hades to rescue me from the police station. But if he's normal, and he jets, that's good too because then I won't live with the pain of love. Because I am immortal, and all mortal men I fall in love with eventually die. That's why that Justin Bieber song I love is so wonderful, but so awfully sad for me. Do you get it?

You don't? Well, I don't either. I hate love.

"What is it?" he asks quietly. We've been walking in silence for a little while now.

"Do you like Greek mythology?"

"Sure. I'm an English major."

"That must be why you like books? Like me?"

"Yeah."

I fumble with my fingers. Then he grabs one of my hands.

We walk on. I listen to that glorious sound of waves

rolling in again. Then I look around us. All I see is a few lights on buildings by the shore. No one is on the walkway at this time—not in a college town in the summer in the middle of the night.

"What would you say, Ash...if I told you that it's real. All of it. In fact, some of those people that you call Greek or Roman "gods and goddesses" are living and doing things like you do every day? Like going to the beach, working in office cubicles, serving at restaurants or...shelving books in libraries in universities?"

His hand twitches in mine a little. His muscles tighten. The creepiness is settling in, and we're almost to that point of no return; I like to call this "tight or flight." He either gets close to me or leaves. Because it's such an important moment, and I haven't had someone close to me in over two decades, my hand shakes too.

"What are you trying to say?" he asks almost in a whisper. He stops walking.

"I'm not only different. I've been here for a long time, Ash. I mean, I've lived on this earth for a very long time."

We face each other and he nods seriously. Then he gesticulates for me to go on.

"I'm pretty old."

"Just say what you're trying to say." Asher closes his eyes and shakes his head. "Just say it. Please."

"Medusa."

"Huh?"

"Medusa," I say with a nod.

"What are you talking about?"

"Medusa. You asked me to just say it. There. That's it. Medusa."

"And? *What about Medusa?*"

"You're standing in front of her."

"Maybe I should take you home."

See. There it is. I told you.

"Yeah, probably," I say, lowering my head.

"Damn it, Gorgi!" I jump from his outburst. "It's so crazy being around you. I don't totally mind." He laughs, but in an odd angry-nervous sort of way. "I mean, even the theater turned out okay—but I keep looking around thinking we might get jumped. You're scaring me."

"I won't let that happen to you ever again. I promise."

"What are you talking about? What about Medusa?"

See. You can tell someone right to their face the real stuff going on, and they still won't believe you. Especially if it involves magic. Nobody believes in magic anymore. Let's not even talk about religion.

In the olden days, he'd have immediately jumped to the conclusion that I'm a witch. He'd be planning with his friends to tie me to a tree and light a nice cozy bonfire under my bare feet. Then again, a few centuries ago, he probably would have considered that the first time I threw him against a wall.

"Gorgi!" he snaps again. He brings my face up, but I avert my eyes. He's trying to search them. "What are you thinking? What are you saying?"

"Don't look into my eyes."

"Serious?"

"Don't look into my eyes, Ash," I say firmly with a nod. This is the worst thing he can do right now.

"Medusa?" he asks in a whisper.

"Yes, Asher," I whisper back. "That's my name." I've turned to the ocean. And the peaceful waves. I'm wondering if I made a mistake. "I came up with Gorgiana long ago. It's from the root word *gorgon*. My enemies used to call me Gorgo. I'm—" I get teary eyed. Damn, don't cry! Stop it! "I'm a monster, Asher. My name is Medusa. I'm that same lady they talk about, the one with snakes in her hair. A monster, Ash. That's me."

He digs his hands in his pockets and turns from me. That's better. At least now I can't curse him with my cursed gaze.

"You're not a monster, Gorgi," he says. He shakes his head. "You're an angel. You're the sweetest girl I've ever known."

I cry. I violently shake my head. Damn, those words are *sooo* sweet! Damn it! I'm such a cry baby!

I get the hell away from him. I run.

I rush in the sand toward the waves. Part of me considers swimming. I could. I could just go out there along the aquamarine horizon—well, it's just a dark shadow right now, but I always imagine it as aquamarine—and see where the water takes me. I've done it before. I can't drown. I mean, I could end up at the bottom, but I'll awaken. Then my body will rise and float. See, I can't leave this forsaken hell you call Earth no matter what I do.

I stop crying because crying disgusts me right now.

Fuck Ash! I don't need him. I don't need anyone. I don't even need you.

I look out at the waves with green shining over the water under my feet. I'm thinking he left me, but I don't have the courage to turn around and see if I'm right.

I'm right. I look back and don't see him behind me. He's gone...

17

EMBRACE

I FEEL SOMEONE GRAB ME IN THEIR ARMS. AT FIRST, I SHAKE him off thinking it's one of those Imada agents. It's not. It's Asher. I smell him. I feel his hard back and muscular arms, his breathing and rapid heart. It's him. He hasn't left me. Usually I would have smelled him coming, but I'm so messed up inside.

Can you believe it? Is he insane? Why didn't he run home? If I'm really Medusa, or just plain crazy, why wouldn't he bolt?

He's holding me by the waves.

"Go away," I murmur quietly.

He doesn't... Shit... I... really don't want him to.

"Stop pushing me away from you," he says.

Me? I'm doing that?

I turn from his gaze. Then I do something weird again, but he lets me. I cover his eyes with my hand. Then I press my lips gently against his. Just a peck. He pecks me back. Then I enter his mouth with my tongue.

I think he saw the green glow, but he's acting alert. I didn't mesmerize him yet. It's now that I recall that he caught a glimpse of my green eyes back at the movie theater too. He didn't leave me then either.

We're French kissing by the waves in the darkest night. It's romantic—in a gorge-horror-freakshow sort of way. I mean it's pitch black but for me, who can't be out in the sun, it's romantic, okay?

"You're an angel," he says quietly between kisses. "Not a monster."

"And you're a nutjob."

A little mean? Well, it's true, isn't it?

I laugh. He doesn't stop kissing my lips. I don't fight it anymore, and I even let my tongue change. It gets narrower and bifurcates. I do this selfishly for myself. See, the more excited I get, the more I turn; the more I turn, the more I get excited. I even feel my wigglies hopping to get out of their nest above my head.

Stay put, little ones! Behave.

They can't run loose. Snakes on my head are probably a bit too much even for Ash at this point. Not to mention that when I'm full-on Medusa, my skin wrinkles like an old lady's.

He doesn't stop kissing me, even with my forked tongue. He even presses me closer. I really know how to pick 'em, don't I?

I'm only kidding. It's so nice. It's just I can't...believe... Oh, that feels good. He's touching my butt. My heart's thumping. I want more.

Calm down, Gorgi.

My eyes open wide, turning his face into an emerald under the starry night. I gaze at his cheek. His rough stubble and his hard chin. I run my fingers along it and through his hair and that wave of blond. He opens his eyes. I quickly turn. He can't look into my eyes. I don't want to hypnotize him.

"What's the matter, Gorgiana? Kiss me."

I shake my head. "I can't anymore. I can't let you see my eyes."

"Why?"

"You'll freeze."

"Like a stone?"

"No, you'll black out."

But part of me wants him to look. Part of me doesn't care if I hypnotize him. Part of me, the part that...keeps getting my bum rubbed by his hand, wants to turn him so I can devour him.

I spin back so fast that he can't see my face, pressing my head against his chest. His heart is beating quickly by my ear. I'm so quick, he can't know my intentions. I cradle his head, looking away toward the shadow of waves. Then, with my free hand, I reach down and unbuckle his belt.

"Gorgi!"

I undo his zipper. I reach down into his pants, careful not to hurt him. I feel his cock. The bare skin is soft and erect. I grab it gently with my fingers and stroke it. Then I feel his hand slip down the back of my loose granny pants. He touches the crack of my ass. That spurs me on to stroke faster. As I stroke, he squeezes. He even tries to enter the crack, but I move away.

"Should we...should we be doing this out in the open?" he asks.

I laugh. I don't mean to be mean, but it's a little late now, isn't it?

"I'm not shy, Asher."

"Move back and I'll touch you too," he says. And he starts to move his hand away from my butt, but I snatch his wrist.

"No."

This isn't for me. It's for him. He actually wants me—as insane as that is—so I'm going to reward him.

"Then kiss me," he says.

"I can't now. I'm sorry."

I'm too excited. I don't trust my eyes and I don't trust my control. As I stroke his cock, my free hand rides up his T-shirt and touches his hard chest. It's cut as hell. That drives me wild. Man, he's amazing. I run my fingers along the ridges of his abs and then up around his pecs. He has short hairs here and I stroke them and run my fingertips along his nipples. I massage him. He groans again. His hard cock quivers. He's close, I think. I stare at the waves and, whereas before I considered drowning myself, now I find the sound and view tranquil. Soothing.

"Please, Gorgi. Face me. Let me kiss you again."

"No, Ash. I'm sorry."

He squeezes my butt cheek tighter and moans. That arouses me more. I have to be careful. My curse makes me irresistible. Not just my eyes, but the touch of my body. I don't want to be Medusa for him. I want to be Gorgiana.

I take my free hand out of his shirt and hold him. I just hug him close. But I still stroke him with my other hand.

He's almost there. His cock is wet. So am I. He's not touching me between my legs, but I'm so aroused. My hair's wild. The vipers broke through the pin a long time ago. I have to finish now. If the snakes come out, as hard as his cock, he's not going to be aroused—he's going to freak way out.

"Thanks for not leaving me," I say.

His hand pulls me so close. Then he squeezes my ass to the point of hurting me. I don't mind. It means I'm driving him wild. I press his body closer than ever as I feel movement on my head, so he doesn't see or feel the wigglies.

Now, I know men. I've lived for a long time. I know what

will finally drive him over the edge. I release his cock and yank down his pants and underwear. Then I pull down my pants and panties too. We're on a public beach and the daringness of this, the gall, of being naked in public predictably frightens the hell out of him. But I know it excites him more.

"Gorgi!" he snaps, jerking for his pants. "We shouldn't do this here."

"It's exciting," I say in his ear. With my free hand, I touch his cock again. And, once more, I lean close to him, pressing my head against his shoulder. "There's no one here. It's okay."

He's quiet and still. That's weird. I hear the waves. I hear his breathing. But he doesn't say a thing.

He's petrified, of course. Frozen. But not by my eyes. By my actions. My long black hair's flowing over my shoulders, moving a little despite myself. And my smell, even though my body should smell rank after not showering for two days. My naked pheromones, cursed for four millennia, are made irresistible when aroused. And now that they're out in the open, with my pants down, they're intoxicating to his nose. I might be able to control my hair, but I can't control that. And then there's my face. He can see my profile. The source of Athena's curse itself. I'm the most beautiful woman to have ever lived.

I rub his cock faster out in the cold night. His hand, in turn, reaches further along the crack of my ass, between my legs, and finds my labia. Now I no longer fight it. He rubs there, stretching my skin. I close my eyes tight from the amazing pleasure. I don't have much control over my hair now. He enters me with a finger. When I open my eyes, green shines like a beacon toward the dark sea.

"Medusa," he mutters.

His free hand is running over my long hair. For a

moment, I leave my pleasure and think that, perhaps, he said my name to humor me. Does he really finally believe that's who I am? Is he so gone that he doesn't feel the slimy snakes in my hair?

But. His finger is inside me now as I stroke his cock, and I feel him rub faster in my perfect spot. I told him not to. I was afraid I'd lose control. I still...might...oh God, I moan in sync with the rubbing of his fingers, as if we're fucking each other. It feels so good. I know my moaning drives him crazy too. Then I say between breaths, as I jerk him off, "Touch me, Ash. Yes, there. Right there. Yes. Touch me."

He presses deeper.

"Hold me close!" I command. "Yes, oh, please fuck me there. Don't stop. Yes. Fuck me, Ash. Fuck me!"

Warm liquid spills on my hand as he orgasms. That takes me over the edge too. My body shakes, and I fall back into his arms in rapture. I feel his body, and a few of my snakes escape my control and brush against him.

Now I know the vipers are out. But he doesn't pull away. He holds me tight.

Then... I whimper.

"Are you okay?" he whispers in my ear.

"Yes." I nod, cradling my head against his chest again.

"Are you crying?"

"Yeah. I'm crying, Ash."

"Why Gorgi? Why?"

"You make me so happy."

18

BREAKFAST BY CANDLELIGHT

I'M SITTING ACROSS FROM ASH AT THIS BEAUTIFUL CANDLELIT table. We're in our own private little booth. The tables in this place are full, but everybody's real quiet, behaving in this swanky restaurant. There are no windows. I don't like that. I'd rather eat looking at the beach I love. But...that's okay. I can watch my date instead.

He's wearing this white button-down with cuff links and black slacks. He's got on a tie, which is cute as hell, especially with his gold hair thrown to the side, and white tennis shoes. That's funny. Boys never look at their shoes, do they? He looks young. That's okay. For an old geezer like myself, I've become accustomed to young men. They look my age, you know. They also grow up eventually, don't they? That is the real, dreadful, seriously fucked-up reason I fall in love with young men. When in love with an eternally immortal woman, young men live longer.

After I throw away that unsavory thought, I gaze down at my swanky sleeveless white dress and gold necklace, which is a gorgeous bundle of thin fourteen-karat-gold chains. The necklace is another relic. It was hidden in my closet. This one was given to me by a duke. Ash probably thinks it's fake. He made sure to tell me he was paying tonight, because this place is expensive. (I haven't told him I'm loaded yet.) Actually, I'm not even sure if he knows I'm wearing a necklace. He's a typical boy, not looking at my dress or my lovely gold high heels. He keeps trying to look in my eyes.

Don't do that.

Or sipping his water. He's doing that a lot too.

I brush my bangs back. The wigglies rest quietly in a bun. But I have makeup on. I shouldn't have done that, but I wanted to look good for Asher.

I have time to think of all this shit because there's something seriously wrong with my date. He isn't saying a damn word. He just keeps drinking his water. I also don't know where our waiter or waitress is. He looks up and smiles a couple of times, but then he turns to the wall. He's been acting strange since that night on the beach. I get it, I suppose. It was weird. But I told him I was different.

"How did you do on your American lit exam?" I ask, fishing for something to say.

"Good. It wasn't hard. I just focused on *The Great Gatsby*."

"That's a good book."

"You like it, Gorgiana?"

"Um-hmm. I remember liking it, but I read it a long time ago. Maybe I should read it again?"

"You can start at the end this time," he says with a smirk.

Ah, funny. Humor's a good sign, right?

"Yeah, I already know the ending."

He nods. Then he turns all quiet again.

He digs in his pocket and looks at his cellphone. He takes a deep breath and stares at this modern art sketch, of pink and black lines, on the wall. Then he touches the white tablecloth, as if it's something to do.

"What about your multiple-choice astronomy test?"

"You're acting like my mom, Gorgi," he snaps.

What? That's rude. It hurts my feelings. I'm sensitive, you know. I mean, if he doesn't want to talk, that's fine. It's just weird to be alone in company.

"Sorry," I say. "I didn't mean to."

"It's okay. I know you didn't. Forget it."

Then he's back to being mum.

Well, while he's playing the silent game and fondling the tablecloth, let me tell you something about astronomy. I *love* astronomy. Many people these days think it's common knowledge that those little white dots in the night sky are big fiery balls called stars. It wasn't always that way. For thousands of years, we didn't know what they were.

I have my own star, you know. It's called the Eye of Medusa. It's a binary star that flickers bright and dim. Perseus is next to it. Of course there are a lot of lies about Perseus. I wouldn't be here if that guy really chopped off my head, would I? Anyway, stars are really cool 'cause I have my own.

Ash coughs and interrupts my thoughts about stars.

"Ash?" I ask quietly.

"Yeah?" he asks, glancing at his phone again. "What's up?"

"Why are you acting like I'm a leper?"

"Don't be silly—"

"Do you two know what you'd like this evening?" interjects a waitress standing over us in this formal suit and tie. "We have a special tonight. Lobster. And escargot as a first course. I really recommend both dishes. The specials are there on the back of the menu."

"Gorgi?" Ash asks, gesturing for me to go first.

"No, you go, Ash." Then I flash a quick glance at the waitress through my thick spectacles. "It's his birthday."

"Happy Birthday," she says.

"Thanks. I'll have a steak," Ash says. "Medium. With a baked potato and vegetable platter." He looks at me and smiles.

"I'll have a steak," I say. "Raw. And that escargot thingy you're talking about. And...we'll have bread with butter. Lots of butter, please. Thanks."

"Do you mean rare?" the waitress asks, furrowing her brow. Here we go again.

"No. Raw. I like rare, but *rarer* than rare. Just pour seasoning on it and serve it to me without cooking it. I mean, it can be warm, I guess, if you must." I know it's weird, but I like it that way. Okay?

The waitress nods slowly. Then she takes our menus. "What would you two like to drink?"

"He's twenty-one today," I blurt out.

The waitress nods smugly.

"I don't know," Ash says. "I'm more of a beer—"

"Try a vodka martini," I say to Ash. "That's what my best friend likes. Martinis. She says they're fucking amazing." Oops. I put my hand over my mouth after I cuss.

Ash laughs. "I'll have what the lady recommends."

"Would you like it up?" the waitress asks.

Ash squints and looks down. I nod. "Yes, he would."

"What about you miss?" the waitress asks.

"Same. With lots of olives."

And she's gone.

I look at Ash and I lose my smile. He looks stern and his nose is flaring. He's pissed. "You're crazy," he says.

I squeeze my hand under the table tightly—so tightly that if I had his hand in mine, I'd break his bones. Because he's not saying that to be nice this time.

Things aren't going well. I should have thought out that night with a lot more care. I acted too rashly on the beach.

But I was so worried he had been hurt, or even killed. He thinks I'm a freak. And I am. But I don't want him running out *now*. But you know, just because a human doesn't run from me the first day I tell him who I am doesn't mean he won't run the next. It's happened before. I think that's where this is going. I should have moved slower.

"I'm sorry," he says, softening. "Don't look so sad, Gorgi. It's just... I'm trying to get used to you."

I shrug.

"Can I be honest?" he asks.

"Please. I respect honesty more than anything in the world."

"I didn't like it when you told the waitress my age."

"Why?"

"I don't know," he says. He throws his hair back and looks across the restaurant. Many of the booths are empty. It's Thursday and late. "I didn't like that."

"Ash," I reach for his hand, but he doesn't give it to me. "We're here to celebrate your birthday. You're twenty-one." I force a laugh with a shrug. "No more fake IDs at bars. Right?"

"I know, but that doesn't mean I want you advertising my age."

"Why?"

"The way you said it didn't make me feel older. It made me feel younger." What is going on here? I furrow my brow and stare at him through my library specs, forgetting my cursed eyes. Luckily, he's looking down playing with the tablecloth. "You're making me feel like a kid, Gorgi." And it's funny, because he kind of reminds me of one when he hangs his head, under his cute surfer hair, fondling the tablecloth.

"I'm much older than you," I say.

"Yes...look, you have to give me time. I like you, but you're so different from anyone I've ever met."

"I am."

"*Very* different," he says with a nod.

Yeah, I am different. Okay. GOT IT.

He quickly puts his hand up. I think I must look the way I feel—really, really hurt. "It's okay, Gorgi. I like that you're different. Man, you're so sensitive." He takes my shaky hand. "I can't believe you call yourself a monster. You're so delicate. I like you, I really do. I just—"

"No more age talking."

He takes my hand from across the table and kisses it. And nods. "Whatever. It means so much that you accepted my invitation tonight, Gorgiana. You know what, say whatever you want."

And that melts my heart. Shit. I take a deep breath.

How can I tell him my next words without pushing him away further? I say very carefully, "I haven't been out on a date in a long time, Ash. This means a lot to me."

"You can be so emotional," he says with a nod, looking away again.

Fuck! That sounds like another insult! What can I do to smooth things over? Let's try the direct approach.

"Are you afraid of me?"

"What? Of course not."

"Most people, when they find out who I am, Ash, are. That's nothing to be ashamed of. Look..." I pat his hand. "Forget it. Act any way you want. I so like that—"

"I'm not afraid of you." He leans back and furrows his brow. "I suppose I'm afraid of what you are, Gorgiana, not you."

"What does that mean?"

"I don't think you'd ever hurt me."

"I would never hurt you."

"I know." He nods slowly. "It's the glasses. It's your hair. I see one part of you and then another. I'm not sure which one you are. Tonight, you're sort of both."

"I am both."

He shakes his head. "I'm not so sure. When you went up on stage and sang on our first date, the whole place went wild. You could have had anybody at that bar. You were so confident. So strong. You were like hypnotizing us."

"It's my eyes," I say, covering them.

"No, it isn't just that. It's your voice. No...it was you. After you were done, when the crowd went wild, you ran offstage. Why?"

"Ash, that's me. I'm like the gal who performs, drops the mic, and silence follows. I grab attention in a freaky bad way."

"No, you don't. I don't think it's what you have inside you. I don't think it's Medusa. I think it's actually you. When you sang, you weren't hypnotizing me with magic. You were hypnotizing me with who you really are."

He touches my arm and tries to push my hand away from my eyes. I look down.

"You don't have to hide your eyes from me," he says.

"My eyes are cursed," I say, shaking my head. "Even if the wonderful thing you just said is true, it's also true that my eyes hurt people."

The waitress comes back. She does that shaking thing, preparing our drinks, hands us martinis, and goes. I sip it. It's too strong. How the hell does Cora do this?

"Hmm, not bad," he says, gazing at the martini in the air. Then he sips some more. "Nice tip. I like it, Gorgi. Cheers." He reaches over and clicks my glass.

"Happy birthday, Ash."

"Thanks." He puts the glass down. "But you're not getting off that easily. When can I see your hair down?"

"Oh, we can go back to the beach and I can show you, if you want to."

He laughs.

"Never. Ash, I mean, hopefully never. They're not something I'm proud of. The snakes are like my cursed eyes. I don't want you to look at them."

"I'm not just hypnotized by your eyes," he says, pointing at me with his martini, "I'm fascinated by you."

"You're not so bad yourself." I reach out and touch his hand. "Tell me. What are your parents like, Ash? Let's not talk about me. Did you grow up around Orlando? Have you always lived in Florida?"

He shakes his head. "San Francisco." He shrugs and sips more of his martini. "I suppose the sun drew me to Florida. And the university. Sunland's a good college, you know."

"It is. What does your daddy do?"

"There you go. Acting like I'm a kid again." *Oh...* "What about your mom and dad?"

"You don't want to know about my mom and dad."

"Actually, I'd love to know about them, Gorgi."

"My father was a carpenter. My mother took care of me. It was a different time. A very different time. Men fought wars, guarding the home. Or they tended fields or sold at the local market. Women took care of domestic things. The home. Honestly, it's so long ago that I can't remember much anymore. But I remember my parents, and we were very happy."

"Where did you grow up?"

"We're really going through this? I tell you what, I'll tell you some of my secrets only if you tell me yours."

He nods, raising his eyebrow. "It's worth it."

"I grew up in Sarpedon. It's an island off the Greek Isles near Turkey. I was born by the Aegean Sea. What did your dad do, Ash?"

"A film producer."

"Really? How interesting."

"Yeah. And a screenwriter. I suppose that's why I wanted to be an English major. My mother was an English teacher." He drinks more of the martini. "What friend of yours drinks martinis?"

"Cora."

Don't tell him about her. Don't. He's not ready for that.

"She has good taste in drinks," he says. "Why a librarian?"

"What do you mean?" I ask with a chuckle.

"Why are you working as a librarian? If you've been around so long, why would you choose a job like that?"

"I already told you why—I love books. I love reading. I'm happy reading alone."

He takes a deep breath and squints at me, scrutinizing me. If I'd let him, I'm sure he'd look right into my eyes. It reminds me a little bit of that bastard Hades. But then his lips curl into that famous grin only Ash has. "Okay. Here's the biggest one. Why aren't I a statue already?"

"That's a myth."

"You can't turn people to stone?"

"I can." Oops. His face turns and winces, but then he quickly flashes a fake grin at me. "If I focus long enough into someone's eyes in trance, I can turn them. Anyone. Yes, I can. I can turn anyone, or even any immobile object, into stone if I stare long enough. But I'm as disgusted by it as you are."

"I researched online. You mentioned Sarpedon offhand before. The web said Sarpedon was an island full of statues. Is that true?"

"I can't talk about that."

"What? Why?"

Veer him off that subject, Gorgiana. Now. Do it quick!

"I can't." I shake my head and stare at other people eating at their booths around us. I move my bangs from my eyes and say, "What books are you reading? It's your turn."

"Steinbeck," he says. "The usual classics for class. *Grapes of Wrath*. It's more what I'm writing. I have half a ton of reports due over the next couple weeks. It's stressing me out, honestly. Summer was supposed to be a break, but I'm diving in to maybe save some money by graduating early. But it's too much work."

"You told me you get good grades?"

"Yeah. But I don't want to talk about studying. If you won't talk about statues, I've got another one. You say you've lived so long, what was the best time?"

I pause. The answer comes far more quickly than my mouth moves. But I pause because I think about how I'm going to explain it to him. How can I get him to understand and make it sound less weird?

"Before I changed, Ash, that was the happiest time of my life. Do you... Do you know why?"

He shakes his head.

The waiter comes with our dishes just in time to stop me.

It's cute how they garnished my raw meat on a plate. And six snails, the escargot, are nicely dipped in lots of searing butter on a metal tray. And talk about butter, she brings over a tray of three sticks of white butter just to make me happy. I really like this place.

"Bon appetite." Ash raises his martini glass. I raise mine. Then he takes his fork and knife and cuts his steak.

"It's not just because it was before I was a monster," I say as I watch him cut his meat. Then I pause as I dig into my raw meat. "It's the sun. You really don't know how wonderful something is until you lose it. Not being out in daylight is terrible."

"I can't imagine. I love the beach."

"I know you do. But you know..." I pull and cut at the tough steak. Their steak knives aren't too sharp here. It's gonna take lots of cutting and chewing. "I've had some good times since, I suppose."

"What was your favorite time *after* the change then, Gorgi?"

"Sorry, it's my turn," I say, shaking my head. "What was your last girlfriend like?"

"Not fair." He laughs. "Your life is far more interesting than mine."

"Not to me, it isn't."

"I dated my landlord last year. She was young. Cute. Simple. Like you. Or...like I thought you were. I'd hardly call you simple now."

"Thanks, I guess. What happened between you?"

"We just weren't into the same stuff. We never felt much of a connection." That's what I was worried about when we weren't talking, you know. But now he's chatty. "Now tell me. Tell me about your favorite memory *after* your transformation?"

"That's easy. It was two hundred years ago. I was living in a remote area in the far north, in Inverness, where I could enjoy the sun. It was sparsely populated so I could come out during the day back then. But cold as hell. Well, it mixes with your question. I met a guy working in a pub. I trusted him like I trust you and told him who I was. We fell in love. We got married outside by the shore. It was..." I smile but turn. It's sad and beautiful at the same time. "Being out there was one of the greatest moments in my life. It was a peaceful time. A wonderful time."

"So it was someone you loved?"

"No. I mean, yes. But that's not the only reason I treasured it. It was the ceremony with the guy I remember and loved. Maybe that sounds stupid? We got married by a priest along the shore during the summer. It was under the bright sun, and the sound of waves crashed beside us as we exchanged our vows. We had to trust the priest too. I can't wear a veil, obviously."

"Why not?"

I take a deep breath. I'm scared again that any moment he's going to get up and rush out of the restaurant.

"My hair doesn't accept any sort of covering. It gets shredded in less than a minute. In fact, it brings more attention. Unless it's worn over my head without touching my hair. But that sort of headdress would look ridiculous. The only acceptable thing is this." And I point at the bun. "Or, I could tie it in a ponytail, but that's a bit riskier."

"Oh, now I get the bun."

"You don't like it?"

"It would be unattractive on anyone but you."

"Thanks...I guess."

"Really," he says with a nod, sipping his martini again. He gets quieter. "You're beautiful however you wear your hair. Behind your getup, you're the most beautiful girl I've ever known."

"That's so nice, Ash. Thanks. Did you like my favorite memory?" He nods. "I thought you'd think it's corny."

"I'm really sorry," he says, putting down his silverware. "Things seem so hard for you."

I shrug. "It's life."

He shakes his head. Then he starts putting fixings all over his potato. I enjoy watching him drop the sour cream, chives, and cheese all over it. He sees me watching, I think. I just like being with him.

"You want some?" he asks.

"Yes."

So he scoops me some potato. Then I gesture to the

snails. He wrinkles his nose. That's when I remember my relic.

"Oh, Ash? I have something for you."

"Hmm?"

"I got something for your birthday." But first I reach into my purse and lay the silver bookmark on the tablecloth. "I have to give you something in return for this beautiful cross."

"You don't have to."

"Of course I do. It's your birthday, silly." I take a small book out of my purse and put it on the table. It's a collection of Shakespeare, circa 1800s. "I loved your bookmark so much. I carry it with me everywhere. I had to give you something in return. Happy birthday."

His mouth is gaping open. The book on the table is leatherbound but looks frayed, it's so old.

"I can't take that." He pushes it back to me. "That looks way too valuable."

"No more than your bookmark."

"Gorgi, the bookmark was my grandmother's. That book looks like it was made before my grandmother's grandmother."

I push it across the table to him. "Please. Take it. We both love reading. You like Shakespeare, don't you?"

"Of course I do."

"Then...please, for God's sake, take it."

He picks up the book and runs his fingers over it. He smells it. Then he carefully opens it. I think I see excerpts from *Macbeth* across the table. I don't read Shakespeare anymore. I don't need to. I have most of his works memorized.

"It's incredible, Gorgiana. Thank you."

"Happy birthday, Ash."

He picks up his fork but then lays it down slowly. "Gorgi,

I don't get something. If you love being out in the sun so much but can only go out in unpopulated places, why are you living here? Why aren't you somewhere out in the Arctic again or something? Somewhere where you can let your hair out?"

"It's warm at night. I don't like it up north. I like seeing a lot of people. I like it busy where I can watch people. I adore the sun, but I love seeing people more, even if it's only at night from a distance in my library. And, anyway, I can still see the sun I love from inside my home. I... I'm sorry, that may sound weird. But people seem happy here in sunny Florida and I like watching them."

"Hmm." He shakes his head. "Well, I really like *you*, as long as you stop talking about my age."

"Sorry. No more of that."

"I thought we'd get closer, Gorgiana. How is that going to happen if you keep thinking you're my grandmother?"

Wait? Is that why he was offended about my mentioning his age? I thought it was just demeaning for him to feel young. He's worried about our age difference? He's worried that we're incompatible because of our ages. Is that it?

That is so cute!

I turn away, this time to keep tears from streaming from my eyes. All I need is to start bawling in front of him again. I feel him take my hand and rub my fingers. "You've lived so long, you say, but after all that time, you still don't realize how special you are? How can that be, Medusa?"

Well, tonight is going better now, isn't it? But he's wrong about that. Really wrong. I'm a monster. I won't tell him about Sarpedon. Not yet. He's not ready. He might never be ready for our secret.

You can't ever tell him.

I know. I know.

19

MY GUEST

I'M WHEELING A LIBRARY CART DOWN AN EMPTY HALL OF cubbies, picking up an occasional textbook left on a desk by kids actually studying. I love this time. No one reads. No one checks out books in the summer. I always get done early so I can engage in my favorite pastime: reading. I wrinkle my nose as I pick up a gum wrapper beside an old copy of *Of Mice and Men*. Ugh. Would it kill the kids to throw away their own trash? Geesh. Then I readjust my thick fake glasses and wheel on. Here's an engineering textbook and a pair of jeans draped over a chair. I hold the pants by a belt loop with the tips of my fingers and toss it in a bin under the cart. Then I make my way into the main hall to park the cart and be done.

It's late—around ten o'clock. It's completely empty in the hall. I mean, there are a few kids sitting by a table toward the back leaning on their elbows and talking quietly. One of them is a weird boy with long curly hair staring at me.

Look away. Go on. Nothing to see here.

Did he catch a glimpse of my eyes? I didn't remove my spectacles. Sometimes, at just the right angle, people are hypnotized from the side. Or, of course, if they stare directly through the lenses, which aren't thick enough for protection. And if I'm upset, it's all over.

But I'm not upset tonight. I'm in a really good mood—because of Ash. I feel like one of these kids again. Like a lovesick schoolgirl.

The guy turns.

Then a pretty girl with long blond hair catches my attention coming up the escalator. She's wearing a red sweater and jeans, but the clothes look like they were just purchased in a store. And she's got boots on. That's weird because it's like eighty degrees outside. She doesn't look like a student, except for the backpack slung over her shoulder. And she's looking right at me and chewing gum.

She walks up to me. Nobody notices me—except Ash.
Stop thinking of him, silly.

"You Gorgiana?" the girl asks with a large grimace.

I nod.

She throws her arms around me and laughs. "I'm so happy to finally meet you!"

"Who are you?" I jump out of her grasp.

"Gracie," she says between chews. Then she says more quietly, while holding a hand over her mouth, "I'm doing incognito shit. Special delivery from Cora." And she winks. But then she squints at my sweater. Her grin turns to a frown over my granny clothes.

Gracie? Who's Gracie?

Cora's best friend, Grace? The girl Cora always talks about? It must be. I never met her that whole week I was in Toronto. She was away visiting friends in LA, Cora had told me.

"How come Cora didn't tell me you were coming?" I ask.

Gracie loses her smile and nods. "It's getting real bad, Gorgiana."

"Call me Gorgi."

"You can call me Grace. Cora told me she can't even call you. But, see, she can call me. And I can keep tabs on you to make sure you're okay. See? But you wanna know the secret? The real reason I came here? You're gonna love it." And she laughs a little too hard.

"What?"

"The beach, bitch!" she cries out loud. Her voice echoes around the library. I look around, embarrassed, as everyone turns. "So, what do you think of my disguise?"

She winks again, pointing at her red sweater and then at her pants.

"I don't think people will buy that you're a student."

"Oh, snap," she says, shaking her head. She looks down. "I still look too old, huh?"

"You look too good," I say with a laugh. "Your clothes are brand new."

"Well, here's the thing, Gorgi. I need a place to sleep. Cora assumed it'd be all right—"

"Of course. You can stay at my place."

"Really? Great!" And she hugs me again. Then she looks at my hair. "Is it true?" She carefully brushes strands. "Are there really things in your head and—"

"Wigglies. Yeah."

"You call them wigglies?" she asks, staring. "Far out."

Then she gazes directly into my eyes. We're only about a foot away from each other. It doesn't matter. She freezes midchew on her chewing gum. She's completely still, staring into my gaze.

Grace is gay? Hmm. Go figure. Thirty seconds straight on, or more, I could petrify anyone, even a goddess. But she looked for only a split second and froze like a guy.

As she's staring, standing stiffly, I'm looking around. No one else is the wiser. But Grace looks ridiculous standing completely still midchew. Then I think, this is bad. Really bad. Not Grace being petrified, Grace coming here for Cora. I thought I was in the clear after Hades captured Apollo? Why would Cora send her best friend to watch over me? Why wouldn't Cora come here herself? And, shit, what does this mean for my new boyfriend?

"Far... out," she says slowly, shaking her head. A minute passes. I quickly look down.

"I'd be happy to have you stay at my place, Gracie."

She giggles and hugs me again, like the tenth time.

"We're gonna have so much fun. So, tell me, how does that freezing thing with your eyes work?"

20

HAVING FUN

I told you Cora's fun, right? Over the centuries, I've been able to count on my best friend's zaniness, with her knocking on my door at any hour of the night and whisking me away to all sorts of wonderland madness. Well, her friend Grace is like a mortal version of that—hyped up on steroids. Over the past week, she's been exhausting me. I have to watch over her and make sure she doesn't kill herself. It's easy for Cora. She has the power to heal her. Not so easy for me.

And tonight's no different. I would have preferred a nice walk with Ash on the beach. No, I had to watch over my new roomie as if I were her mom.

Right now, I'm hopping up and down under the moonlight like a fool, with a bunch of bodies, under multicolored strobe lights as this really bad heavy metal music blares through the speakers. It's cloudy by the shore. It could rain. I don't think that'd stop anyone from dancing. There's a live band, but no one really cares. It's nearly two in the morning, but I doubt they have last call. It's a beach club. No one can talk because no one can hear anything. It's like, if you're not drunk or on something, it's annoying. I'm on energy drinks and whiskey-sour shots—a special brew, thanks to Gracie— but it's not enough.

Here comes Grace. See her? Her blond hair flinging up and down, sweat dripping down her face. There are so many people, their bodies creating heat around us. My hair is safe, tight in its bun.

"Hey babe!" Grace slurs in my ear, grabbing my arm. "Having fun?"

No, not really.

She tugs on my shoulder and points at a guy and winks. The guy is coming in and out of view in the strobe lights. He's moving like a professional dancer. His T-shirt is wet with sweat, and I can see his body underneath, ripped as hell. He's dipping down, doing this limbo thing. He's got a half-goatee without a mustache. And he's got a crew cut. The girl he's with, who's wearing a respectable skirt, is gone. Now he's dancing next to a guy.

"He could be gay," I shout in Grace's ear.

She laughs and shrugs. "He's wasted. He probably doesn't care! This is so fun, Gorgi! Go over and say hi to him with me. Come on, let's go say hi. He looks like fun. And he's hot, right?"

"I like Asher."

She rolls her eyes. "Come on. Don't be dull. Let's go say hi."

She pogos over there.

The band stops, but the lights don't. Multicolored rainbow lights are still shining around the giant dance floor. I'm hoping everyone will just go home now.

Nope. Here comes the sound of techno drums blaring again. Honestly, there was enough noise coming from a hundred bodies jumping up and down.

I've had enough. I stop jumping and try to make my way

out of the dance circle to a bar. A girl hurls her body into me. I shove her, a bit too hard, and she lands over three other people. Then I get to the outdoor bar, looking out at the sea. I'd love to walk on the sand, even alone, but I look back, worried about Grace again. It's been like this every day since I met her. She's a complete lunatic.

A surprisingly preppy-looking guy walks by the bar. "Can I buy you a drink?" he asks me.

God, aren't my thick glasses enough? I don't want to do anything with anybody right now.

I shake my head.

"You have nice hair."

Fuck. Get the hell away from me or I'll show it to you.

After I don't say a word, he finally buzzes off.

I use my super-eyes to pinpoint Grace. She's dancing with that guy she was pointing at. He has his arms around her. People are watching them dance.

I get a text.

Having fun?

It's Ash. I lean against the bar, shake my head, and type *No!*

Good. He sends a laugh emoji. *Hey, but why not? What's wrong?*

Grace. Are you studying?

Going to bed. It's two in the morning. Goodnight, angel. See you tomorrow.

Can't wait.

He sends me a kiss emoji. Cute. God, I love him. But then he follows that with a heart and a snake emoji. Ha ha. That's not funny. I send him a green nauseous face.

Goodnight, Gorgiana.

God, I think I'm in love. Really. I've been in love before and it's like... It's so nice. Isn't it?

Yes. It's nice. But you might want to take a look at Cora's human nutjob who's being pushed and shoved around the dance floor.

Shit! What's going on now? Three burly guys are surrounding Grace. One is touching her chest. She slaps his hand. She smiles, but she's totally gone. Then another pulls her long blond hair, and she winces in pain.

A couple of girls from the audience shout at them to stop, but there's too much noise. Two of them grab her and lift her into their arms. They're running off with her as if she were a piece of fucking luggage!

My eyes flash green. A few people by the bar look over. I quickly cover them. I sniff the air, but I can't watch her by smell. The whole area is too full of human sweat.

My feet are moving faster than my thoughts. I... I don't know what I'm going to do, but I know if they lay a hand on her, I'm going to rip their fingers off. Grace is an idiot, of course. She hardly deserves my rescue. But any woman in distress gets me riled up. You know that.

My hair bursts out of its bun, and I feel relief as it waves over my head. A few wigglies, still narrow, brush along my cheek. I think they're trying to calm me down. I'm not in full-on Medusa mode *yet*. I'm doing everything I can to not change further in public as I rush across the dance floor. But those jerks grabbed her! Those assholes literally kidnapped Gracie in front of my eyes!

I'm pushing my way around bodies. A few dancers bounce off me, being shoved into people.

No. I'm not going to move around people; they're going to move around Medusa. I shove everyone out of my way, clearing a straight line for the beach.

Grace's legs are dangling over the shoulder of one of the burly guys. He's carrying her like a bag onto the quiet, dark beach. He slaps her ass and I hear her scream.

I'm past the last body, now in hot pursuit on the sand.

It gets darker further away from the club. Then, of all things, it starts to rain. It's hot outside, but it's cloudy. And water's pouring over me. My hair is in full-on thick viper mode now, thick cobras twisting about my head.

I'm going to take each one of them, every single one, tear their flesh off, rip out their eyes, and decapitate them. They'll be so broken up that I won't know whose body part belongs to whom.

Where are they going? They're heading to the water. It's almost as if they plan on throwing her into the sea.

The guy carrying her finally drops her on the sand near the waves. Then another big guy pulls up her T-shirt, exposing her bra. She struggles to move away. Then he pulls up her bra and runs his hands along her naked boobs.

I'm ten feet away. My hands are clenched tight, ready to break their bones.

But then I hear laughter. It's Grace. She's laughing.
What? Why?

The guy over her leans down and kisses her on the lips. She turns her head from him. That's when she sees me. Her eyes bulge and her smile turns to sheer terror. She loses her mirth and quickly shakes her head.

"No! No, Gorgi! No!"

I throw the guy off her, hurling him ten feet. All the other guys surrounding her back up. They haven't seen my eyes, but it's likely they've seen my hair—they then scatter and run off in the sand as fast as they can. Except one. The guy who carried her is on his knees beside her, and he looks right into my eyes. With one glance, he freezes.

"Stop it, Gorgi!" cries Grace. "Stop! Don't hurt him!"

Grace's screams reminded me of the sound of a woman in distress. They were like the girl in the library. But now she's asking me to stop? Why?

They were going to rape her! And then, what? Throw her into the sea? I've seen it done before.

One of my snakes runs around the guy's neck and starts choking him. It's easy. I'll simply snap his neck so Grace isn't traumatized too much.

He starts shaking, struggling to breathe.

"He's my friend! Stop! Stop it, Gorgi! We were just playing around. We were just having fun!"

My viper drops him. He falls on the sand, clutching his throat and gasping for air.

I clutch my head with my hands. What's happening? *Friend?* What's she talking about?

"We were fooling around," Grace says. "It was for fun. Jesus, don't kill him! We were messing around. We were going to make love by the shore. They were carrying me away from the crowds."

"*Friend!*" I shriek at her. She covers her ears as sand is thrown around her by my rage. "*Love!*" She cowers from me, clutching her naked chest. "*What kind of a sick game is this!*"

"That's Tom," she says, turning from me and gesturing to the guy with a trembling finger. "I met him a few days ago at The Crave." She laughs nervously. "I'm...fuck, I'm so fucked up right now, Gorgi... I think I took too much stuff. Sometimes it turns me on when I'm with a lot of guys. I just wanted to have sex with all of them." She laughs again.

I'm not finding any of this funny. In fact, I'm doing everything I can to not lunge at Gracie and kill her.

Just do it. Just kill her.

But this is Cora's best friend.

Her body is glowing green from my eyes. "I totally forgot about you. I forgot about your past and all that stuff you told me about and—"

"*Go home alone!*"

"I'm so sorry," Grace says, shaking her head.

"I should kill you!"

Kill her!

"I'm sorry, Gorgi."

"You think it's funny when a girl's raped? You like being played a victim!" And I point at the man still on the sand. The guy's awake and he kicks his legs back trying to move as far from me as he can. "You think it's funny to act like you're getting attacked!"

But I cover my head for a second. I'm so confused. My hair is jumping everywhere. A few vipers have already curled around Grace's neck, ready to snap her too. Others are jabbing at the dickhead on the floor.

I'm... I put my head in my hands and shake it.

"I'm sorry."

"Sorry? *I thought you were fucking gay!*"

And then she laughs. Can you believe it. That is so much worse. She actually laughs at me.

I really hate her. I want to kill her. It would be so quick. Centuries ago, in the midst of my rage, my monster would have. I'd have snapped her neck. It'd be curtains for her in seconds. But this twitchy little drug addict is Cora's best friend. And she's way too far gone to be lectured.

Now she's laugh-crying on the sand from the stress of seeing Medusa.

The guy tries to stand up.

"*Don't ever do that again!*" I scream at him.

He stumbles. But somehow he manages to get up. He runs, trips again, then sprints up the hill away from us.

I take a deep breath. Then I touch my nose. My glasses are gone—fuck! I lost them somewhere in the sand. I only have two of those pairs of special fake lenses.

I quickly dig in my pants pocket and dial Cora's number on my cellphone. Grace relayed instructions to never call her under any circumstances. At this point, I don't fucking care.

It rings and rings as I stare at the dark waves in the sea.

Music is still blaring behind us, and colored lights are reflecting off the fog. Stupid Grace isn't laughing anymore. She's whimpering under me on the sand like a baby.

"Hello," Cora's very tired voice answers.

"Take this piece of shit home."

"Gorgi? What's the matter?"

"Take her back. You hear me? I don't want to be anywhere near her. You understand me, Cora? I can't watch over her. She was supposed to watch over me. She's out of control."

"I told you to not call me."

Her command makes me step back in the sand. In the thousands of years I've known Persephone, I don't think I've ever shouted at her before. It's not because she's a goddess. I just really love her.

I hear a grunt from a man in the background over the phone—probably Gabriel.

"She's sick, Cora!" I cry. "I almost tore apart some of her playthings she was going to screw on the beach. They were playacting that she was in distress. She looked like she was getting raped! You know what that stuff does to me. You know my thing about that. If you want me to lay low and not be found, you'll take your friend home. I can't stand her! I don't want to be anywhere near her? You hear me?"

"Yes."

There's silence on the other end of the phone. Then I realize I'm still in monster mode. That's why I'm yelling. I don't have control over myself.

"You there?" I snap.

"Don't call me again. I love you more than anything, Gorge, but your line is being tapped. It's not safe. Okay? Don't call me again."

"I can't do this."

"Put the bitch on the line."

I hurl my cellphone at Grace, who's still crouched in the sand, bawling like the little baby she is.

"I fucked up, Kore. I really fucked up bad... Yeah. I know." She laughs again. I can't believe this. Are they laughing at me? But then Grace looks up at me and her whole body trembles. "She's going to hurt me. I know it. I just know she's going to do it."

My face is drenched. I didn't realize it, but the rain is pouring down. It wasn't bothering me before when I was Medusa. I look back and see people up the incline still dancing like fools under swirling lights. They don't seem to mind the water. Apparently, they also had no idea someone was almost gang raped. Or pretend gang raped. Whatever sick game Gracie is into.

"I'm sorry," Grace says, crying again. "I'm so sorry. Yeah. I know. Oh, come on... I'll, I'll just come home. Gorgi's right. I should come home. No. I have to. No." She shakes her head and glances at me again. "Oh...okay, Cora." And she takes a deep breath. Then the bitch chuckles again.

I'm getting dizzy. I didn't drink a lot, but that's the problem. This sick concoction of stimulants and alcohol is getting to my head.

Grace drags herself from the ground and reaches with an outstretched hand to give back my cellphone. Her head is hanging down as if she's bowing to me.

"Gorgi," says Cora on the cellphone, "no more clubs. Okay? Grace will behave, I promise, but I can't take her back. This is for security. Sorry."

"Okay."

"God, Gorge, hang on, 'kay. I'm doing everything I can."

"I know."

"Bye. It'll be a while till we can talk again. Do not, until I give you the clear, call me again. Unless it's a full-on emergency. Okay?"

"Sure, Cora."

"Sure. Yeah. Sure."

"Is Gorgiana okay?" I hear Gabe mutter in the background.

"Bye," I say. "Sorry to wake you."

Cora chuckles. "I don't sleep anymore, babe." Then she hangs up.

And Grace is, of course, still crying on the sand.

"Come on," I say.

"I am sooo sorry,"

"Shut up."

She walks near me and reaches for my hair to try to touch it. I quickly swat her hand.

"Where's your glasses?" she asks as we head back up the hill. She's clutching her ripped shirt over her chest as we walk in the rain.

"I don't know. Lost."

"You're so nice. I'm sorry."

"Stop apologizing."

She laughs. "Sorry. I mean, not sorry, I guess." More laughter. "I mean, I'm so fucked up, Gorgiana... You're a lot like her, you know?"

"Who?"

"Cora. But you're nicer."

21

THE ONE

"Where are we heading?" I ask quietly, looking out the window of his pickup truck. I brush my bangs from my eyes. My hair's tightly wrapped in a bun, of course.

When I turn, he puts a finger to his lips and smiles. He's already driven me far out of Sunland. Now we're driving this one-lane windy road, and it's woodsy with shadows of trees everywhere. I look at the dash. The digital clock reads midnight. Then I glance back at Ash.

"You've been to this mystery place before?"

"Yep."

He's acting chipper. That's good. That should make for a good night.

"It's nice that you can adapt to my weird times."

"I met a night owl, I suppose," he replies with a shrug.

Ooh!

"Don't say that word."

Ooh, I hate that word. I shudder at just the sound of it. *Owl.* Oh, how I loathe owls. Owls disgust me.

I turn from him. Then I lean against the door and stare out the passenger window again.

"Did I say something wrong?"

"I can't stand owls."

"Oh," he says with a chuckle. "I don't mean to laugh, Gorgi. You have so much different stuff I'm learning about you. By the way, where are your glasses?"

"I lost them running after ditz Grace. My other pair is still in the library."

"I like it."

"Well," I say, scooting back in my seat and gazing straight through the windshield, "don't be getting any silly ideas like actually looking into my eyes."

I run my hand along his arm. He's wearing a white-and-blue checkered button-down with jeans. It's more rustic, I suppose. Of course it looks good on him. Anything looks good on him. I'm wearing the yoozh: my brown fluffy sweater and baggy pants. But he's right about my eyes. I have to be careful where I gaze. There's already been like three close calls with Ash.

"I haven't camped in a long time," I say. "I brought some stuff I think you'll like. Gracie made some cookies. Even though she's absolutely crazy, she knows how to bake."

"She is crazy. I don't think I like her."

"I really don't like her. Still, the disaster last night was good in a way."

"Why?"

"We're able to spend the night together alone." I shrug. "After last night, she's so scared of me that I'm sure she'll stay put at home—at least tonight."

He squeezes my hand and nods.

We drive down a dirt road that parallels a lake. We're here, I think. The lake is really a dark blotch surrounded by shadows. The shadows are trees and bushes. There's nobody out. We pass another parked car, but that's the only sign of civilization. And yet we're only about an hour outside of campus.

He parks the car. Then he clips off his seatbelt and looks at me.

"I'll get the stuff," he says with his to-die-for smile.

"It looks nice. I'll get my picnic basket."

"No, I'll get it, Gorgi. You just relax."

I open the door and walk over to the dark lake's edge, stretching real tall. There's a full moon. The stars are prettier out here in this rural area.

I walk right up to the edge of the water. Then I look at myself in the moonlit reflection. God, this sweater is awful. Its ugliness is just too ugly. I can't believe I didn't fool Ash. Do you see this thing? How can Asher stand it? My hair would look better free too. Maybe I'll take the sweater off for Ash. But I can't let them wigglies go free. No, I can't do that. Especially in case I get excited around him.

Giggles.

I look back and Mr. Handsome has his hands full. I run over to help him, grabbing my cute wicker picnic basket.

"Thanks, Gorge."

"Looks like you know exactly where to go?"

He nods and takes out a foldable chair, along with a bunch of other stuff, which he lays down on the dirt. Then he cocks his head back. "I went with some friends here last year. We could have done the beach, but you told me about last night. It's quiet here and—"

"Lovely. It's beautiful, Ash."

He nods. Then he takes out all these plastic pole thingies to get a tent constructed. I open my picnic basket. I take out my roast beef sandwiches and Grace's baked cookies.

It doesn't take Ash long to erect the tent. Then I watch him build a fire. It's a real small fire. We don't want it too bright at night—it'd mess up the view. Not to mention, it's not too cold. But it wouldn't be camping without one. I don't tell him that I could probably light a fire about three times faster without all his fancy stuff—see I lived outside in the woods for eons. When I was an outcast, I had to live alone in the woods. He takes out a rug and drapes it by the fire. I move the food there. And then I sit beside him, tent behind us, fire in front, as we gaze out at the lake. In the sun, of course, it'd be better. But my eyes are adjusting, and the water is reflecting the full moonlight. It's pretty. He leans back against more blankets and puts an arm around me.

I take a whiff of the fresh air. I smell the special perfume I have on for Ash—a smelly fruity thing from Grace. She insisted I use it for him tonight. Hell, I think after last night, she'd give me everything she possesses. He's got a nice fittingly woodsy cologne on.

We munch on sandwiches. The fire crackles.

After we finish, I lean into his arms…and, well, it's nice—real nice, you know.

"Maybe we should stay tomorrow too," he says. "I can skip class."

"I can't," I say with a sigh. "I'd love to, but I have to work. You should go to lecture. And I don't trust Grace alone. She'll probably burn down my house."

"But you should enjoy the sun. Last time I was here, no one came by this spot all day. You can let your hair out—for real, Gorgi. I think it's terrible you can't come out during daylight. At least the morning sun would be nice." He touches my neck and then presses the bun. I'm sure if it weren't wrapped, he'd feel movement. "I can't believe you have snakes hidden in there."

"But I do. Which is another reason why we won't be staying here tomorrow, mister. I don't want you to see them. And stop touching them, please."

"Okay. But can I kiss you?"

"Yeah. Of course, you can do that."

"How? Gorgiana, I can't look into your eyes. How can our lips touch if I can't be near your eyes?"

"Easy. For one thing, most people close their eyes when they smooch. But, just in case—" I slowly turn. He can probably see my profile. I close my eyes. "Close your eyes. We both will. Then we just touch. Like this. That's how it's done. But I'm really serious. Keep your eyes closed."

He nods. I turn, move his arm, and cheat, gazing at his face. My eyes turn his features green. That's from desire. And I can feel the wigglies hurting my bun trying to burst out. I touch his face and his cute stubble. His eyes—

"Don't open them! The only other way is blindfolded. Do I have to do that?"

"Sorry...but, why? What's the worst that happens? You freeze me for a minute? You said you can't turn me into stone."

I lean forward and kiss his cheek. Then I kiss his closed eyelids. Each of them.

We're touching lips. I enter his mouth and our tongues touch. It's like last time, but sweeter. Gentler. There's no rush fearing that something will take him away. No one can see us out here. So we have the whole night to ourselves. So my tongue stays whole—barely.

"But why don't I blindfold *you*, Gorgi?"

"I'd never let a man blindfold me." I sound angrier than I intended. He nearly opens his eyes again. "Don't open them. I can't let anyone restrain me, Ash. I can't, because of my past. Will you keep your eyes shut?"

I let go and touch his lips, harder this time. Then I reposition myself, straddling my legs over his and facing him straight on. I run my hands inside his shirt. Then I lift his shirt and sneak my head under it. It's like his shirt acts as a tent.

"You can open them now," I say with a giggle inside his shirt.

With my green eyes, I watch as my fingers glide along his musculature. His skin twitches from my touch. My fingernails get sharper. I have to be careful that I don't cut him. I run along his nipple.

"I'm gonna take your shirt off. You're gonna have to close your eyes again."

"Do whatever you want," he says.

I'm getting too excited. My fingers are close to my eyes, and even this close up I can pinpoint each finger as it runs over the ridges of his tight green abs. I'm falling into predator mode, and my eyes are getting super sharp. My ears are pricked too. I can hear birds sleeping. I hear their breath. I even hear two alligators lurking about a thousand yards across the lake. But there aren't any humans around.

So I can have sex with him, right? I can remove his clothes and have him right here in front of the lake. Is that wrong?

Uh...no. Until he sees your snakes.

I hesitate to remove his shirt. That cue could be enough to drive me over the edge.

He does it for me—with eyes still closed, of course. Good boy.

I touch my lips to his again, now running my hands along his bare chest.

"Perhaps we should stop."

"Why?" He laughs.

"You just asked for a kiss," I say, between kisses. "This is going too far."

He surprises me by grabbing my body hard and pulling me closer to him. He kisses me more passionately than ever.

"Ash..."

I feel him removing my stupid granny sweater. I don't have my usual ugly button-down blouse underneath. I have a cute gray T-shirt on. So I help him by pulling that off too. Now I'm pressing myself, with only a bra, against his naked chest as he's kissing me.

Maybe I should make love to him?

"You're amazing," he says, running his hands along my back. He presses against the clasp of my bra. I know he wants it off, but I hesitate. I snatch his hand back.

"Can't I look now?" he asks. "God, I want to see you. I want to see your eyes."

"No. Do this. But keep them shut."

I take his hands and run them along my face. I feel his fingers touch my moist lips as I kiss them. Then he fingers my soft cheeks. Now if I lose control, he'll be feeling ugly crow skin. That'd make him toss me off for sure. But I'm not that far gone yet. And, anyway, when I'm that deeply gone, the man usually doesn't have a clue what's going on anymore anyway.

"You're so beautiful."

I'm rocking over him a little. I've been doing that. I didn't even realize it until now, but I'm moving up and down over his cock.

"How do you even know I'm pretty?" I ask with a laugh.

"I...seriously, you're the most beautiful girl in the world."

"And the deadliest."

That hardly stops him from rubbing my back. And it bothers me a little. It's like, he doesn't realize that he's fondling an A+ predator, as if he's petting a tiger or cobra. He doesn't get just how dangerous I am. I was hoping my words would serve as a warning. It tells me that, even though I haven't entranced him with my eyes, I've mesmerized him with my body.

"We should stop."

But I'm still slowly rocking up and down over his cock. My body is not obeying my words. I feel his hands roam near my bra strap. I know he wants it off, but I push his hand away again. When my boobs are out, there's no more discussion.

He nods and stops touching me. I'm surprised. Few men can ever stop at this point—like, no one.

"If you want to, Gorgiana, sure. I didn't come here for this, I came here just to be with you."

I want to cry over that. I want to bawl my eyes out. But that would make him run to the car. That's so sweet!

That's when I get it. This guy isn't a crush. He's the one. "The one" is so rare to find. Sometimes I'll go for a century without knowing one. But this is "the one." This is a man that could love me, if I could love him back. Well, I do love him. And I'm thinking, somebody who can withstand this temptation—the greatest succubus in the world—has to be in love with me. Right?

I hope so.

My lips reach over again. Just a peck. But then...we can't stop kissing. And I'm moving on him all over again. And it feels like we're kissing more passionately than ever.

"I love you, Ash." But it sounds almost like a whimper. Then...one last kiss, it has to be, and then...I make myself turn my head and lie still with my face on his chest. "You can open your eyes now, lover."

"Are you okay?" he asks with a chuckle, holding me tight.

"Never better. Happier than I can remember."

"Oh, Gorgi. You're irresistible." He kisses my head. "You know that?"

"Yeah, I know that."

"I felt one of your snakes."

"What!" I ask, jumping from him. But then I quickly lie back on his chest, so he doesn't see my green eyes.

"I felt something move on your head."

"Oh, God, Ash. No. It's so gross."

"Dirt and mud is gross, Gorgi. But when you go camping, you look to sleep on that. Right?"

"I guess," I say snuggling closer to his chest with a sigh. "But my hair is super disgusting. Your similitude doesn't fit this predicament very well. We're talking about slimy icky snakes."

"They don't bother me. I don't mind snakes. My sister's the one who hates them."

"Her impression of me all makes sense now."

He laughs and shakes his head. "She doesn't dislike you. She doesn't like snakes because of what happened to us."

"What? She was bitten by one?"

"Yeah. Well, sort of."

"*Really?*"

I feel him nod. But I'm still leaning against his chest.

"She and I used to hike with our parents in Yosemite. When she was, like five, we were out on this trail. Dad was off nearby, walking with Mom near a trail by the water. You could see this amazing bright view of Half Dome, where we were playing. I didn't know at the time, but I went back to the same spot many times later."

"Half Dome with the reflecting granite is very pretty."

"Yeah, well my sister and I, we were little so we were perfectly happy rummaging through leaves. Anyway, she and I were stirring leaves with sticks. Tons of yellow leaves had collected over the trail. My sister walked to the lake's edge. Then my voice shrieked before I even realized what had happened. I saw blood along my arm. And this really huge snake slithered away back into the bushes. My sister came over and became frantic screaming at the sight of my arm. Then Mom and Dad ran back."

"Even when you were little you were bitten by a snake," I remark glibly.

"Yeah, but the weirdest thing is they still didn't bother me. After Mom and Dad freaked out with Sandra, they had me see a doctor, or whatever medical practitioner they had in the middle of nowhere back then. But my sister was the one traumatized. Every time Sandra saw a snake after that, she freaked out."

"She cared about you. It bothered her more than if she had been bitten."

"Yeah."

"Perhaps she's not so bad. No wonder she didn't like me."

My body shakes from his laughter. "She might not have cared for Gorgiana the librarian. But she liked Gorgiana, the Medusa. She was in awe of your voice."

"Yeah, well, she really wouldn't like my hair."

He reaches back and kisses my neck. "She'd like you when she gets to know you." He touches my hair again. "I can feel your hair quiver."

"Stop touching it then, Ash. Please. You can be weird and like it, but I never will."

"I want to take the bun down."

"Please, Ash, no." I sink even deeper into his chest and move my head farther from him.

"You're not being fair. You said you wanted me to be Ash. I want you to be Medusa."

"But Gorgiana and Medusa aren't the same. All you'll be feeling is Medusa. My snakes are part of my curse. They're like my eyes. They're not who I am."

"I think you're Gorgiana and Medusa. I like you both. When I first saw you in the library, I knew there was more to Gorgiana the librarian than meets the eye. The outfit works.

People don't look at you. But I did. I saw a beautiful, intelligent, fascinating woman. That's why I went over to you that first time. Then there was the Alcove."

"Don't stop, Ash," I say with a laugh. "Please go on."

And I'm back to grinding again. Fuck. I can't stop. My head's still buried in his hard chest, but I'm moving on him again. Shit, I don't know how I got back to straddling him, but I did. So? Sue me. I can't control myself. Shameful? Whatever. I'm a monster. I'm also a woman with a very attractive man.

"Tell me more," I say.

"You're funny," he says.

"I'm funny?"

"Yes, very."

I'm about ready to jump off and take a walk. I don't know what else is gonna stop me from fucking him at this point. Or maybe I can jump in the cold lake and bathe as if it's a cold shower?

But I've trained my new man. As I look at Ash, he turns from my gaze.

But he's also a man. His fingers are working my bra strap again.

I laugh. He can't unclasp it. So I sit straighter over him, my eyes glowing, his whole body green, and reach back and take my bra off.

"Don't tell me you're not going to let me look at those too?" he asks, pained.

I laugh harder. I turn my head and close my eyes. "Go ahead."

But he doesn't just look, he runs his fingers along the curves of my boobs. Then he touches my nipples.

"Amazing."

"You mean, what an amazing rack?"

"Yeah. They're you. Just like your wigglies."

Fuck it. I undo the bun over that. I don't think I'm thinking straight, to be honest. I think I'm mesmerized just like Ash is.

"They're out of the bun, all right?" I say. "Just don't open your eyes."

"Feel?"

I dip down closer to him. Then I feel my body shake. I've been brave about him leaving. But now? When I desire him more than anything? It'll kill me if he touches my hair and runs.

He runs his hands along my hair.

Are you worried they'll bite him? Not Asher. I'm not about to have him relive his childhood memory. Hell, I'd jump into a raging fire before hurting this man. But I'm still so nervous that he'll bolt.

"Feel them?" I mutter nervously. I start working his pants. I unzip and pull them down under me.

"Yeah."

"You want to run now?"

"No, Gorgi. I don't."

I yank his pants down to his feet. I kiss his cheek and lips. He moves his hands back over my boobs.

"Ash?" I say. He's pulling down my pants now.

"What?"

"I become very wild when aroused. If we're really going to do this, please do not look into my eyes. And don't touch my face anymore. Or my hair. Okay? Please promise."

"Why?"

"Just don't do those things. It's the only way this can be done. And..." how do I tell him this one! "No sucking my boobs."

"What?" he asks with a chuckle. "Why?"

"Seriously."

"Any other rules, Gorgi?"

I answer by straddling my panties over his naked cock. He reaches for my butt and squeezes. I get up for a moment and look behind me at the dark lake. Then I pull off my underwear and kick it from my feet. I straddle him again. He looks at my breasts. Quickly, but gently, I move his head to the side.

"Careful. No looking."

"You have too many rules."

But I know how to end his complaint. I slowly sink down and position my body until he's inside me. And now, as I grind like before, I'm fucking him. He's facing the lake. That's okay. It helps remind me to turn from him to look at the lake too.

He's touching my breasts. I'm holding his chest too. My hands are on top of his hard ribs. With a little squeeze, I could break his chest or fracture his back. That's another secret I'm keeping from him. In this predatory state, I have to use every ounce of concentration to not hurt his body. Trouble is, that's gonna keep me from paying attention to my hair. And, in fact, some of the naughties are touching his chest and face. Does he feel them? He doesn't say. His eyes are closed.

"God, Gorgi, shouldn't we do this in the tent?"

"No," I say. "There aren't any other humans near us."

"How do you know?"

"I... I can smell them. I can smell everything, especially now. It's heightened so much that I know where every animal is by the lake. There's a deer. About three are up the hill deep in the forest. The closest animal is a squirrel sleeping in the bushes about twenty yards from us. I can even feel where the closest fish are swimming."

"You smell them?" He's breathing more heavily.

"Not the fish themselves. I hear the sound of the movement they make in the water."

It's turning me on even more talking to him. I love talking to men when having sex. Another weird thing about me, right? Well, I'm talking to you right now. Typically, men don't say much. But when they do, I can hear heavy breathing. That arouses me more.

"That's incredible."

Sometimes, like—just now—did you hear it? Did you? I hear a groan between his words.

"I see the image in my mind," I say. "And, no... none of that's incredible. You are incredible."

I reach down and touch my lips to his again. We're back to French kissing. Between kisses, I say, "I probably couldn't hear them much right now though. But the closest human, I guess, is about five miles from here."

"How come you can't hear them?"

"I'm too busy fucking you."

"Yeah. Keep doing that."

I laugh. So does he.

And there's no more talking. I'm too far gone into a trance myself. I'm bouncing hard on him now. Up and down and it's only getting heavier.

"Yes, Ash. Yes."

He opens his eyes just a little bit under the green light. I quickly cover them with my hand. I almost fall on him, losing balance, making sure they're covered.

"Close your eyes."

Because my snakes are full grown. They're cobras when I'm this transformed. And if Ash looks, he's going to lose his arousal. Hell, I would. The vipers are snapping, but they're obeying me. My fangs are out too. So I can't reach down and kiss him anymore.

In the olden days, this would have been my true hell. When I was first cursed, it would be like this. I'd find that rare true love, *the one*, and make love to him, only to tear him to pieces. This was the greatest delight of that bitch-witch Athena. To make me live an immortal hell totally and completely alone. Part of me wonders if Ash still thinks this could happen to him. Never. I'd never hurt him.

He's lying there with his head turned from me. A snake or two passes along his eyelids, I can't control them anymore, but I think he's too aroused to care. Oh, God, it feels so good! I'm...

"I'm coming, Ash. I'm coming. Don't stop."

I feel him orgasm inside me. That takes me over the edge.

I fall to his side, ashamed. My stupid snakes are still moving all over his body. My face, if Ash looked—I shudder at the thought!—would look like Grandma, so I hide my face in my hands.

But I peek. He's not looking at me. He's still obeying me with his eyes closed. He just turns a little.

I run my tongue along my teeth. My fangs are receding. When it's safe enough for me to peck his cheek, I lean over and kiss him.

"Was it too weird?" I ask. I'm not sure I want to know.

He shakes his head. "But," he says, "will you ever let me look into your eyes, Gorgi?"

"Why? I guess. You can now, I suppose. If you really want to so badly."

"Yeah. I really do."

I lift my head from my hands and face him. He opens his eyes. For a flash, a faster moment than is visible for any human, he grins. Then he turns solemn. His face freezes. I turn from him and lean my head against his chest, listening to his heart rate slow a little. I wait for him to awaken. A minute later, I feel him put his arm around me.

"Do you remember what my eyes looked like?" I ask. I'm turned from him and he's spooning me.

"They were amazing."

"Liar," I say with a chuckle.

I feel him touch my cursed hair. They've become thin and receded, but they're still moving. "It's a part of you. It's beautiful."

He's absolutely crazy, isn't he?

22

MORNING, FOR REAL

WHEN I GET UP QUIETLY AND SLIDE FROM MY LOVER'S embrace, I see bright light shining through the cracks of our tent. I slept naked in his arms for the rest of the night, so I rise in the nude and walk outside. I look back and Ash's shirtless chest is still gently undulating, quietly up and down, with his cute nose and mouth taking small breaths in and out.

I lift my head and sniff the wilderness air. There's still no human nearby. But there's a gator about twenty yards to my right. He's slowly walking to me by the shore. I don't mind. I told you, I love those creatures. We have a lot in common.

I ignore him and make my way across the dirt and leaves, barefoot, to the edge of the lake. Then I gaze out.

I feel like I did when Cora stood with me at her house. This lake is small but, under a cloudless sky, just as lovely. The blue-green water reflecting the sun's rays, surrounded by green marsh and trees is... well, there are no words. It's what I imagine heaven to be—or the closest my damned soul could ever get to being there. The sun is warm. And I have to squint as it's shining right into my eyes.

I feel Ash put his arms around me. I'm not going to act surprised. I felt him leave the tent a minute ago. Didn't you? Now he's holding me as I gaze out at the lake.

"You were right," I say. "It was worth it to stay the night and see this in the morning."

"Yeah."

"What do you think of my hair?" I run my fingers through it. "I guess if you're not rushing back to the car, it's not too scary in the sunlight."

"I felt them last night, Gorgi. Seeing them hardly bothers me. Nor does seeing your absolutely perfect body in sunlight."

And he leans down and kisses my cheek.

"You make me so happy," I say with a nod.

"Your dark hair outside a bun is curlier than I imagined. Gorgi, I'm imagining you wearing a dress. You'd look Greek. You'd look stunning in a Greek dress."

"Medusa was Greek, Ash. Yes. Snakes and all."

Then I'm remembering my going-away party hosted by Cora. I wonder if that's why she had me dress up in that peplos and look the way we once were. Cora must like seeing me the way I once was too.

"*Jesus!*" he cries, jumping from me. "*Watch out!!*"

The alligator is five feet away. It growls. They rarely do that.

"It's okay," I say with a laugh. "He's not going to bite you when I'm here. Put your arms back around me."

"Why is he growling?"

"You don't want to know."

Ash obliges. He puts his arms back around me. Then, although he's still trembling with fear, he's back to kissing my cheek.

"You're irresistible. Even in front of an alligator."

"And without clothes, right? But stop. You're making him jealous."

Of course, I already told you when I'm naked, my pheromones are irresistible. They're just more insidious than my eyes. But I think having slept together all night is enough to enable Ash and me to control ourselves. Anyway, I just want his company right now.

"I'm going to put some clothes on. I'll be right back."

"If you must." But then he snatches my wrist. "Is it safe here?"

"You mean with the alligator or with me and my hair moving in the sunlight?" I ask with a laugh.

"That's not funny, Gorgi."

He kisses my lips again. He laughs as we smooch.

Then his hands drift along the crack of my ass, and I touch his naked chest and stomach. Oh...that feels good. Unlike me, he's got shorts on. But, fuck me, he's turning me on again touching me. My hands drift down to his shorts, seemingly by themselves.

"I better go get dressed," I say, tearing myself from his lips. "Excuse me, Asher."

"I'll come with you," he says, gesturing to the alligator.

"No." I shake my head. "It's okay. You're safe. Watch." I kneel right beside the alligator. Then I touch its nose and pet it. It growls again. "It won't hurt you."

"Can I do that?"

"Are you crazy? He'll bite your hand off." I laugh at his expression. "I'll be right back."

23

PALLAS

THE DRIVE BACK HAS BEEN UNCOMFORTABLE. I HUNG A TOWEL over the passenger window and another between me and the windshield so no one sees my hair in the car. Isn't it great being a mythological beast? Well, we're driving back during the day, and I can't chance a stray glance. There's even a shade over Ash's side to shield us from prying eyes. Ash suggested we just wait till nightfall, but I wanted to get back and check on nutzo. I kind of feel bad, you know. I've been so mean to her since the beach. I don't blame myself for hating her, but that doesn't mean I had to treat her the way I did. If I were a human girl, I'd be shaking at the sight of my stupid snakes too. I don't know, maybe it's the time spent with Ash or something, but I want to make up with Gracie when we get home.

Ash turns the corner into our neighborhood, and I'm happy to be home.

But then I jump in my seat. The window that Hades had fixed at the front of my living room is broken again. Is there another intruder?

Oh no. What about Grace?

Ash barely stops the car before I throw open the door. I hear him shout behind me because I didn't cover my hair and, though it's near sunset, the sun's still out.

Calm down Gorgi. Ditzy Grace probably had another stupid party.

I hope she's okay. Why did I leave her?

I don't bother with my front door. I don't need to. Whoever broke in made a nice hole large enough to fit my body through.

"Grace! Gracie! Are you here?"

I charge into my living room hoping she's sleeping on the couch, but there's a note on the carpet, shining green under my eyes, stopping me:

Dear Gorgo,

Tell Kore. Tell her I request one thing, and one thing alone, if she wants to ever see her friend again. You. If you come to my location by sunrise and turn yourself in, I will exchange your life for the human's. Imada may even consider burying you as a sufficient sacrifice to make peace once more. But if you do not meet me, her friend dies. I give you and Kore one night. By sunrise tomorrow, if you do not appear, Grace will be sacrificed.

Imada shall have its sacrifice, whether by the blood of Medusa or the blood of Persephone's best friend.

With hatred, your most blessed creator,
Pallas

I hear footsteps behind me. My vipers are moving like crazy around my head, searching everywhere, snapping all over the place. I whirl around. Asher puts his hand out to avert my green gaze. It's too late. With a full view of my eyes, he freezes. I don't have time to care for my dearest cherub.

Rather, I rummage through my pants pocket and yank out my phone. But I don't need to call, Cora's already calling.

"Oh my God, Cora, did you hear? They took Grace."

On the back of the note there's an address. It's somewhere in Arkansas. Dellon's lair? Probably. I don't know the actual spot.

Cora's quiet, which is really weird. For a moment, I wonder if Imada broke our connection.

"Where can we meet?" I ask.

I hear crying on the other end. Shit, can you believe that? When's the last time Persephone cried! Like never. I never hear her cry. Never. I'm the crybaby.

"I can't, Gorgi," she says. "I can't. I have to protect Gabriel and Moros." She takes a deep breath. "Gorgi, they're asking me to choose between you and her. I won't do that. This is up to you. Maybe you should just stay home."

"I'll go."

"Why? Why would you do that? You can't stand her."

"Why'd you send her here, Cora? She was supposed to be your informant to protect me. All she's been is trouble. All I've been doing is protecting her."

"Grace is the only person, other than you and Gabe, that I trust."

Ash wakes up from his trance. He quickly turns, thinking he can still avoid my eyes. Then I catch him in the periphery staring at my hair. Yeah, it's in full-on slimy cobra mode now. Gross. And even though he and I have become much closer —as you well know—he hasn't looked upon my thick snakes in their full glory like this before.

His gaze wanders around the dim room. But it's weird because he keeps looking back and then quickly looking away. His neck muscles are tight. He's clutching his hands. And he's breathing funny. Basically, he's finally freaking out.

He runs out of my house.

Fuck. Now? You knew it would happen eventually. Could there be any worse time?

"What should I do, Cora?" I ask, turning back and staring at my charred wall.

"I won't love you any less whatever you decide, Gorge. It...it has to be your choice. It's up to you." But saying those words seem to kill her. "If you go, you'll be in so much danger. But I have Hades on your tail. The plan is for him to follow, intervene, and save her before they exchange you for her. But I can't guarantee he'll succeed. It's really too dangerous. Like I said, you should just stay home."

"I'll go there. I don't know what else to do. I don't see a choice, Cora."

Ash is back on my threshold. He's running his hand through his blond hair and staring down at the living room carpet.

"They took Grace," I say, cocking my head back.

He nods. But he still has his head down.

"I'd do it, but there's only one problem, Cora. I don't know how to drive."

"Press the gas pedal and steer the fucking wheel, Gorgi!" she snaps. Cora never shouts at me. Like, never. "Come on... It's not hard to drive. Look, I have to go. I'm making arrangements for defense here at home. Soldiers are walking my grounds right now. Can you believe that? It's that bad. Things are coming to a showdown. Whatever your decision, I love you. And I'm worried about you. I'm so sorry I got you mixed up in this."

"These are *our* troubles, Cora."

"Yeah, well, you just be careful."

She hangs up. I take a deep breath. Then I turn back to my man. He's near the door with his hands still in his pockets.

"Will you finally leave me now?" I ask.

"What?" He's still staring at the ground. He shakes his head. "I'm... sorry. I... I haven't—"

"Seen my hair in full form?"

He shakes his head. "Your skin."

Ugly? Old? Shit, I know. Medusa is a hideous monster. There's no way to explain it until humans see me for what I really am.

"Wrinkled skin and snakes," I say with a nod. "That's Medusa, Asher."

"No." He shakes his head. "Just your face. I didn't expect... You never told me that changes. I told you... I want you, the whole you. Gorgi and Medusa. I'm just shocked. Sorry."

I walk up to him, but before I touch him, I touch my head. Thank God, the snakes are thin again. My cheeks are soft.

"Turn around. My face is me again."

He turns, but he knows not to gaze into my eyes. I take his hand and glide it over my face. Then I put my arms around him and lean my head on his shoulder, like we did that first special time at the beach. Then I squeeze him in my arms.

"What are you going to do?" he asks.

"Save Grace." I don't tell him what that might mean for me. "I'm scared, Ash. I'm really scared. Please hold me."

He embraces me tightly by the door.

24

CONFESSION

I will do what I have to do. What I've done my whole wretched life. I always have. But I can't leave Ash. He's in grave danger hanging with me and I should ditch him. But I can't. Well, the problem is, as you well know, I'm a homebody. I don't know how to drive. Never learned. Stupid, right? But without a car, how am I supposed to drive eight hundred miles and be in Arkansas by sunrise? And if there's one thing I know about Pallas Athena: when she threatens to do something, she does it.

I'm assuming the bitch has Grace at Dellon's hangout. Or at least nearby. But I don't know. I took a bus in the area, but I had no idea where the exact location was. Anyway, I haven't ditched Ash yet. He's driving me. I know what you're thinking. I'm being selfish, right? I could have just taken his car and hoped for the best.

That would have been better. Cora's right. How hard can driving be?

Maybe...shit, maybe. I don't know. Maybe I need him with me. I'm messed up, you know.

We know.

"I'm sorry," I say, staring out the passenger window. It's like what Cora's been saying to me since summer. Now I get it. Because now I'm doing to Ash what she thinks she's been doing to me. It's okay to look out the passenger window with my naked eyes because it's nightfall. And we're already far from civilization.

"Sorry about what?"

I kick off my sandals and stretch out my legs, covered in tight black leggings, propping my feet on the dash. Then I run my fingers through my long hair and take a really long, deep breath. The thin little wigglies are not dormant. They're twitching, nervous as hell. Ash might notice. I'm not sure he cares anymore. Not after what he saw in my house. Then I stare at my fingernails. I never paint my nails. See, when I get excited and they lengthen, the paint chips off.

"'Bout what, Ash?" I ask wryly. "Oh, I don't know. How about ruining any chance of you going to school tomorrow? You're not gonna make it to morning lectures." He shrugs, staring at the highway. "Or...asking you to drive me a thousand miles, all night, to Arkansas? Or... how 'bout risking your life over a super-psycho-bitch goddess who wants to kill me and anyone I'm close to? Or—"

"Who is Pallas?"

I tuck my legs back under my seat and stare at the lines on the highway, lit by our headlights, zooming by. There's lots of shadows of trees on my side of the freeway. I'm not sure I want to tell him.

So I don't. I've been on this earth long enough to know that most people forget the questions they ask if you don't answer.

"Who's Pallas?" he repeats.

Should I tell him?

"You won't believe me."

He laughs. "I'd believe anything at this point, Gorgi."

"The goddess Athena is also known as Pallas. You know, Minerva is the Roman name for Athena. Athena is the founding goddess of Athens and the queen bitch of the whole world."

"I've read Homer. Somehow, I don't recall the name Pallas."

"Hmm." I stare into darkness. There's a dim green glow along my window now that I'm talking about my archenemy. "Take a look again. Athena was raised with a nymph sister in Libya. One day, as a little girl, Athena had a fight with her. She impaled her nymph sister with a spear. In honor of her murder, and to hide the crime, from that day forth, Athena called herself her sister's name: Pallas. She altered the story and said the two of them were just playing. Athena did what she always does, she lied. She lied, schemed, and used others for her own selfishness. She even had a large statue made of herself, The Palladium, said to protect the city of Troy."

"I've heard of the Palladium. So, you don't like Athena? I thought Athena was a good goddess?"

"I despise Athena with all my heart, body, and soul. She's the goddess that cursed me."

"Oh."

I watch trees flash by my window. We're passing through a forest. It'd be nice if it was sunny.

Ash yawns.

"Are you sure you can drive this late?" I ask.

"Yeah. But it is the middle of the night. Why didn't you ever learn to drive?"

"When cars first came out, there were accidents all the time. There still are. I don't want to risk hurting anybody."

"It's not hard, Gorgi. But don't worry about it. So, Pallas, or Athena, wants to capture you in a trade with Grace. Why?"

"You believe she's a goddess from ancient Greece?"

"I saw the snakes on your head." He looks toward me but darts his eyes from mine. Then his eyes roll.

It starts to drizzle outside. He turns on the windshield wipers.

"I believe you, but why does she want to capture you?" he asks.

"We've been at war for thousands of years. Not just Athena and I. Cora, Hades, and I are against many gods. Some immortals, like my best friend Cora, are on our side. Arachne's another monster like me on our side. I haven't seen Arachne in years. She's a friend wronged by Athena too. Even Sara, Cora's mother, Demeter, is sort of on our side."

"These gods and goddesses are members of your family?"

"No. I told you, I was born a human like you. I lost contact with my family three thousand years ago when Athena transformed me into a monster. I went on Cora's side after she rescued me. It wasn't hard because Cora's arch-enemy is Athena too."

"How did she rescue you?"

Oh, no. Don't go there. End this now! Don't you dare speak of it, Gorgiana. I'm warning you.

I turn back to my window and fold my arms. I hope that, maybe, he'll ignore his question.

"How did Cora save you?"

"Persephone. Cora is the goddess Persephone."

"Okay. How did Persephone save you?"

Don't tell him!

But he won't run. He's seen who we are.

He doesn't know who you really are. He doesn't know Medusa. Remember how he acted when he saw your face?

He's seen me. He knows me now.

Remember his reaction?

"I don't want to lose you," I whisper. I brush my eyes and they're wet—of course, because I'm ready to stupidly cry. Because, you know, I like doing that.

"You don't have to tell me."

"For the danger I'm putting you in, I owe you." I touch his hand. But my hand's shaking. I'm really scared. "It's about my home in Sarpedon."

"You told me you couldn't tell me about that," he says with a nod.

He squeezes my hand, which is adorable. I slowly take my hand back.

After I tell him, he'll probably slam on the brakes, throw me out of his car, and make me walk home. No. If he does, it's okay. I'll leave. Honestly, I'll just go. He'll be safer that way. I'll still have to somehow get to Arkansas though. Maybe I can borrow his car and wing this how-to-drive thing.

"You don't have to tell me, Gorgi."

"It's rare to find someone I care about. Especially for someone like me. You know, I go around as Gorgiana the librarian, not just in Sunland, but I've done it for centuries. I've been a gypsy, a nun, even a simple farm girl. I mind my own business. I stay to myself. I can go so long without ever talking to anybody."

I look over. He just nods as he stares forward.

"Every once in a while, I find someone special. When I do, it's always the same fear, that they'll run."

"I won't run."

You know what? I'll throw all my chips down. I'll confide in him. I like him so much and I owe him. I'll tell him the good along with the horrid.

"I've fallen in love with you, Ash. I know we've only known each other for a little while, but I know when a guy is right. When he's the one. There are so few men out in the world like you. And once, there was a time I didn't trust any man. But I know I can trust you."

"I really like you too, Gorgi."

Well, that was easy, wasn't it? No doubt it would be. But my hands are trembling. Because he still wants to know about Cora.

He reaches for my hand again. Shit. That's sweet as hell. I pull away. I say, "I don't mind it when I tell you I love you and you don't say you love me back."

"What does that mean?" he asks. "I care about you."

"You don't understand," I reply, quickly shaking my head. "No human being should love me. Especially one that's pure and such a bright light as you." I'm choking up. "No one should love a beast."

"I told you, you don't have to tell me if it hurts you this much."

I nod and turn my whole body, facing the passenger window. I intend to just stare into the darkness as I say the rest of my words, but my cursed green eyes light up the cabin. I cover them so the stray rays don't affect Ash. That's all I need is for him to freeze and drive us into a tree.

"Sarpedon." The word comes slowly out of my mouth.
Don't—
Shut up. I'm done with you. I'm with Ash now.
He will leave you.
"I've told so few people, Ash. But for the risks you're taking, and for you to understand why Athena's doing this, I must tell you."

I don't turn. I just open a finger of light through my hand and look out. Even that lights up the cabin. We're on a bend now, and he's turning the car. We're passing a semi-truck. The driver probably sees our car glowing green inside.

"It was so long ago. I think I remember more the

memory of it than the actual occurrence. Just fleeting images. You know, an immortal mind is still like a human one, and there's only so much we can cram in there. Anyway, it was a horror. It was the worst time of my life." I chuckle. "It's funny because before my transformation, I told you, it was the best time. I walked in peace in Athena's temple. I was a model priestess and I had so many friends. It all ended when the god Poseidon visited me. When he raped me."

I let that simmer. Ash, being the amazing guy he is, of course touches my shoulder.

"Is that it?"

Not even close, mister.

"Poseidon visited me in Athena's temple. At first, he wooed me. But he knew I was celibate by duty. Sex on temple grounds was the worst offense to an Olympian god. I resisted. Then he did the unthinkable. He ravaged me in the temple.

"After he destroyed my life, I ran. I was in the worst panic of my life. I ran and fell before Athena's altar and confessed to her, begging for her forgiveness. After a couple hours of kneeling and crying, she visited me in her temple with the god Apollo. At first, she spoke with her usual fake sugar tongue. I almost thought she was going to forgive me. I should have known better.

"Apollo is a champion of vipers. He bound my legs with snakes. Then they both picked me up and dragged me to a water well. Well, it wasn't a water well. It was a pit of snakes.

"I don't recall my transformation. But I recall waking up the next day in daylight in the snake pit. Surrounding me were hundreds of these vipers slithering all over my body. Then, unlike now, I was terrified of snakes, like your sister. At first, I screamed, touching my head, because I thought they were in my hair. Then I realized in darkness the full horror of Athenian justice.

"I wandered for many moons in the form of Medusa—the same disgusting thing you saw in my home. I didn't know how to transform back into a human. I didn't know it was possible. Cora taught me later. I certainly didn't know that I could roam around at night without the snakes showing themselves.

"I learned to live alone. On my isle of Sarpedon, I found cave dwellings inside the rocks of cliffs. There alone, mainly at night, I hunted fowl and wild boar. I could sneak up to animals while they slept. Hunting came easy for me.

"In time, I visited human dwellings again. Not inside, of course—believe it or not, I feared what humans thought of my appearance more than they feared me. I was more like an outside prowler. Sarpedon was a small island. It thrived as a shipping port. A couple thousand citizens lived along the shore away from the less populated farmland and the cliffside where I resided.

"One day, I can't tell you when, two teenagers came snooping around my lair. It was a young couple, a boy and a girl. The girl entered the cave first. I didn't know yet that my power worked through arousal. If only the boy had come down first...if...if only the boy had come first. Well...he would have simply frozen.

"The girl descended with her torch. She saw me sitting by my fire. Again, I hadn't changed back to a human, I still didn't know how. Only the girl hadn't been prepared, like you."

"She screamed," Ash interjects with a nod.

"Of course she did." I peek out between my fingers. Even more green. I close my eyes and cover them again. "Her boyfriend pulled out a sword. I think I was as surprised as the girl at how fast and ferociously I mutilated him. I recall stepping back against the earthen wall... I remember, I recall this so well still...stepping back against the wall and staring at the girl, with her hands over her mouth, shaking and screaming at the body of her dead boyfriend by my bare feet. Some of his fingers and both legs were scattered in a pool of blood under her."

I stop at that. Not because I'm about to cry, but because it's so disgusting. Ash just keeps driving.

"I wanted to cover it up. I wanted it cleansed. I didn't want to see his body anymore but, more so, I didn't want to hear the girl's terrible screams. I didn't want to be reminded what I had done. No...I didn't want to be reminded what I was. Her screams told me what a beast I was. I didn't want to know. I still hear them. Then my rage over my transformation made me lash out at the innocent girl. Quicker than I imagined, I killed her too."

Ash's hand's not even shaking. He's just ever so slightly inching the wheel and staring at the road.

"At first, I felt less lonely." I chuckle. "The death of my first victim almost made me happy. You can't understand, I'm sure. But I was so miserable in loneliness that even that brief contact with humans was something, even that hideous act was a closeness, however repulsive. But then, like you're thinking now, thoughts of their ruined lives settled in. That little part of me that was just a seed growing —Gorgiana, the one who could care—thought about that. I thought of the two lives I had destroyed. And damn it, Ash, it only made me more miserable.

"People investigated. That destroyed my guilt. For anyone daring to walk into my cave to check on what happened was promptly eliminated. I learned to be even faster at killing, because it blinded me to my act. Soon they brought in hoplites—soldiers in armor—who were experts with the sword and shield. Some were from the city state of Sarpedon, others were mercenaries, others came for the sport of trying to kill the mythic snake beast. A few even boasted coming from the young war-state of Sparta. I killed them all. But they came with a new pain. The hoplites struck back at me. Even though I always won, they cut me with their swords, tried to douse me in fire, or tried to smoke me out and then fight me with an entire army. It didn't matter how many there were. No one could stop me. Even if they captured or managed to kill me, it was temporary. Athena had made me an invincible devil.

"I started collecting things. I disposed of the bodies, but I took their objects and cherished them. I called them relics. They were remnants to keep me company and remind me of the people I had killed. Women's earrings, shields, spears, even clothes became mementos. I was so confused at the time that I felt like they didn't represent victims, they represented lost objects from friends.

"But my conscience and hatred for myself grew. And as my guilt grew, Gorgiana was born, that shy nobody, that alter ego that wanted nothing of Gorgo. The one that hoped the monster didn't even exist. Pain over my enemies became a strange catharsis for Gorgiana, a way for her to accept what Medusa was doing. She felt as if the terrible pain was an even better fate than suicide."

I'm not done, but I pause. I haven't gotten to the bad part yet.

I fold my arms and stare outside the window again. But the whole car lights up green. I quickly cover my eyes. Honestly, I feel as if I'm talking to myself, to you, and Ash isn't even listening. But on the off chance that he is listening, I shall finish my horrid tale.

"It was then that I learned of my power to not only put people into a trance, but to literally transform them. I realized that if I stare at someone, or even a thing, for longer than thirty seconds to a minute, a man, a woman, even a god or goddess, could turn forever into stone.

"All the people in Sarpedon fled. My story sailed through the Greek Isles and thousands of locals, some who were once my friends, fled the island. That left me completely alone. And for years, perhaps decades—I didn't count—the only people I had contact with were occasional ignorant strangers visiting the island. But some were mad, wanting to meet Medusa. Now when they came, I didn't tear them to pieces. I turned them to stone. Then I collected whole bodies. They became the greatest relics of all. A garden of statues that I spoke with and used as my imaginary friends."

I look to see if Ash is paying attention. Boy, is he now. He furrows his brow and shakes his head.

"That's the secret of Sarpedon. The myth of Sarpedon and my stone statue collection is not a myth. It's real, Ash. It happened only there, for a short time, but the number of specimens I collected was enough. The damage was done. And centuries of acting for good...it isn't enough to ever erase my sin against so many innocents. That's what I didn't want you to know. Any human, whether good-hearted or evil, was transformed into a statue. The statues became my only friends. I didn't care about the price. They were my friends."

I don't cry. There's nothing more messed up than this. But I don't weep. I'm too overwhelmed to cry.

Ash doesn't say anything. He just keeps driving.

The funny thing is, if he didn't know me as well as he does now, I could have told him easily. See, he wouldn't have believed a word of it. But knowing me, like you know me, makes this far more repulsive. There are many soulmates in my past, one or two that I stuck with until they died, that I never told the story of Sarpedon to. Some were my husbands. But I'm telling Asher now because he's being brought into Athena's trap. I feel like I owe him.

"And that is why, when I said I love you, I didn't mind that you didn't say you loved me back."

I look at him. He says nothing. So I finish.

"Cora saved me. See, the goddess Persephone is a monster too. She understood my pain and she saved me. Now, as we go to Arkansas, Athena wants justice. She wants to jail me for an eternity in the earth. And perhaps, now that you know what I did, we should let her."

It's silent. Just the sound of the engine's steady hum. Occasionally, Ash turns the wheel.

I told you not to tell him.

Outside now are dark fields. My eyes lose their green. My stress is over. It's been replaced by a calm melancholy. An acceptance. Now he knows. He's seen me. And now he knows me. He knows everything. Let Athena's justice be done. I deserve it. Just as I deserve Asher's.

"How did Persephone save you?"

"I told you Pallas was a nymph. She was one of the first. The nymphs hated Athena after the death of their champion warrior, Pallas. That hatred festered into a hatred of all of Olympus, even though the gods' home of Mount Olympus resided above theirs. Centuries later, Harmonia, a descendant of Pallas, became the first nymph ruler and queen. She was elevated in power by Hades—a god that hated Mount Olympus more than anyone.

"Harmonia's daughter was Nephrea. Nephrea had two daughters. One was a foster daughter: Persephone. Cora loved Nephrea, her foster mother, more than anyone in the world. And when Cora watched her disgusting family of gods slowly destroy Nephrea's people, the nymphs of Azure Blue, Cora sought revenge on her gods. She caused a flood that destroyed Mount Olympus. But that same flood destroyed her beloved nymphs' home.

"Cora, my blessed Persephone, came to me a century

after the destruction. She came a few years after my terror in Sarpedon. If anyone could understand solitude and misery, it was Cora. Cora had lived alone, like me, for a century.

"She lived with me in Sarpedon for a long time. I was so messed up in the head. I was completely gone. Half the time, I didn't even know what I was doing. It took seemingly an eternity to get me to let go of my relics and my so-called friends. Only Cora was my real friend. And I was hers. She was fucked up too, and we helped each other back then, I suppose.

"Anyway, this is the mess we're in now, Ash. It's a feud that's been going on for thousands of years. Athena wants to punish me for Sarpedon. She plans to imprison and bury me forever. And she has every right. Justice would be for me to be buried. She also wants to punish Cora for Olympus. Cora deserves punishment too. That's Athena's side of the story, and that's why she kidnapped Grace. But you heard what she did to me. She ruined my life. Just as her family ruined Cora's. True justice, Ash, would be to get rid of all of us."

And then I'm silent. So is Ash.

I hear the hum of his car. I watch the shadows pass us. And I don't want to talk anymore. I don't even want to talk to you.

"Why did you tell me this?" Ash asks.

"I... I'm so scared that harm will come to you. You're not a part of my problems, and I brought you into them. You deserved to know what's happening."

He shakes his head. "You told me that after you left Sarpedon, you never hurt anyone good again."

"So? My sins will never be forgiven. Who is good? Who judges the good? Shouldn't I never harm anyone at all? I stopped killing those I thought were good after Cora saved me, sure I did. I had killed only a handful of innocents when

I'd first changed. So? So what? How am I absolved if even one pure-hearted soul was killed thousands of years ago? After I killed thousands of so-called *bad* people later? Anyway, doesn't it take the murder of one good soul to ruin me? How can I ever be a good person?"

I lean against the passenger window and close my eyes. This is the middle of the day for me. But I feel so tired.

Why'd you tell him! Why! Oh, why? You're so stupid!

I know. I don't know what came over me.

I feel a hand touch my back. Then I feel shaking. At first, I think it's his hand or the car. Then I realize it's me. His touch sends tears streaming down my face.

Justice is coming. Finally, I shall meet my sentence. But I will accept it. But Asher? No. I won't let Imada touch him. I tell you, if Athena lays a finger on him, I'll use every part of my will to tear her apart. You see how my friend Cora and I are alike?

I hear his voice, I think. I open one of my eyes a crack. The green is gone. My whole body is curled up against his car door. All I want to do is hide. Sleep.

He pulls the car over and leans beside me. But I don't want to turn. All I want do is curl up into the dark shadows outside like a snake.

"Gorgi," he says quietly.

I shake my head.

"Gorgi," he repeats, rubbing my back again. "You've endured so much. You've paid such a horrible price for something that wasn't even your fault. But it's only worse when you torture yourself like this."

I shake my head. I'm still leaning away. He rubs my back some more. Then I hear myself stupidly whimper. And all he does is touch my back and wait for me to stop crying.

And so... Asher isn't throwing me out of his car. He's a complete loon. God, I love him.

So shall come pain. He will die and I will be left alone again, whether tomorrow or in a few decades. When that day comes, will you come and comfort me? Why would anyone comfort a damned soul, Medusa?

"Please get back on the road, Ash," I say between tears. "Please. We have to save Grace."

25

ATHENIAN JUSTICE

My phone buzzes against my leg, startling me. It's still dark outside. I open my eyes to my gorgeous boyfriend holding the wheel with one hand while focusing on the road. I dig in my pants and take out my cellphone. The contact is "Aner."

Stop the car. Go the rest of the way ALONE.

"Stop the car, Ash."

"What?" he asks. "Why? We're almost there."

"My contact is telling you to drop me off. I told you before, you'd have to drop me off early. This is the spot."

"But we're still five miles out, Gorgi. The sun will be up soon. How will you make it on time?"

"I'll run. I've done it before. Turn the car around and go home. If all goes well, I'll make my way back to Sunland and see you tomorrow."

He stops the car by the curb on the highway. We're the only car for miles, and it's pitch black outside. He takes a deep breath. Then he yanks off his seatbelt and jumps out, runs around the car, and opens the door for me. When I get out of the car, he grabs me into his arms.

"There's no time for hugs," I say, looking down. "You know I love you. Get out of here, pronto. Head back to Sunland."

"You don't have to look down anymore, Medusa," he says, lifting my chin with a smile. And he can look at me because it's dark. But then his voice turns grim. "Is this really it? Don't tell me you're just going to give yourself up?"

"I'm going to fight. Cora said Hades will be here. But I have to do this for Cora. Grace is her friend."

I look to the horizon. There's a red light rising ahead of the sun.

"Gorgi, I..."

I touch his lips with my finger. "Shh. I know." I touch his hand, stroking his fingers. "Do me one last favor, 'kay. Look away. I have to change. In case we don't see each other again, I want you to remember me like this, as Gorgiana, not Medusa. Don't look at me as I run."

"You have too many rules."

I shrug and look down. Then I nod.

"I'll see you back in Sunland," he says, cupping my chin, serious as hell. Then he leans down, closes his eyes, and kisses my lips.

"Sunland," I say. I've never liked the sound of my home better. I nod. "I can't wait, Ash."

"I love you, Gorgi."

He kisses my lips again. It hurts. "I love you, Medusa," he repeats. "You're an angel." He gives me another kiss, after that lie. I could kiss him forever. I mean—

Get him out of here! Now. He should never have come!

"Ash, I love you. Go. Hurry. Leave now."

I don't change yet, on the off chance that he looks back. But the moment his door shuts and the engine starts, I dig my fingernails deep into my palms. I feel sticky fluid and sharp pain. I squeeze harder. Then I think of Grace and the danger she's in. I mean, I hate her, but even Gracie, a drug-addicted mess, doesn't deserve "Athenian justice." My wigglies are dancing on my head. My teeth are tingling. My nails are cutting deeper while enlarging. And now the snakes on my head are hissing.

Asher drives off, nearly peeling out on the dirt road.

The surrounding shadows of trees and bushes are becoming as clear as day with my predatory eyes. I smell a deer about a half mile out near a water hole. The doe's fawn is sleeping nearby. There's a farm up a hill two miles back. And the silo, Dellon's hideout, the one I thought I'd be trapped in forever, the one I rampaged and killed a hundred agents in. I now recognize the rendezvous point just five miles ahead.

I growl. Then I break out in a sprint, running as fast as any coyote or cougar from these parts.

It doesn't take long to get there. I recognize it. It's a desolate dead field of wild grass with just a handful of trees. There's a pool of water. I remember bathing here. Then I recognize the abandoned silo and Dellon's lair, under a gated concrete slab. Two spotlights light the field in front of a fence, along with yellow light shining from the headlights of three black SUVs, a grounded helicopter and, of course, that huge black semi they used to hijack me. Are they planning that again? Or burying me in the depths under the concrete block?

Athena's standing in a black sports jacket over slacks. Her hair is long and curly, like mine. It always is, which I can't stand because I hate any similarities to her. And she's wearing leather boots. A pile of silvery chains is at her feet —those are for me, I think. Her clothes look expensive, as if she swiped them from a fashion runway. It's gauche and totally her.

Surrounding her, with rifles slung over their shoulders, is a group of soldiers in black uniforms. Some are hiding behind shrubs and in branches of trees, but I locate each and every one of them.

Standing beside Athena, with her hands tied behind her back, is Grace. Grace looks awful. Her mascara is running. She has red marks on her cheeks and blood on her lips. They fucking hit her. Can you believe that! That spurs me to run faster.

I'm still a mile out, by the way. All of this was perceived through smell.

I leap over a ten-foot-long stream, then over bushes. I spot a sniper hiding by a tree to my left. He sees me. I doubt he knows I see him. He doesn't fire. But as I pass, Minerva reaches into her pocket and answers her phone.

As I'm about fifty yards from them, they can see me. Every light in front of the silo moves in my direction. But a far brighter yellow is peeping over a hill, on the horizon, from the rising sun. Under all this light, I stop and stand— stooped in a crouched position—ready to attack. Yet before my creator, my body shakes.

"You made it, Medusa. And right on time." Athena's not hollering. She's speaking softly, but she knows I can hear her. "The trade is simple, beast: you for the human. Come here slowly and I'll release her. But slow. My men remember the last time you were released."

"What's the catch?"

"No catch. Only you. Come here and Imada chains you."

My eyes fall on Grace.

"Hi, Gorgi," Grace says stupidly, flashing a rueful smile. I really hate her.

"Her too. Cora gets her human in exchange for you."

"You bitch! Look at her face. You hit her."

"Give us your wrists, Gorgo," says Athena. "We've brought invaluable Mandrigelian chains to bind you." She points to them, now not far from my feet. "Jailing you will end your blight on the world. I will imprison you. That's all we want. Then I will free Grace. Ever since I created you, I've wanted to destroy you. Hubris brought your curse, then your sin hurt the innocent. Athenian justice wills you to be buried forever."

"If I go, will you let her go?"

"Yes."

"I don't believe you."

It's then that I smell a hundred soldiers, about three miles to the east, snaking their way toward us. Athena notices too. She turns and looks in that direction. With her goddess eyes, which are even better than mine, it's possible she can see them. They just appeared out of nowhere. By air? It's Project Orcus, I'm guessing. My backup is, this time, on time. How will Athena run? She must know he's arrived too. She's scheming. She's got something awful worked up in her head.

Grab Grace and just run!

I know, but she's so fast. She'll catch us.

There's no other way. Grab her! Do it now!

Athena always wins. But she must know this time if she kills Grace, she'll get Cora's wrath. And as much as I fear Athena, she fears Persephone, though she'd never admit to it, even more.

Wait. What's that familiar woodsy smell? It's not the trees.

I vaguely recognize it. It's cologne.

My wigglies turn in the direction of the scent. Then I hear a car approaching from the same direction. My head snaps to my right following my vipers, who are already sniffing.

Oh, no...

I feel sick. It's another black SUV driving to the compound, and inside, there's a smell I'd recognize anywhere.

Ash? They've got Ash!

"*You bitch!*" I shout, whirling my head around. With my yell a rush of wind brushes over the grass surrounding me. It kicks up wind over her and Grace's hair. "Let him go. I warn you!"

For the first time in my life, I glare right into Athena's eyes. I don't care if she hurts me. All I care about is Ash.

"Him too," Athena says with a nod. "Turn yourself in and—"

"Don't touch him!"

"I knew how you felt about the male. I had to hedge my bets. Don't worry. Just walk forward and he'll be unharmed. Give us your wrists."

The SUV stops close to us. Then my greatest nightmare comes true. Asher is hauled out of the SUV at gunpoint. Unlike last time, at the movie theater, he's wide awake.

"Sun's up," Athena says, reaching for me. "Come here and give me your wrists now."

"No, Gorgi!" cries Ash. "Run! Get out of here! Run!"

But he stops talking as the guard in shades, beside him, presses the rifle hard into his back. I growl at the guard like a lion. I could attack, but I don't stand a chance of saving him before the soldiers shoot him.

"Easy, beast," Athena says, reaching for me again. "You're frightening my men. Move slow."

Ash shakes his head. But I let one of the guards snap a simple handcuff over my wrist. Then a bunch of other men rush over and lift the silvery chains—Mandrigelian chains, thousands of years old and stronger and lighter than steel— up to me.

But there's a gunshot. It echoes throughout the valley. My vipers turn, sniffing the air. It's not just one soldier. It's a hundred, rushing the fields. Then I hear machine gun fire.

Soldiers around me fall, being picked off by a spray of bullets. One is struck in the head.

I move to protect Ash from the bullets. Another soldier is shot in the chest. Athena's hit in the arm, but the gunfire seems to do little to her. A stray bullet hits my leg. It burns and I fall to my knees.

Athena grabs a knife from her pocket. Then she lunges forward and snatches Ash from behind. She lifts the knife to his neck. I leap at her, grabbing her arm, pulling it from him.

More shots are fired and, by my side, Grace's neck is hit by a stray bullet. Grace falls to the ground. Another bullet comes for Ash. I step in front of it and it strafes my flank. More terrible searing pain.

But Athena still has a knife to Ash's neck! My entire weight is literally hanging from Athena's arm, fighting to pull the knife from Ash's throat. But she's too strong. She looks into my eyes, meeting my gaze as if to challenge it, as if to show me she can.

"Let him go!" I plead. *"Please! Please! No!"*

"This will be punitive damages for your crimes, my pet," she says nodding. "So it shall be."

"No." I'm begging. "Please. Don't!"

She runs the blade along Asher's throat. He falls limp in her arms.

"NO! NO! NO!"

My cries are so loud that Athena drops Ash's body, covering her ears. I fall to the ground and grab for him. Then I hold him in my arms, covering his throat with my hand, but blood keeps pooling. My cobras slither across the hole, trying to stop the bleeding.

"Let's go," Athena orders, looking down on me.

She turns and rushes, with a few guards, to the helicopter. The chopper blades turn faster, kicking up more grass and dust. But from the corner of my eye, I see more of her guards shot down by stray bullets.

"What about the beast?" A soldier asks, gesturing to me.

"Leave her. But bring the chains back into the copter."

Ash looks up into my eyes. His eyelids seem so weak.

Oh, Ash!

He sees my green eyes and he freezes. But that's okay... it's...it's okay because I know it will calm him. It will make this easier for him. I've done it before with those I love. It stops their pain, especially when they're about to die.

Is Ash about to die? Oh, my God!

The blood keeps pooling. I can't stop it from pouring from his neck.

I hear his heart flutter and skip. He's frozen looking into my gaze, but his body is still alive and fighting. His lungs have too little air. I reach over and put my lips over his. I breathe air into him.

His side is hit by another bullet. That's so cruel! But the army is spraying shots everywhere in the fields, trying to kill all of Minerva's goons.

My snakes move back and forth over my head in the gust of wind as the helicopter rises over us. The queen bitch is escaping.

"Ash. Ash."

His heart stops.

"Oh, Ash." I run my hand through his hair. "Ash!"

My snakes see soldiers approaching behind me. I don't care.

I'm crying. Ash's body is immobile in my arms and I'm crying. Worse—Grace is lying beside him immobile too. I didn't protect her. Everything went wrong. Everything was a failure. And it cost my boyfriend and Grace their lives.

Is Ash really dead?

I... I sniff about me. I'm breathing heavily. My eyes search the field. If there's any soldier left, any enemy close enough to kill, Medusa will tear him apart. But everyone's been cut down by gunfire, and I've been shot in my side and my leg. I finally succumb to searing pain. I fight to keep my eyes open. And then...

26

THE BASTARD

My body sits up gasping for air. I look about me. I'm on a field. There are bodies lying motionless everywhere. Soldiers in green, not black—they're all dead—are combing the fields. An occasional shot still echoes in the dead valley. And every time I move, it sends sharp pain through my body.

Some guy's standing over me. I squint. It's Hades. He's looking down with red eyes in a green T-shirt and camouflage khakis. I lunge at him. It's a weaker attack than I intended, as one of my legs gives out from the bullet wound, but I want to tear him apart. The weirdest thing, the oddest, is that the god doesn't fight back. He lets me run my sharp fingernails, like small knives, over his skin and draw blood. Then I cut a gash along his cheek. My snakes snap too, biting and cutting his chest. I keep attacking him. My fangs even gnaw at his neck and tear off some of his flesh. Finally, as if swatting a fly, he tosses me off of him.

"Enough!" he shouts.

I look around but I don't see Ash's or Grace's body anywhere.

"Where are they! Where are my friends? Where are Ash and Grace? At least let me mourn their dead bodies!"

He puts a hand up to silence me in his usual pompous way.

"How could you do this!" I cry. "Why didn't you just let them take me prisoner! Even if they jailed me, that'd be better. Why'd you move in and allow them to be killed!"

"Taking Athene is more important than you. Even more important than your friends. And, might I remind you, Medusa, I didn't bring your male friend here. You did."

"I helped you. I even killed for you!"

"Yes, you did. And I let you cut me."

"You deserve it!"

"Perhaps," he says with a nod. He takes out a handkerchief from his pants pocket and wipes the gashes on his face. "Maybe. But now I've come to ask you if you'd like a ride to Toronto."

"Toronto?" I shout, crouched, ready to throw my body at him again. My heart's thumping so hard it's trying to burst out of my chest. Sweat is dripping down my face. My fangs are cutting at my lower lip. I'm barely able to control myself. The only thing stopping me is Hades's eyes. They're shining redder, and my memory of his infernal family's power is enough to stay my hand.

"We're going to see if Cora can revive your friend and hers," he says.

I squint at him. But then I look away as crippling pain runs along my side and leg. I try to shake it off.

"What if she can't?"

"Minerva and Imada are on the run, Medusa. Thanks to you. We've never had them this close. And all the soldiers you see lying on the field are their agents. We're getting closer and closer to taking her prisoner and winning this war."

"You used me again."

"Yes."

"Well, Athena's too smart." I stand up straight. "She probably already thought you'd attack."

"No. She would never have guessed I'd sacrifice your boyfriend and Cora's best friend to save you."

I growl at him like a lion. I lean forward threateningly but, this time, the bastard doesn't flinch. He squints his red eyes at me. I recall Dellon striking me with the back of his hand. That stops me from charging again.

"She wouldn't have gambled on my letting them die," he adds, turning from my gaze. "Now..." He gestures to a plane with helicopter blades on vertical shafts. "Please get in the tiltrotor, Medusa. Kore can revive people newly dead, but the process gets harder the longer you wait. Your friends don't have much time."

I turn my back on him. My legs, without any conscious volition, limp toward the sleek green military aircraft. I hear the asshole creeping up behind me. And accompanying us are a few soldiers in green camouflage uniforms wearing dark opaque shades.

"I know why you're doing this," I snap, without turning. "In your sick mind, you think that you'll need my services again. Well, I'm never helping you again. Never! Whether you save Ash or not."

"Actually, I'm doing this for Cora."

He's such an asshole.

We climb up a ramp at the backside of the airplane. There's a red glow inside. And there are green-uniformed troops inside. My snakes are finally receding and transforming back into my hair. See, I don't feel anger anymore. I feel pain. And, damn it, I feel sad. I feel horrible.

Don't you?

Is Ash really gone? Is he, Gorgi?

I think so.

There's a step on the ramp onto the plane. Hades actually tries to grab my hand to help me over it. Can you believe that?

"You don't care about me!" I shout, swatting his hand. "You don't care about Persephone. You don't care about anyone. All you care about is—"

"The world? Is that so bad, Medusa?"

"Yes. Without heart, it is. And it's not our world, it's *your* world in your mind, you arrogant son of a bitch!"

Some soldiers show me a seat against the wall of the plane. They're still wearing sunglasses to protect themselves from my eyes. I sit down. A soldier shows me a seatbelt to strap into. I show him my middle finger.

Hades stands over me for a moment. Why is he still here? The ramp starts to rise.

"You should know that the raid was also planned to save your friends," he says. Oh, that makes me feel better.

"Fuck you."

He gestures some sort of hidden signal to another soldier meaning take off, I think. Then he leaves the craft before the ramp closes.

I feel the airplane rise.

Closer to the front of the aircraft, near the pilots, I see two bodies in white sheets. I jump up and run up to the front.

"Miss," a soldier says, "please sit down and put your seatbelt on while we're taking off."

I kneel next to the two body bags and unzip one. It's Ash. His eyes are closed. Blood is still dripping from his neck. His skin is paler than I've ever seen before.

Oh, Ash. This is my fault. It's all my fault.

27

THE DOCTOR

Everything feels slow. I mean, every movement. Everything. Even though I'm running. I rush to the front door of Cora's mansion, and it seems as if time itself has fallen to a crawl. Four soldiers rush behind me carrying the two white body bags. Our legs are sloshing along Cora's wet circular driveway. It's drizzling and foggy outside. And my cursed hair is blowing like crazy from the propellers still moving on the helicopter-plane.

I pound on the front door with my fist. Then I wait, playing with my fingers and tapping my foot against Cora's front entrance. I glance back at the 'copter. It looks so bizarre in the center of Cora's posh circular driveway. The pilot landed as close as he could to the house—on top of a large marble fountain—and water is pouring from under the plane. Two camouflage armored Humvees are parked beside the house. And just beyond that, beside a private road, is a tank. Yeah, an actual tank. Cora wasn't kidding when she said she had increased security.

Where are they? Open the—

Hashan throws the door open. He's wearing his usual

black suit and shades, but he doesn't have his usual stoic face. He looks frantic. He quickly turns at the sight of my eyes. He opens the doors wider, and the soldiers behind me rush the body bags inside.

"Where is she?" I raise my nose. I feel a snake brush across my cheek; it's smelling the air too. "Where's Cora?"

"There's little time, Gorgiana," Hashan says, shaking his head. "Bring them into the living room. We prepared it. Come on. Hurry."

I catch a glimpse of Moros halfway up the stairway. She's wearing a cute brown smock. She waves at me, even though my hair is full-on thick-snaked Medusa. She's seen the snakes before, but they were small. But I don't seem to frighten her. She doesn't look scared—she looks serious. I'm not sure how much she knows, but all the soldiers patrolling the grounds are terrible enough.

The living room has been transformed. They've cleared the furniture and set up two hospital beds with white sheets and wires and machines. The soldiers carefully carry the bodies down two steps into the room.

Gabriel's standing in the living room next to a white grand piano. He signals for the soldiers to put the bodies on the beds.

"Where's Cora?" I ask Gabe.

"I'm here." Someone from behind whisks me into her arms. I smelled her, but I'm so riled up, I didn't locate her.

"Oh, Cora."

"Gorgi, I heard all about it." She's all choked up. That makes me want to cry.

"Can you do it?" I ask. "Can you revive him?"

"I think so. But the more time that passes, the harder it is." She turns to the soldiers. "Unzip them." Then she cocks her head to Gabriel. "Gabe, get Moros out of here. Take her to the other side of the house. She can't see her like this."

He nods and runs past me. But before he goes, he glances at me again. No, he's looking at my hair. See, I avoided the living room during the day when I stayed. It's a sunlit room, with floor-to-ceiling windows facing the lake and the front yard. And even though there's fog outside and you can't even see the lake from the backyard, there's little doubt Gabe saw my snakes—especially in my current mood.

The soldiers unzip the body bags. And that's terrible because Ash's head is turned, and I catch one of his lifeless eyes half open.

On the back deck a guard with a rifle slung over his back is running by.

Cora stands beside the two beds.

"The bitch cut him along the neck." I stare down at Ash's pale face.

"And bullet wounds in his arm and side," Cora says with a nod. The soldiers who brought in the bodies are now standing with their backs facing the windows. Hashan is the only one in the room other than me looking at Grace and Ash. "And you. You were shot too, Gorgi."

"I'm fine."

I'm not fine. It burns in my stomach and I feel sick. But I don't care. I only care about Ash right now.

Something really bizarre happens as Cora continues to examine Ash. Three men wearing blue surgical gowns walk into the room. They start turning on machines by the beds.

"There was so much shooting, Cora," I say. "The dick ambushed her and sprayed bullets everywhere, hitting all of us."

She nods. She moves to Grace. Then she falls over Grace's body wailing. God! I'm so focused on Asher that I'm cold to what Grace's death means to her. This is her best friend. Cora's eyes shine like red flashlights over Grace's dead body. "Bullets are everywhere," Cora says, shaking her head. She takes a deep breath. "Here's a hole penetrating the skull." She's not only talking to me. One of the surgeons is standing beside her now. "It went clear through. This one was probably the fatal one." The surgeon nods. "But here's another penetrating the chest. This one hit her heart. Another at her hip and pelvis."

Tears are streaming down her face. That's terrible because it makes me wonder if she can do this. Does she doubt herself?

"Can't you just touch them and heal them?" I ask.

"No."

"Some bullets have to be removed, madam," Hashan says, standing behind us. "Or they'll stay embedded in their bodies after they're revived."

"And then they could drop dead the moment they open their eyes," Cora says with a nod. "Especially this one at her heart." She backs away for a moment, shakes her head, and wipes her eyes. "Shit."

"I'm so sorry, Cora," I say.

Cora stares at me with her bright red eyes. "Why are you sorry?" She turns to Hashan. "Let's give the doctors a moment alone to do their job."

"But why are doctors here?" I ask. "They're dead. I don't understand."

"The surgeons will check what shrapnel needs to be removed, Gorgiana," Hashan answers.

Cora tugs at my arm. I shake my head. She insists, tugging me harder by the elbow.

We walk down a hall into the kitchen.

I didn't notice until now that Cora's wearing the simplest clothes: just a T-shirt and pajama bottoms. I don't think she's changed since she was wakened by this nightmare this morning.

When we get to the kitchen, Cora leans her head in her

hands and runs her fingers through her long blond hair by her large marble island. I can hear the commotion behind us.

Little Moros and Gabriel are sitting at the small dining table. They're not looking at Cora; they're watching me. I must look a mess. I mean, I was shot and there are bloody cuts in my muddy leggings. Or... It's probably my cursed hair again.

I rub Cora's back.

"Stop being nice," Cora says. "I might not be able to revive your friend. If I can't, you won't be comforting me ever again, Gorge."

"What's wrong, Mommy?" asks Moros.

Cora still has her head in her hands. "Nothing, dear."

"Is Auntie Gracie going to die?" Moros asks.

Cora jumps up from the island and glares at Gabe. It takes me a second to get why she's so angry. She glares at him with burning red eyes. She scares me. But it's obvious she's shone her fiery eyes in the house before. Gabe doesn't even flinch. And Moros sits calmly too.

"You told her!" Cora snaps at Gabriel. "I can't believe this. You fucking told her what happened to Grace?"

"She already knows," Gabe replies. "The whole house is guarded like a fortress. She knows what's going on, Cora."

"She didn't know about Grace. I don't even know if I can revive her. Why did you tell her, Gabe! Her body is riddled with bullets. And Gorgi's boyfriend wasn't just cut up, he was shot too. They might not be able to prep them well enough for me to save them."

"You've done it before," Gabe says, shaking his head. "I know you can do it. You've done it with bodies in ashes."

"Well, I'm glad you have confidence in me. But there are two bodies, not just one. One might not make it."

"They'll make it." Gabe asks, "Are you afraid it will hurt?"

That comment enrages her. I step back. I've known my friend for a millennium and, boy, she has a temper. Her red eyes are super big right now. She stands silently with her brow furrowed, just glaring at Gabe. But before she opens her mouth again, everyone turns at the sound of a group of soldiers outside running by the kitchen windows.

"Seriously!" Cora shouts. I jump. *"Afraid! Are you fucking kidding me, Gabriel!"*

In a normal house, everyone in the kitchen would be running for their lives right now. Not here. Gabe actually stands up as if challenging her.

"What do you think I am, an infant, Gabe? I'm not scared of pain. I'm worried it won't work."

Cora once told me that there was no pain greater in the world than the pain of reviving someone back to life.

Moros slides off her chair and runs to Cora. Then the little girl surprises her by throwing her arms around Cora's waist and legs.

"Its okay, Mommy. You don't have to do it, if you don't want to. If it hurts."

Cora closes her eyes tightly, takes a deep breath, and gently pushes Moros from her. "I'll do it one at a time. But it's going to be hard, Moros. Very hard."

28

SURGERY

Since that showdown between Cora and Gabe, it's become really quiet. Too quiet. Even little Moros, a really wild little tyke, is totally quiet.

Cora's still leaning on the island and running her fingers through her hair. Moros and Gabe just sit at the table staring at a wall. And I keep looking out the window.

The heavy fog keeps shining green. That's my eyes. And that's why I'm turned away from Moros and Gabe. I'm so worried. I keep illuminating everything in green.

Occasionally, a soldier sprints down the walkway near the window, and I have to turn from him too. Something bad's going on outside. I hear far-off gunfire.

Who cares? Ash. God, worry about Ash, Gorgi. Can Cora heal him?

I know. God, I hope so.

I hear metal clanging. It's the occasional noise of metal instruments clanging over metal tables and murmuring coming from the living room. There's no way Gabe or Moros can hear it. It's really faint for human ears. But I'm sure Cora hears it. I think that's the other reason she keeps burying her head in her hands and not talking to anybody. My stupid ears keep perking up every time they talk about Ash. But it's usually medical jargon, and I have no idea what the hell they're talking about.

"How long do we have to wait?" I blurt out to no one in particular. "This is torture."

"They're going as fast as they can, Gorgi," Cora answers.

"I'm sorry," Gabe says to Cora. "I was just worried about Grace."

"Fuck off, Gabe," Cora says quietly. "I don't care about your dumb insult right now."

That's not nice. But that's Cora.

Cora looks up from her hands at him. Her eyes are still shiny red, but she flashes him a rueful grin. That's Cora too. And Gabe, the angel he is, nods. Then little Moros gets up from her chair, sits on Gabe's lap, and puts her arm around him. She weeps quietly in his arms.

Hashan rushes into the kitchen. "They've done all they can," he says. "It's time, madam."

Cora looks up at me and nods. Then she walks over to Gabe and Moros, puts a hand on the girl's head, and says, "I'll bring you back Grace, Gabe." Then she looks into my eyes. "And your Ash."

Cora leaves the room as though she's going alone.

No way. I follow right behind her.

Back in the living room, one of the guys in surgical gowns walks up to her. He has blood all over his blue gown.

"The man is prepped but the woman has a lot of metal lodged around the heart," he says. "We've done all we could, but we stopped at the heart. There's too much damage. If that heart becomes whole with all that debris, it's unlikely she'll survive."

"You should have removed it then," Cora says. "It will

have to be completely regenerated. Show me where most of the metal is, we're running out of time."

The surgeon walks over to the table and points at Grace's pale, naked chest. I jump as Cora thrusts her hand through Grace's ribs and digs inside her thorax. Blood sprays and pools around her chest. Cora digs and digs, with her head turned away, yanking out pieces of bloody flesh, seemingly randomly. Then she pulls out her bloodied hand and points at Grace's head.

"The bullet went through?" Cora asks, shaking pieces of her best friend's heart from her fingers. "Nothing else needs to be removed?"

Cora acts tough but I've never seen her fair skin so pale before. And she stumbles a little as she walks closer to Gabe. I feel sick too.

The surgeon shakes his head.

"Clear the room," Cora says to all of them. "Everyone except Gorgi and Hashan. The rest of you, get out."

All the soldiers and doctors leave.

Cora lays a hand on Ash's chest. I snatch her wrist.

"No, Cora, do Grace first. Please."

"You know I came to you in Sarpedon. When I heard the tale of what my family had done to you," Cora says. "I felt I owed you. Now I owe you again. I got us into this mess. This young kid should never have been hurt." I'm about to speak, but she puts a hand up. "Look, Gorgi, Ash has a knife wound to the neck. He stands the best chance of awakening."

I shake my head again, but Cora yanks her wrist from my grasp. She stands over Ash. She wipes her bloodied hand over the white sheets, then she places it over Ash's neck. She takes a deep breath and closes her eyes.

Then she cries out in pain.

It's so hard for me to watch her suffer. I know, you think I'm this terrible monster, right? You're remembering me going on a rampage at Dellon's lair and wondering why I'm suddenly so sensitive. It's because I was Medusa then. Now I'm Gorgiana. And Cora is writhing in so much pain. God, it's terrible! Even if her pain were the only reason for her hesitation, I'd believe she had every right to fear it as I watch her thrash up and down, struggling to breathe, over Ash's body.

She lets go of him and clutches her own neck. I grab her hand from her neck, and I hold it in mine. She squeezes my fingers so tightly I think she'll break my bones. I think if I were human, she would have.

Then I watch the miracle unfold. Her other hand, still touching Ash's neck, closes and seals the cut, as if it were never there. The bullet wounds close too. But as the wounds close, Cora collapses over Ash.

"Cora?" I shake her. "Cora."

Ash's eyelids flicker!

But in the midst of my joy, my snakes smell something stinky, but familiar. It's not just the putrid smell of blood; it's something else. Something I loathe. It's like this old grandma smell...

29

____

THE PROTECTOR

As Cora sleeps and all is quiet, I hear a gunshot. Then another. Then an explosion. These aren't far off; they're right out the window. People are shouting outside. But, in the midst of yells, I hear Gabe's voice. My ears perk up. "*Stay away from her! Stay away!*"

A little girl screams. It's Moros! There's an explosion so close that it shakes the house and rattles the windows. To my left, I see smoke rising from nearby trees, darker than the surrounding gray fog. A guard that was outside patrolling the deck brandishes his automatic rifle and jumps over the rail, down the hill, into the trees.

"*Momma! Momma!*" Moros cries.

"Cora!" I say, yanking at her, but she's unconscious lying over Ash's body. "Cora! Wake up! It's Moros!"

I run. Just when I see Ash's arm move in my periphery—a glorious movement I would have given anything in the world to watch a moment ago—I ignore it and run up the double stairs and down the hallway, following the little girl's screams. I think they're still in the kitchen.

I must be too late. There's no way Athena hasn't killed

them. But how is Athena even here? Maybe my nose is wrong. Maybe it's someone else. Perhaps the scent is a memory of fear or some other old lady. Perhaps Imada is here, and only humans are threatening Cora's family?

"Daddy! No! Daddy!"

I hear something crash against a wall. Then the sound of wood cracking. Glass shatters.

I'm near the kitchen. My cobras are searching in all directions. My green eyes are shining over the walls. The light travels through a window and bounces back, reflected on the outdoor fog and smoke. I'm clenching my fists. One more turn toward the dining room and—

"No!"

Athena is standing in front of a couch holding Moros's little body over her head. Gabe's body is lying motionless under a glass window. Dead? I don't know. Moros is screaming and jerking in Minerva's grasp. The goddess props her knee against the sofa. I think she intends to break the girl in half.

The witch turns and looks at me. So does Moros. For a moment, the little girl grows a smile on her face as she gazes upon me. This is super strange because I am in full-on Medusa mode, wrinkled and crouched over with fangs and slithering, hissing snakes on my head. And at the sight of Athena, even stranger, my monster trembles.

Athena squints at me and then the bitch smiles.

I shake my head.

No!

Athena opens her eyes wide and screams. Her blue eyes rapidly turn red and shine on one of her sandals. Her foot is bleeding; a shiny red kitchen knife has punctured it.

This is my chance. I leap with all my might, the greatest long jump ever attempted, one that might even put good ole Jesse Owens to shame. I grab Moros midair, curling the girl into my body like a pill bug. Then I crash into the wall across the room with her safe in my arms. Looking back—no, smelling back—I'm aware of Minerva crouching over her foot, yanking the knife out and hopping up and down on her other leg. I'm holding Moros against the wall, shielding her with my body. Gabriel wisely made a run for it after stabbing Athena. Now he's on our side of the room. He runs to Moros and scoops her in his arms. But our victory is short lived. Athena will nurse her wounds for only so long.

Athena spins around and scowls at, not me but Gabriel. I suppose she hates him even more than me right now. Of course, there's no choice but to fight. But I've been in this position many times before. I have no chance against her.

"Leave them alone!" I shout, standing in front of them. My voice, always perversely sweet and Gorgiana, even when I've turned to Medusa, somehow sounds a little menacing for the first time before the goddess.

"You protect nymphs like Kore? Persephone's always made friends with strange things. Nymphs. Vermin. Now snakes like you." She looks down again at her foot. She shakes it and closes her eyes. "A nymph cuts me again. But you, nymph-man, shall be the last one. I promise you that."

I'm breathing heavily. Staring. Sniffing. Panting. Waiting. I don't dare let down my guard, even for a second. All my attention is focused on protecting them. But that leap I did for sweet Moros is nothing compared to what this goddess is capable of doing.

"How did you even get here?" I ask.

"I hitched a ride on your plane," Athena says. "You do recall I can change into an owl? But listen." She pauses and turns her head, smiling. The sound of gunfire and explosions is everywhere. "Hear that? That's Imada. I was ready for your capture to fail, Medusa. I hoped you and Cora's friend would die if it did, because that left these two vulnerable. You see, now there's no one to protect Cora's family. Only a confused ugly gorgon."

I growl at her. My ancient fear is gone because, at this moment, little Moros is shaking and clutching at my leg. Athena laughs. I want to tear the bitch's lips right off!

I charge, hurdling over the sofa, throwing my body at her. My snakes bite. My sharp claws hack.

I'm hurled back across the room, crashing through another glass wall! And it...*really*...fucking hurts! Why am I always going through windows?

I clutch my head. Then my body. I'm on Cora's upper wooden deck. My wigglies are licking my wounds. That wall didn't feel like glass. Shit, it felt like a brick wall.

Someone screams. I whirl around and look inside the house. *That bitch is grabbing Moros by her long hair!*

I rush through the glass wall and grab Athena's arm, but it's like when I held her knife away from stabbing Ash. Even leaning with my whole body, I can't move her arm. She flicks me off like a bug, and I slide across the carpet, knocking down a lamp and crashing into the wall.

Then there are gunshots, but they're not outside. Things are exploding inside the room. A lamp bursts into pieces. More windows are blown open.

Two soldiers in green run through the hole my body made through the window. They fire on Athena with machine guns. The goddess takes, like, a whole round of bullets. Somehow, she still manages to rush a soldier through the gunfire, bash his body against the wall, and then fight off another.

She leaps after Moros again! She raises her hand to strike the child. One strike could kill her. I rush to her, but before I reach her, Athena is tackled by a figure moving at incredible speed. She's knocked down and slides against a wall. Then the assailant, in a green uniform, flicks his wrist in her direction and her body is again tossed against the wall by some invisible force.

Athena rises in a fighting stance. She lunges at him. They fight so fast it's hard to track, even for my A+ predator eyes. But I can smell the attacker. I'd know that smelly smell anywhere. It's Hades.

I run to Moros and Gabe again, but they're fine now. Cora has her arms around Moros. Gabriel is hugging both of them. Athena might have planned the perfect attack, but it had one flaw—time. Apparently, my hopeless battle with her wasn't for nothing.

I hear dishes break as the two gods start smashing everything around them in the adjoining kitchen.

"Thanks, Gorgi," Cora says, rushing by me.

Cora rushes across the room and joins the melee in the kitchen. Then the three gods hurl each other back and forth against the walls. They all crash through a wall, and I hear the fighting continue in the adjacent rooms.

Moros is crying now. I look at Gabe. And, of course, with all the excitement he looks right into my eyes. He freezes. It doesn't stop the poor tyke from remaining in his arms crying.

The violence in the other rooms is terrible. It sounds like they're literally breaking the house down. They keep slamming each other against walls.

"Medusa!" shouts Hades. "Medusa! Come here!"

I run out of the kitchen and down the hallway.

Of all places, they've led each other back to where Ash and Grace were. It wouldn't surprise me, in Athena's sick plans, if she led them there to kill the two humans again. But both bodies are missing from the tables.

"Medusa!" It's Hades again.

Cora is holding Athena by one arm. Hades is grasping for the other. When he gets it, they drag the goddess, kicking, to one of the beds. They throw her on the bed and each one holds an arm down.

"Medusa!" Hades shouts again. "Come here quick!" They're staring at each other with bright red eyes.

"Turn her," Hades says, fighting to breathe. He cocks his head at me. "We have her pinned. Turn her, Medusa. Do it now!"

"No!" cries Athena, squirming on the bed.

"You had your chance," Hades says to her, panting. "You overstepped your bounds. Now you must be bound. Turned to stone."

"If anyone should be bound, it's you, Uncle!" Athena shouts. "And that harlot who destroyed our home." She looks over at Cora. "He still loves you, you know. That's why he's willing to destroy the world over you."

"There's no destruction of my world as long as the two of them live," Cora says.

"Nephrea's long dead, lunatic," Athena replies. "The two of them barely have any nymph blood left. We've already destroyed the Ambrosia line. That man is just a mutant, like your snake friend. But whether they die or not, the fate of this world shouldn't be based on precarious madness." She turns to Hades. "And you know it. She's unstable. She makes friends with spiders and snakes. Animals. Monsters. How can you help her if you care about this world!"

"You made Gorgi into that beast!" Cora cries.

"Because she dared to call herself better than us. Because there once was a time when that was a crime. When there was order and justice in Gaia. When there was respect for gods. Before you sank Olympus into the sea!"

"Shut her up, Medusa," Hades says, cocking his head back at me. "Enough of this. Turn her to stone."

I shake my head.

"Gorgi," Cora says. "You have to. She ruined your life."

"I worshipped her," I say.

"She had Poseidon rape you!" cries Hades. "Then she transformed you into one of Apollo's snakes. Now be done with her so I can bury her in the ground where she belongs!"

"Your home?" Athena asks. "That's where you belong, God of the Underworld!" And she spits in Hades's face. She winces as he throws his whole body against her arm.

"Thirty seconds," says Hades to Athena. "Just thirty seconds, Athene. That's all it will take for even you, a goddess, to be stilled and stoned forever. And I'll never have to hear your fucking drivel again."

"Freeze her, Gorgi," Cora says with a nod. Athena loosens from her grip, but then Cora pins down her arm. "Please. Hurry. I'm weak. I don't know how long I can hold her. Freeze her. Turn her to stone."

I come to the bedside, and Athena squirms even more. She launches her whole body up against both gods, but she is thrown back down on the bed.

"No!" cries Athena. "Get her away from me! Get her away!"

I look into her eyes. She closes them and screams.

"Pry open her eyelids," Cora says to me. "She won't be able to fight your fingers. Open her eyes, Gorge, with your fingers. Do it."

I obey my friend. Even Athena's eyelids, the eyelids of a goddess, are almost stronger than my fingers. But I can't keep them steady. I gaze into her red eyes, and a green glow surrounds her.

"No! Please!" cries Athena. "Please! Don't do this!"

"Bitch!" snaps Cora. "Come to my house and try to murder the only people left in my family? What makes you think you're any better than this girl who you cursed?"

Athena's writhing, struggling to move her head from my grip. But we have her in our grasp.

"You destroyed your true family, Persephone," says Athena.

I look into her bulging eyes and see something on Athena's face I've never seen in my entire life. Fear. No... terror. It's the same feeling she's instilled in me since I was a little girl working in her temple.

"Please, Gorgiana," Athena pleads. Tears stream from her eyes. "No. Please, don't do this to me." She's never called me Gorgiana. Like, never.

"Hurry," Hades says. "Stare and be done with this, Medusa. We can't hold her forever."

I hesitate. Cora turns and looks at me, nodding. I look back into Athena's eyes. I ready myself to look upon her for the last time.

"Please!" she pleads. Her tears make her eyelids slippery. Their strength is nearly equal to the strength in my hands. I pull them again. And I glare deeply into her eyes. "Please, don't, Gorgiana."

Sarpedon, Gorgiana. Sarpedon. Cora destroyed every statue for you because you couldn't do it. You couldn't do it yourself because you thought they were your friends. And you couldn't face the truth.

And I forbade you to ever stone anyone again.

I turn my gaze from Athena.

"*She destroyed your life!*" shouts Hades. "*Does she not deserve the same fate?* Look back upon her and help rid this world of this beast, Medusa."

"I can't," I say.

I shake my head and walk up the two steps away from her. There's complete silence. I don't even hear Athena squirming anymore. It seems like everyone is in shock.

"Thank you," Athena mutters. Then I hear the goddess whimper.

"I swore to never turn anyone to stone ever again," I say.

"You did it in Sarpedon!" cries Hades. "You froze innocents and spoke to them in madness. Now you can't do it to your jailor? The goddess who ruined your life? We will hold her down and you can finally take your revenge. Now do it!"

I shake my head again.

"Do it! Turn her to stone!" cries Hades.

"There must be another way," Cora says gently.

"She's weak," Hades chides me. "She's always been weak."

"And you always use others to do your bidding," Cora says. "Leave her alone."

It's so quiet. This is bizarre, but Athena's stopped fighting. She's crying as they continue to hold her down on the hospital bed.

"Don't let go of her, Kore! This will be so much harder. If we can't turn her to stone, she'll escape." Then he turns to me. I'm standing with one foot on the steps to the living room, ready to leave. "I want you to think about this for a moment, Medusa. Think hard. Think about what you're walking away from. There will never be a chance like this again."

"She has thought about it," Cora says. "Now leave her alone."

"Think about how you're showing mercy to the one who's sentenced you to hell," Hades says to me. "You will never be pretty. You will never see sunlight. You will never be normal. And it is all because of this woman lying before you. She is the one who sent my brother to defile you. She, the goddess you worshipped, turned her back on her priestess to curse her. And why? Imperious jealousy. That sickening arrogance of my family that once ruled this world. Now you can be an instrument of her own justice. Turn her to stone, Medusa. Petrify her. Give her what she deserves."

"She's already petrified her," Cora says, oddly looking down at Athena with pity. "Look at her." Tears are streaming down Athena's face.

"*I mean an actual frozen fucking stone statue, Kore!*" shouts Hades.

"No," I say, shaking my head. "I won't. I'll never do that again."

"Thank you," Athena says, almost in a whisper.

"*Fuck!*" cries Hades. He moves from her arms to her neck and starts strangling her. "For this! This thing! I hate you more than your creation, niece. Look upon what you've birthed." He raises her head toward me. "Look! Look at her hair. Gaze upon her! Look at her snakes. It's the same filth you spread to the world. That is you! Your filthy curly hair! I watch over Persephone and I watch over our world, it's true. But if her prophecy ever comes to pass and she does destroy the world, I won't blame her. I will blame only you, Minerva. You gorgon! I'll blame you!"

He releases her neck. Athena gasps for air. Then he shoves his hands back over her wrists.

"Tyler," he cries. "Captain Tyler!"

"Yes, sir," says a soldier rushing into the room. I didn't even know there were soldiers standing outside the door. He stands at attention and salutes Hades.

"The women in the room have decided to make things kind and pleasant for our prisoner. This makes it all the more difficult for us. I'm going to need chains. Lots of them. We're gonna have to bind this goddess the old-fashioned way."

"Yes, sir." He rushes out.

"You are under arrest," Hades says to Athena. "Anything you say can and will be used against you in a court of law.

You have a right to an attorney. If you cannot afford an attorney—and now that I've confiscated all your holdings in Spain, it's very possible you won't be able to—"

"Oh, will you please shut up," Cora says, rolling her eyes.

"Kore," Hades says, "tell me you'll agree to at least remain here until I get the chains?"

"Fine." She cocks her head back to me with a smile, for once. "Gorgi, the soldiers rushed their bodies upstairs for protection. Hashan is guarding them now in the guest room."

Their bodies?

"Is Ash alive?"

Cora hesitates. *Oh, God, why does she hesitate!*

She's distracted as Athena jerks her arm. But Athena's only shifting her body. She's not struggling anymore.

"I hope so," Cora says with a sigh, tightening her grip on Athena's wrist.

That's enough for me. I make a run for it to Cora's stairway.

"Gorgi," Cora says, turning. "Thank you."

"Oh yes," Hades replies, "thank her. A thousand thanks. Congratulations, Medusa, you managed to save the world through clemency. Only to curse us tomorrow."

"You're such an asshole."

"But everything I say is true, Kore. She'll find a way to get out. Won't you, Athena?"

"I was wrong about her," Athena says. "I was wrong."

"Gorgi's better than all of us because she's not a goddess," Cora says.

"Speak for yourself, Cora," Hades says. "She might have just destroyed the world."

"Then this world deserves its end."

30

FANGS SOMETIMES GET IN
MY WAY

I HURDLE FOUR OR FIVE STEPS AT A TIME, RUNNING AWAY FROM Cora's giant royal bedchamber. I pass down a hall and throw open the door. I know where the guest room is because this is where I stayed last time.

Hopefully? What the hell does that mean? What am I going to do if Ash was taken away from me and everything was all for nothing again?

Great, everything is going well for us against Imada now. We captured Athena. Great. So? What about my lover!

You should never have let him drive you.

Really? Duh. Just shut up right now, please.

As I fling the door open, Hashan greets me, with legs wide apart, pointing a pistol at me. It's then I remember what Cora said about him, how everyone thinks he's this stoic lamb but nobody knows how much of a real badass her stiff butler really is. He's wearing sunglasses but still freezes as he stares right at me. I'm in full Gorgo mode at the moment. I turn from his pointed gun.

Grace and Ash are sitting together on the bed with their heads down. But they're awake! They're breathing.

They look so weak. Ash looks up. I run to him and scoop him up in my arms.

"Gorgi," he says with a chuckle. "Gorgi."

"Oh, God, Ash, you're alive. You're alive!"

"Seems so," he says in my arms. I'm pressing him so tight. "Gorge, you're hurting me. Can you let me go?"

"Oh, yeah. Sorry."

"Your hair looks pretty gnarly, babe," quips Grace. "It's really cool." I quickly touch my head. Oops, my long snakes are still out. I reach for Ash and hold him tightly again, so he doesn't look.

"Thanks for saving my life," Grace says, touching my back. "Hashan says you came for me."

Didn't I just come for Ash? Honestly the past day has been so rushed it's becoming a blur. Oh yeah, I did come for her. Why did I do that? I really hate her.

Ash pulls away from me, but I don't let him. I pull him close again. "I'm still changed, Ash. Don't look at me."

"It's okay, Gorgi," he says with a chuckle.

"It really isn't," I say, shaking my head. "But thanks."

"Can I at least touch your lips?" No. Because then I'll bite him with my fangs. It's fun being a monster, isn't it? "Just let it pass for a moment."

"Yeah," Grace says, "you really don't want to see this shit."

She's such a bitch. I mean, she really is. I think I really hate her. Why does Cora hang out with her? And why did—

Ash manages to get out of my grasp. He's pressing his lips on mine. But my fangs? What about... Oh, that's nice. Now I'm pressing my body close to him, not because I don't want him to see my hair, but because I want to feel his body close. And I do. I squeeze those thick arms and press against him.

"Get a room, guys," Grace says.

I let go of Ash for a moment and purposely stare at Grace. She freezes with a stupid smirk. Sorry, she deserves it.

"Hey, is she—"

I'm back to kissing him. He touches my head. I mean, now it's just wigglies up there but still, even now, probably due to arousal, they're moving too much.

"Don't, Ash."

"I see you're feeling better, madam?" says Hashan, awakening. Oh yeah, he's still here in the room.

I nod. I mean... Yeah. But the snakes are probably gonna thicken again just from this stud's tongue.

Oh, touch me there. Yeah, please, go ahead right there. I... I really couldn't be any better, really.

"Are they *still* at it?" Grace laughs. "Hashan, I'm going to go see if Cora's okay. I take it the coast is clear outside?"

"You'll have to ask Ms. Gorgiana."

"She's a bit too preoccupied at the moment."

31

BYE

I walk outside wrapping my arms around my body. It's real early and getting cold. But I don't care. As you know, it's a treat to just be out in sunlight. The sun's risen and the clouds have dispersed, and I'm out on the long deck with the view of the lake and the rising sun. It's simply lovely. It's turning fall and in Toronto, unlike at home, that means winter will bring snow.

I look out along the lake. For a moment, I shudder considering how this could have all been destroyed had things gone differently. It's so horrible how quickly the world can end. It makes me take a deep breath and just stare for the longest time, feeling grateful for the lovely view of the lake.

The birds are chirping. There's a gentle breeze under the warmth of the sun.

I smell Cora coming. She's walking from the house, down the lower deck steps, with her arms folded. Even in a long red raincoat with her blond hair tied back, she looks pretty. I don't feel pretty.

When close enough, she says with a chuckle, "You're

dressing like Florida." She touches the blue throw I'm wearing. "It's cold. You want to borrow one of my coats?"

"No, I'm okay."

Her bright blue eyes shine in her pale face. Then she takes me up in her arms and gives me a hug. "Sleep well?"

"Are you kidding? In your place? Wonderful. Especially with Ash." I wink at her.

Cora chuckles.

"Hashan was up and said you wanted to meet me here alone again?"

"You're leaving, Gorgi. I wanted to thank you."

"You already thanked me a thousand times."

She nods and stares out at the lake like I was doing. Then she falls silent. After a big sigh I ask her something I've wanted to all night.

"Did I do the right thing?"

"No." *Oh.* But she turns with a rueful smile. "But you did what my mother would have done. You had every right to trap Athena for an eternity. You didn't. Because you're like Nephrea. You're Gorgiana. That's why I love you so much."

"I'm not Gorgiana, Cora. I realize that now. I'm Medusa. Your family stole that name from me too."

She looks at me and nods, looking serious. I mean, of all people, it's always been Cora who's respected my using that gorgeously hideous name. And I didn't mean to sound angry about it.

"What'd you want?" I ask. I shake my long hair back. The wigglies stir a little under the sunlight.

"I wanted to say goodbye. I told you. And I wanted to ask something of you."

"Two martinis, madam," Hashan interjects, holding a silver tray over his arm with two drinks. With a sweet smile he hands me a martini. "Gorgi."

"It's red," I remark.

"Pomegranate, upon orders of Cora Cartwright," Hashan says.

"Cartwright?"

"Aha," Cora says with a laugh, grabbing her martini. "That's the other thing I had to tell you. I fucking married Gabe. Can you believe that? Why not. If the world's going to end..." She raises her drink in a toast. "I might as well enjoy being the wife of the most amazing man in the world—next to your Asher."

I sip my drink. It's a bit early, honestly, to drink. Actually, it's way too late for me. It's nearly bedtime.

Hashan leaves. Then Cora's back to staring out at the lake. I don't like that in a way. She's been so serious lately.

"Hades wanted me to talk to you," Cora finally 'fesses, after another sip. Ah, that's the reason for the drinks. "He said you hate him too much for him to ask you."

"We both despise each other."

"Right, well, I've lived long enough in this world to know he's a good man to have around. But I hate him too. He wants you to still help us. We've captured Athena and bound her under a base at Groom Lake, but Apollo's on the loose again. You won't have to do much. All Hades asks is that you still report to him. It will be a way to protect you and Ash too. If you're willing to help, great. But you don't have to, Gorgi." She smiles. "Or, Medusa."

"I don't want to help him. When he freed me, he used me to kill Imada. I don't want to be used again."

"But you wanted to harm the guards that imprisoned you, didn't you?"

"Yes. But I don't want to commit violence anymore. I really never did."

"You just asked me to call you Medusa."

"Medusa and Gorgiana are one, Cora. Medusa wasn't a

monster until your family made her one. She was a model priestess. I'm a person like everybody else."

"I'm so happy you finally see that," Cora says with a nod, touching my shoulder again. "Yes, you are. Actually, you're better than anybody else."

"But you can still call me Gorgi, if you want to."

"Whatever you want, Medusa," Cora says with a giggle. Then she sips more of her drink. "Shit, it's too early for a martini, isn't it? I should probably start acting like a wife, shouldn't I?"

"How about acting like a mother?"

"Fuck no." She jumps back from the rail. "You crazy? Do I look like I could ever be a mom?"

"You are, Cora. To Moros."

She smiles slyly like the old Cora I love.

"I'll help if I can," I say. "But I don't want to be used again."

"If you'd been around him as long as I have, you'd know that that's all he ever does. That's why I left him. I'll tell him you said yes. It's not like there's a choice. You have to pick one side or the other. And you're already on mine."

"Yes, Cora, I am."

"But I want to offer one more thing." She raises a finger. "If you want to, instead of going home, you could stay here. Gabriel and Moros love you. Of course I love you to death. And there's perks of being here." She runs her free hand through my hair. "You can step out in the light every day."

"No thanks."

"Why?"

"Grace lives here."

Cora laughs. "She is a little shit, isn't she? Well, the invitation will always stand."

That's when I look down and see a toddler under me. Did you smell her? Yeah, I smelled the little sneak coming down the deck. She's got this mischievous grin, as if she did something really wrong. That makes me smile. Then she points to my hair and giggles.

"Moros," chides Cora, "it's not polite to laugh at Medusa."

"But her hair's funny, Mommy."

Cora turns back to the lake and leans over the rail.

"Who's Medusa?" asks Moros.

"Gorgiana," Cora says to Moros without turning. She sips more of her drink and just stares out at the lake. "Gorgi's also named Medusa, sweetheart."

"Medusa?" Moros turns to me. She looks up with her brow furrowed and her lips curled. "But I thought Medusa was ugly?"

"Moros. Moros," Gabe hollers to the little tyke. He walks to the deck wearing a button-down with slacks—real formal. He's probably doing his job at home right now. He hit it off real well with Ash, by the way. Of course, Ash is like fifteen years younger, but Cora's right. They're two of the most amazing men in the world.

"Did you hear Mom say Gorgi is Medusa?" Moros asks Gabe. "Isn't that silly, Daddy?"

Gabriel smiles sweetly as hell at me—while avoiding my gaze, of course. "Let's leave the two of them alone."

He grabs her hand. I watch them as they walk hand and hand back down the deck.

"The two of them are wonderful, Cora."

She's got her elbows over the rail staring out at her view. She raises her red martini glass and says with a sigh, "More wonderful to me than anything else in the whole world, Medusa."

32

YOU

I'm wondering what's wrong with Asher. Did you notice? The whole plane trip back in Cora's private jet he hasn't said a word. When we landed, his car was in the parking lot. Cora had his truck shipped back to Orlando from Arkansas. So he drove me home—completely silent. What happened? Huh? You tell me.

I look down at the sink. I touch his relic. The silver cross is shiny on the sink. As of late, I like to have it here to look at when I'm getting ready. Because it seems lately, when I'm getting all dolled up, it's always for Ash. His gift is so cute.

Look at me in the mirror. Go ahead. See my hair? My black hair's nice and long, dangling down my shoulders. Pretty. Under the yellow light of the room, you can't see my wigglies and I look normal, right? See my mascara around my eyes? I did that with Cora's makeup. I wanted to put it on for Ash.

Is he in shock? Is that it?

"Are you all right, Gorgi?" he hollers from my living room.

Am I all right? Well...*are you all right?*

"I'll be out in a second."

He must be in shock. If I were a sophomore in college who had just fallen in love with a monster, gotten in a gunfight, and then, like, died, maybe I'd be in shock too. But we slept together last night. Remember? We made love in Cora's guest room.

I remember...

Some of the mascara around my eyes is runny. Is that it? I've never been great with makeup, you know, but I wanted to look good for him on the way home. My cheeks are tanned and smooth—I look cute. I'm wearing a white T-shirt. It looks like a real fancy shirt. It's Cora's.

I throw my hair back. Then I gaze deeply into my eyes.

I gaze at you. Beautiful, aren't we?

Yes.

So what's up with Ash?

I don't know.

When I was really fed up, really sick, you remember what I used to do with you? You remember... I used to stare into your eyes. I'd spend, like, ten minutes staring straight into your eyes hoping to turn myself into stone. I figured being turned to stone would be like dying. Hey, don't get all worked up about that, you know I've had a hard life. The first time, looking into my reflection in a pool in Sarpedon, I was hopeful. Of course it never panned out the way I wanted, did it? I just kept staring into your eyes. How come you're always so quiet, Medusa, anyway?

Giggles.

"You mind if I watch some TV?" he asks from the other room. "There's a game on."

Why would I mind? I was hoping you'd stay.

"We have to talk," I say, cocking my head to the closed door. The words came out before I even thought of them. They sound dreadful.

"Sure. What's up, Gorgi?"

Why does he sound happy? After everything he's been through? I don't get him. I don't get men at all.

I take a deep breath, touching the handle of my bathroom door. And then...deep breath. Here goes.

Ash is sitting on the couch, crouched over on his elbows, watching a football game. "What's up, Gorge?" he asks, staring at the screen. "Why have you been so quiet?"

Me? Me quiet?

He drags his eyes from the screen and smiles at me, but he quickly gazes down.

"Nothing."

"There's something you wanted to tell me?"

"No. I mean, yes. Yes, there is, Ash. We need to talk."

He smiles and pats a place on my sofa. I walk over.

I've got butterflies all over my stomach. It's like the wigglies were swallowed and are moving around in my stomach.

I sit next to him. Being next to him, his scent, his male essence, his "Ash-ness," drives me wild. My hair's jumpy. I quickly touch the top of my head. That's all I need right now is for my hair to get big and crazy.

"Ash, I guess I'm worried about what we're going to do next. I mean, you and I."

He turns off the TV and faces me while staring down at my white T-shirt. He's looking at my boobs. Where else are his eyes going to go? But somehow, it makes me think of when I presented them *au natural* last night, his perfect face right next to my eyes, his eyelashes brushing against my soft cheek. And then his lips grazing my face. His body pushing up against mine. And his hard, ah...it was nice.

"I go back to studying," he says and points at me. "You go back to your work as a librarian. Simple."

"But it's not simple. I'm not normal. I'm weird."

"No, you're not normal," he says with laugh. I don't think it's very funny. As soon as he sees my frown, he loses his smile. "You've hypnotized me since I saw you in the library, Gorgi. That girl with the thick glasses put a spell on me even before she looked into my eyes. That girl who won't look at you, but can bring a whole house down. You're amazing. There's so much to love about you, and so much I want to learn and love more."

"That's sweet." But I turn to the TV. It's off. I just stare at the blank screen. Then I throw my long hair back and look at his face. "That's why you were so quiet today, huh?"

"I wasn't quiet, you were. But as long as you're doing all right, I don't mind."

"Are you sure? Snakes and all?"

He answers by running his fingers down my hair and pulls my head closer to his chest. It sends tingles down my body. I bring his hand to my lips and kiss it.

"You're weird, you know that?" I say with a nod and snuggle closer to him. "You're so weird for still wanting me. I'm afraid... I guess, I was afraid you wouldn't, Ash. That I'd be saying goodbye. That's...that's why I've been quiet, I guess, you know?"

He lifts my head, closes his eyes, and kisses my lips. Then he pulls me close again.

"I'm so happy when I'm with you, Gorgiana. I love you."

"I love you too." More smooching. And...a bit more. And...

"What should we do today?" he breathes between touching my lips.

"Well, it's the early afternoon. It's time for bed."

He laughs heartily.

I hit him in the shoulder. "Hey, it's not funny!"

"Sorry, but it really is."

"Well, tonight," I say, running my finger along his chest,

"I thought, if you want, Cora told me she left Gabe's car in the parking lot at the airport. She said we could borrow it. Have you ever driven a McLaren? It's a fast automobile."

His eyes open wide and he freezes. Oops.

When he wakes, I kiss his lips. And then we're smooching again. Life sucks, you know. But somehow, it's not so bad in a lover's arms.

"You're amazing, Gorgi."

Sure.

Hey, you can come with us to the airport, if you want to, Medusa. As long as you stay quiet.

THE END

Gorgiana and Cora continue their Greek mythological mayhem in the 21st century in "Furies":

- THE GUARDIAN, a novella
- NECTAR OF AMBROSIA , a novella
- CORA

ALSO BY A.L. HAWKE

PARANORMAL ROMANCE

- MY EVIL EYE
- THE GUARDIAN
- NECTAR OF AMBROSIA
- CORA

- ALONDRA
- HAWTHORNE UNIVERSITY WITCH SERIES I-III
- HAWTHORNE UNIVERSITY WITCH SERIES 4-6
- THE HAWTHORNE UNIVERSITY WITCH HOLIDAY COLLECTION

- SHADES
- HAUNTING JOY
- PHANTOM MASQUERADE

FANTASY: THE AZURE SERIES

- HARMONIA
- CORA: RISE OF THE FALLEN GODDESS
- AZURE BLUE
- CORAL RED
- PRINCESS SOJOURN

SCIENCE FICTION

- CANDY SAVANT SERIES

Books available at https://alhawke.com/books

PARTING WORDS

What did you think of *My Evil Eye*? By placing a book review, you can inform others of your thoughts and help spread the word about my book.

Want more? Periodically I like to send news regarding current or new projects. If you'd like to be privy, I encourage you to sign up to my email newsletter. Your information will remain private and you can cancel any time.

Sign up at www.alhawke.com or scan the following QR code:

ACKNOWLEDGMENTS

Thank you to the following beta readers for making My Evil Eye a far better story: George B., Monique S., and Breonna H. Thanks, once again, to my amazing copy editor Stephanie Marshall Ward. Thank you to Alexa B. for proofreading my story. And, of course, Regina Wamba, thank you for creating an another amazing work of art for the book cover.

ABOUT THE AUTHOR

A.L. Hawke is the author of the bestselling Hawthorne University Witch series. The author lives in Southern California torching the midnight candle over lovers against a backdrop of machines, nymphs, magic, spice and mayhem. A.L. Hawke writes fantasy and romance spanning four thousand years, from pre-civilization to contemporary and beyond.

Visit A.L. Hawke at www.alhawke.com

Email: contact@alhawke.com

www.ingramcontent.com/pod-product-compliance
Lightning Source LLC
Chambersburg PA
CBHW050834190726
48286CB00007B/2088